AN ELEMENTAL FEMALE

Sylvain's wrists and hands were still browned from summer, the skin kissed to a golden color. She had a fresh scent to her—or perhaps it was just the cold, crisp day? Or that she wore no perfume and so seemed more elementally female?

If he tugged a bit, she would fit nicely against him. A good height of a woman to hold—not so small that he had to stoop to kiss her, and not so large as to be cumbersome. An easy armful.

And what would she taste of?

Sweetness? Spice?

Then Terrance remembered that he had kissed her once—or did his memory betray him? Ah, yes, now he remembered. Two years ago or so . . .

She had tasted of peaches.

BOOK YOUR PLACE ON OUR WEBSITE AND MAKE THE READING CONNECTION!

We've created a customized website just for our very special readers, where you can get the inside scoop on everything that's going on with Zebra, Pinnacle and Kensington books.

When you come online, you'll have the exciting opportunity to:

- View covers of upcoming books
- Read sample chapters
- Learn about our future publishing schedule (listed by publication month *and author*)
- Find out when your favorite authors will be visiting a city near you
- Search for and order backlist books from our online catalog
- Check out author bios and background information
- Send e-mail to your favorite authors
- Meet the Kensington staff online
- Join us in weekly chats with authors, readers and other guests
- Get writing guidelines
- AND MUCH MORE!

**Visit our website at
http://www.kensingtonbooks.com**

BARELY PROPER

Shannon Donnelly

ZEBRA BOOKS
Kensington Publishing Corp.
http://www.kensingtonbooks.com

For Hilary—
Thanks for the time to get it right.

One

"Well, of all the bloody . . ." Terrance let the curse drift away as he went down on one knee. Dunscombe lay dead. Shot. And not in the duel that ought to have taken place. Should he be relieved that he would not be facing a pistol himself this dawn, or irritated at the man for turning an affair of honor into a mess? Or simply happy that it was not himself lifeless in the dawn? He scowled at the uncomfortable mixture of swirling emotions, then pushed them aside as irrelevant. And quite useless. As usual.

His horse, skittish at the coppery smell of blood, snorted and danced a step away, but Terrance held fast to the reins, ignoring the nervous tugs as he stared at the body, still not quite able to take in the sight. He had seen death before—how could one not in the parts of London where sin ruled. But he had never seen the life gone from someone known to him. And it shook him more than he wanted to admit.

Thankfully, no one was here to see such a weakness in him. It would certainly have ruined his reputation as a care-for-nobody. But what did he do now?

He had not been a friend to Dunscombe—the man had been too much the braggart for his taste. And too damn cruel. But he could not bring himself to simply leave the fellow. There was also Lady Dunscombe to think of still. Though he doubted she'd be grief-stricken, this would be a shock. Only, cowardly as it was, he did not want to be the one who took her the news—it might give her reason to start clinging again to him.

So what did he do?

Leave, stay? Wait for someone else to arrive?

His mind stumbled across the questions, as tangled as if snagged in brambles.

Blazes, but he ought to have drunk more last night—or less. However, he'd wanted a steady hand and a careless manner this morning. He had never fought a duel before.

His mouth crooked. It looked as if he still had that experience before him—and the pure joy of life surged up from his blood to warm his skin before sinking deep again.

Only the faintest guilt stained it.

If he had not come to Dusncombe Abbey, this might not have happened.

Becoming aware of the wet grass soaking through the knee of his buckskin breeches to chill his skin and the incongruous and cheerful trill of a lark, Terrance rose.

Something had to be done about Dunscombe. Unexpectedly, he found himself sorry for the poor sod.

The man lay facedown in thick turf. An ugly hole, its edges dark with blood, tore the gray fabric of his greatcoat just below the six rows of shoulder capes, which stirred in the breeze, almost giving the appearance of life. Judging by the lack of bloodletting, the man must have died at once, before his heart could pump more than a beat or two.

Who the blazes had shot him?

The wound had the look of a single ball from a pistol, not a shotgun's blast from any shooting party. Poachers set snares. Gypsies kept to the weapons they could afford—clubs or knives. And he could not imagine Dunscombe pulling the trigger himself by any means. The man had held himself in too high a regard, and even with all his boasted athletic skills he never could have managed a trick such as shooting himself in the back.

Ought he turn the fellow over?

His stomach clenched at the thought of staring into Dunscombe's blank eyes. Besides, there could be no mistaking that the abrasive personality once titled Lord Dunscombe no longer animated the remains of flesh and bone. Someone else would have to make the verdict official, however. His part in this blasted affair ended now. Or at least it would as soon as he could hand the news to the next person he saw.

Stepping to his mount, he stroked the gelding's neck, not quite certain if the gesture steadied his horse or his own hand.

The mists that had cloaked his ride to the field that lay south of the Norman tower and west of Dunscombe Abbey stirred, lifting and thinning with the breeze into gray swirls. The sky had lightened, thought the weak sun had yet to warm the day. It looked a typical Somerset autumn morn—cold, damp, and dismal.

Bloody all, but he ought to have stayed in London. His mouth crooked at that. When had a Winslow ever kept away from trouble?

Which is how he had ended in Lady Dunscombe's bed, and that, in turn, had led to this damn field. Well, with her husband gone she was now a rich widow. And he hoped to hell this would at last give her a new direction for her attentions, other than toward him.

A flash of regret stirred in him at the memory of ample breasts in his hands and her softness wrapped around him. But then he thought of that last scene with her—the tears, the petulant demands, the accusations.

Well, none of that mattered now.

Rubbing his temples, his mouth dry and sour from last night's brandy, he glanced around the field again as if that would show him a way clear of this tangle.

The field—a clearing in the woods, really—seemed eerily still in the thinning mists—a bit of unploughed, unclaimed land, too small and rocky to farm. He could not recall who even owned the land, but it had by tradition become the locale for illicit meetings, such as an illegal duel, which required utter discretion.

Bloody idiot notion these duels.

Pity that he and Dunscombe had not settled this last night with fists. Damn Cale for stepping in to second Dunscombe, insisting he would act for Dunscombe, if need be. Yet another protocol of dueling that Terrance had not known: seconds had to be of the same rank as their principals, in case they had to act on their behalf. Which is how he had ended up with Ashlin Perriman—Dunscombe's foppish nephew—as his own second.

Those details had not seemed relevant last night. But now he wondered if Perriman or Cale had their own reasons to want Dunscombe dead. Had one of them shot him? Who else, after all, had known of the meeting, other than the principals and their seconds?

Well, it wasn't up to him to sort out any of that.

Leading his nervous mount away from the body, he decided he would ride to Halsage and notify Samuels, the innkeeper of The Four Feathers. He, in turn, could notify the local constabulary. The village lay half a mile closer than Dunscombe Abbey, and someone from there could deal with Dunscombe's mortal remains while he rode on with the news. Lady Dunscombe—or Perriman himself, now that his uncle lay dead—would then have to manage from there.

After that, he would find himself a soft bed to sink into and not rise for the rest of the day.

Blazes, how long had it been since he had slept? A day? Two? The events of the past few days—the trip to Dunscombe Abbey, the tearful confrontation with Lady Dunscombe, the argument with her husband—blurred into images that left his head pounding and his shoulders tight.

Perhaps he ought to swear off anything in petticoats.

Near the woods at the edge of the field, he tossed the reins over his mount's head. Then a glimmer of sun slid through the swirling mists and glinted on something in the grass.

He hesitated, then stepped forward. Bending down, he reached into the rough grass, unevenly cropped by grazing animals, and his gloved fingers closed around the hard, curved handle of a pistol. He straightened with it in his grip.

Silver filigree gleamed on the mahogany stock and on the wicked length of the barrel; there could be no mistaking the deadly shape and elegant balance for anything but a dueling pistol.

He lifted the barrel closer and the sharp sulfuric bite of gunpowder filled his nostrils, confirming his suspicions. Fired. Recently, too. Dragging off one glove, he wrapped his fingers around the metal of the barrel—not fired so recently as to leave it warm, however.

Turning, he glanced back at Dunscombe's body.

Ten paces, he guessed. From the woods to Dunscombe. An apt enough dueling distance. Someone really had done more than dislike Dunscombe. Someone had hated him enough to lie in wait and murder him.

The morning chill deepened, slipping under Terrance's coat and neckcloth to wrap around his throat like a cold hand.

A pheasant startled up from the shrubbery, and Terrance spun around, pulse fast now, as the bird's wings beat the air in a frightened flurry. Lifting its head, Terrance's gelding nickered an inquiry. Terrance heard the hoofbeats then—someone approaching at a slow canter. He turned toward the sound as the horse appeared from the woods, already slowing its pace as its rider dragged on the reins and then halted the animal, awkward and abrupt.

Terrance at once recognized the thin figure on the flashy chestnut—Ashlin Perriman. Who else would wear a yellow-stripped waistcoat, of all things, and a blindingly bright green coat to a duel? He would have thought protocol would have had something to say about dark colors being far more appropriate.

Perriman shared his uncle's blond coloring, but nothing else showed their blood ties. Where Dunscombe had been a tall, athletic man—even in his early fifties—with a hard face and rough manners, Perriman padded his coat for broader shoulders, affected a lisp to match his almost feminine features, and aspired to the refinement of a London dandy.

He sat his horse badly as always, but the sight of his uncle dead seemed to startle him from his usual slouch into rigid shock. His face drained of color until it looked whiter than his breeches and boot tops.

Terrance strode toward him, pistol still in hand, leading his horse and glad enough to be able to give this over to a relative.

"Perriman," he called, trying to get the fellow to focus on something other than the sight of death.

Twisting, Perriman's hand jerked and his horse tossed its head and danced under the suddenly tight rein. After a glance at Terrance, he looked back at Dunscombe, then at Terrance again, before blurting out, his voice reedy, high, and breaking, "Gads, but you shot him!"

Impatience flooded Terrance. "Don't be an idiot!"

Perriman seemed not to take in the words, for he stabbed a shaking hand, gloved in pale green, toward the pistol in Terrance's grip, startling his horse again. "You murdered him!"

Jaw clenched, Terrance sought to check his temper. Then he ground out, "Oh, for . . . this isn't some two-penny sheet story! And I . . ."

"You'll hang for this!"

Scowling, Terrance strode forward. "Don't be so bloody stupid. I didn't . . ."

"Stay away from me. I . . . I mean it!"

Terrance stopped and glared at the man, his eyes narrowed and his temper almost lost. "Blazes, but I'm half sorry someone didn't shoot you instead! Now, if you don't mind, I'm going to . . ."

"What—shoot me?" Perriman's hands tightened even more on his reins and the flashy chestnut flung up its head. "You're a murderer!"

His voice rose to a shrill pitch, setting his sweating, prancing horse to small half-rears, and Terrance had to hold tight to keep his own mount in order.

Suddenly, Perriman's horse swung around and, haunches bunched, galloped into the woods. Terrance was hard put to judge just who had bolted—Perriman or his high-strung chestnut.

"Damn fool," he muttered from between clenched teeth.

He almost let the man go. But then the frantic shouts drifted to him, "Murder! Murder's been done!"

"Oh, blazes!"

Flinging down the pistol, Terrance swung up on his gelding. If he didn't stop this flow of hysteria, the fellow would cause no end of trouble. Digging in his heels, he dropped the reins and his horse sprang after Perriman's.

The animal's stride lengthened. Hooves thudded against turf, and then shadows engulfed them as they gained the woods. Leafless branches slapped at his face, raw as whips. The wind stung tears from his eyes, and tore off his hat. He leaned closer to his horse's neck, letting the animal weave a path between oaks, ash, and apple trees. And he hoped like hell he didn't happen across any rabbit holes—it had been too long since he had hunted these woods as a lad, and he no longer knew the safest paths.

Why in blazes could not someone else have come across Dunscombe's body first? Why had he thought to arrive early for this damn duel!

But he knew the answers—he had wanted to be there, composed and nonchalant. He had wanted to have already hidden every tremor at the possibility that he faced his own mortality.

So much for putting on a good show—it had left him looking as if he had shot Dunscombe. Well, he ought to know by now that his course never ran easy.

But he wasn't about to allow a prancing dandy such as Perriman to make matters impossible. No, he'd muffle the man's delirium before it got out of hand.

With a burst of light, woods gave way to an open lane and

fields already left barren for winter's kiss. Terrance drew rein, his horse plunging to a halt, blowing hard, but still dancing and ready to run. In the now-lifting fog, Perriman's green coat and his horse's red coat flashed down the lane to the left as the horse galloped hard away. Perriman, too, had lost his hat in his mad dash, and he lay forward as if clinging to his horse's neck to keep from falling, letting the animal run wild.

If Perriman held to the lanes, that was the long way back to Dunscombe Abbey.

Terrance smiled.

Wheeling his mount, he dropped the reins again and spurred the horse to a gallop. Two strides later, the gelding handily jumped the hedge set between lane and pasture and set off again. Perriman's horse might know its way home on the roads, but Terrance knew the countryside. He had grown up riding these fields, for Winslow Park lay not five miles away. And if he cut through the edge of the woods there, he could reach the crossroad before Perriman did.

At least he hoped he could.

Then he would pound some sense into the damn fellow with some hard words or hard fists if need be.

Another hedge loomed before him and his mount tore over it, jumping flat and clever. Hooves pounded packed dirt as Terrance let the gelding open his stride. The woods that marked the edges of Winslow Park rose up, and he galloped into them, then jumped his horse across a stream and turned left.

As he had expected from his memories, another hedge lay at the top of a sloping rise. It would be a straight quarter-mile and then he'd be at the crossroad.

With a click of his tongue against his teeth, he urged his horse up the incline. The gelding had slowed, but responded now by digging in with his hindquarters. Fast at brush, slow at timber. His horse had hunted enough to know that without any help from him, but the gallop had half blown the gelding by now. Still, he had enough to best Perriman's flashy but narrow Hyde Park mount.

His horse pushed off before the hedge, jumping from further back than wise for a wider jump. They cleared the Hawthorne.

And from midair, Terrance saw the yawning ditch on the far side.

Too late.

The hedge had hidden it from view, else he would have checked his speed and ridden to jump close enough to get them safely over.

His horse saw it, too, for he felt the gelding stretch. His mount twisted, struggling to clear the ditch, and Terrance's legs tightened as he willed his strength to his horse. He could do no more.

In the next instant, hooves struck soft dirt.

The impact shuddered through the gelding and into Terrance, and for two heartbeats he thought they'd made it. Breathing hard, the horse managed one stride up the side of the ditch, but the effort cost too much, and as he gained the top he stumbled, went down on his knees, and fell.

Ground rushed up. Earth slammed hard into Terrance. He tasted dirt, and the scrape of it stung his cheek. In the next breath, a weight crashed onto him—his horse, half rolling, pushing him into the soft ground with a heavy grunt.

The gelding struggled upright, and as he shifted his weight to rise, something snapped and cracked in Terrance's leg. White agony shot through him, tearing loose a strangled cry from him. Then he lay still in the quiet morning, sweating in the chill, his lungs empty of air.

Pain sharpened everything: the gelding, now on his feet and steaming, shook himself like a wet dog, then glanced around, seeming almost surprised. Wind brushed cold across his cheeks. Terrance dragged in a breath that did not quite fill his empty chest, and he fought the panic of not being able to find any air. It would come—keep it shallow for now. His face burned. His arm ached. His leg hurt as if someone had stuck a hot poker though it. His stomach churned, but he had not enough energy to turn and spill out its contents.

Blackness edged his vision. Shutting his eyes, he clenched his teeth to fight it. And he focused on the one thought that might keep him conscious—just what bloody idiot had dug a ditch there since he'd last been home?

Sylvain Harwood heard the hard pounding of galloping hooves, the heavy crash, the desperate thrashing. Then silence filled the air, and she stood still, listening.

She really ought to be home, not out at dawn, for she had promised her mother just yesterday not to spend all day in the woods again. But Trace had been gone from his bed in the stables this morning—no doubt courting the vixen who had caught his fancy. And she could not leave him loose—not with cub-hunting season begun to train the young hounds for hunts.

A three-legged fox, after all, did not have a chance, not even against young cub-hounds.

Thankfully, Somerset boasted few packs of hounds, and most seasons—autumn through spring—slipped quietly past.

But a galloping horse set her worrying. Thank heavens she had heard no shrill from a huntsman's horn, nor any bay from a hound—but who else would be galloping in the woods that lay between her home and Winslow Park?

And why had she not heard the hooves gallop away again?

Her brow tightened at that. And her curiosity stirred.

She had to at least take a look. Really, she did. What if Squire Winslow or some other neighbor had taken a spill? It would not do to leave someone lying there who might need aid.

Still, she kept her steps cautious as any fox's, and she kept the hood of her cloak pulled forward. No need to show herself unless she really was needed. That would only cause talk, after all. Such a nuisance to have to start becoming a young lady—but she had promised to make the effort. And it really would not do if tales were carried back to her parents that she had been out in the woods at dawn with only her old green cloak thrown over her faded brown woolen gown.

She saw the horse first—a handsome big gray with a darker mane and tail—as she came out from the edge of the woods and peered over the hedge. It stood on the far side of the ditch, its head down as if exhausted, and dark leather reins looped loose. One stirrup—leather and iron—lay the wrong way over the seat of the saddle. Mud and dirt stained the gray's side.

Not good signs.

The horse lifted its head and glanced at her, but otherwise stood still.

She frowned at him, a suspicion already forming and a fear now tight in her chest. It could not be—not really. He was not supposed to be at home, after all. But when had Terrance Winslow ever done anything that was expected of him? And who else always seemed to court such disaster?

Pulling her cloak tight, she skirted the hedge until she found a spot wide enough to push through. Then she slid down the ditch and scrambled up the other side. She glimpsed him on the ground then, half hidden by the mists that still hugged the earth, his brown coat and buff breeches almost blending with the torn earth around him.

Fear iced her muscles, stopping her.

His body stretched out near the top of the ditch, with his right arm flung out and actually angling down into the ditch.

Heavens, please no!

Folding her cloak about her, she came closer. The gesture calmed her and kept her from reaching out to him. If he knew of it, he would not care for her comforting. No, he was not a man who liked cosseting. Nor did she have any right to offer such a thing. They were but friends after all. Neighbors only. And a wise lady would remember that.

So she took inventory of him by sight alone.

Like all the Winslows, he had a straight nose and square jaw, now marked by a smear of dirt. Both looked unbroken. He had torn his coat and a ragged tear lay across his left thigh as well, exposing a thickly muscled leg. But Terrance Winslow had always seemed a man made all of muscles—broad and tall as an oak. A man too full of restless impatience and energy, and that, she thought, was what really got him in trouble.

He had found his share of that yet again, it seemed.

Thick black lashes lay against his pale cheeks. His short black hair stood up in disorder, but she saw no blood. No head injury, thank heaven. She ran her stare across him again, one hand pressed to her stomach. No blood. No bones poking out from places that ought to be covered by flesh and skin. Her fear eased.

The tight set of his mouth also told her that he had to be conscious, even if his eyes were closed. So he could not be too badly injured. And he certainly would be in a temper to have come to grief over a hedge and ditch, like some green novice.

She could almost smile at that.

Except her stomach still knotted and her hands quivered under her cloak.

She knelt at his side, still not touching him, but grateful to feel the presence of him—that stir of something like a strong wind that always came with him.

And with the fear easing came a spurt of anger—would the man never learn to take better care of himself?

Tilting her head, she stared down at him, then asked, her voice calm enough so that it betrayed nothing of her feelings, "Well, what have you broken this time?"

Two

It took effort to open his eyes—the pain made it seem to take years. But the sound of her voice drew him with its soft cadence and low, melodic tones. He knew that voice—and hearing it could almost make a man believe in angels.

Almost, but not quite. Not when the devil seemed to have hold of his leg and was twisting it.

"What makes you think I've broken anything? And who in bloody all dug a ditch here?" he asked.

Sylvain Harwood tilted her head. "Your father did this winter past. To keep the cows from pushing out through the hedge. I doubt he expected either of his sons to be galloping about like a madman."

With a groan, Terrance closed his eyes again, ignoring her comment. Cows! He had taken a fall, and had lost the chase after Perriman for a few cows. It was almost laughable.

Forcing his eyes open, he struggled up onto one elbow. "Where's Drake?"

"Drake? Your horse? He is just over there, and in better shape than you." Twisting, she gestured to the gray, who had recovered enough to take an interest in the grass and was now quietly cropping his breakfast.

Struggling to keep himself propped on one elbow, Terrance winced as pain jabbed up his leg from his calf. "Help me rise."

"Why? So you can mount up and fall off again?"

The faintest disapproval laced her tone, and he could not let that pass, so he fixed his stare on her and scowled.

She stared back at him, her expression interested but not the least shocked or anxious, nor anything else suitable to the sensibilities a young lady ought to display.

And a blessed relief it was, too, that she lacked enough delicacy to faint or have a nice bout of hysteria.

A green cloak enfolded her body, but she had put back the hood so that he could see her narrow face and short golden red curls. She looked a fey creature, with that pointed chin and those wide, blue-green eyes. What in blazes had the ancients called those woodland creatures who transformed from trees into young maidens? His two years at Cambridge failed him. But he knew her well enough to guess that she'd wrinkle her nose in disgust at a comparison to any sort of nymph.

"You still running wild? I would have thought your family would have you tamed by now."

Wrinkling her nose, she made a face at him, and then said, "I should think you could sympathize with the difficulties of being the odd one out in a family."

He gave a laugh, then winced. "Well, I am getting back on, but I am not falling off again. And how in blazes do you always manage to have twigs in your hair?"

With an impatient gesture, she ran her fingers through the short curls, missing a hedge leaf. He almost smiled—and he wanted to pluck it out himself.

Folding her hands before her again, she tilted her head. "I am not helping you up if it is just so you might win a bet, or some other mad lark that will get your neck broken."

"Is murder a mad enough lark for you?"

Her eyes widened and her lips parted, then she frowned. "Just who has been murdered?"

"Dunscombe. Shot in the back."

Her frown deepened, pulling a line between sandy eyebrows which now flattened. "So you were galloping to the abbey to let them know about this?"

"No. I was galloping after Ashlin Perriman, who saw me standing over his dead uncle with a pistol in my hand."

The frown cleared. "Oh. Oh, I see. You have landed in the mud, even more so than usual."

"Usual? I—" He bit off his protest and checked his sudden rise as a warning twinge from his leg reminded him not to move so quickly. Then, back teeth gritted, he ground the words out. "Are you going to help me?"

"What? Go after Ashlin? Why? You cannot hope to . . ."

"Lord, you are the most . . . most . . ."

"Impertinent? Uncooperative? Unconventional?" Sandy eyebrows lifted, she smiled at him. "That's the usual list."

He did not smile back. "The most irritating female."

"I am not irritating—you are irritable. You always are when you break something. And if you would rather, I can just take myself away again." Standing, she dusted her hands.

He grabbed hold of her skirt and cloak hem. "You are not going to bloody leave me here with a bloody broken leg."

She nodded, as if he had just explained the obvious. "I knew it."

Distracted, he glared up at her. "And just how is it that you knew it?"

"When you broke your arm falling out of Mrs. Dermont's window, you were in a mood for a month. And that time you broke you wrist when you overturned . . ."

"I never overturned anything! And if you're referring to that race to Bristol, the blasted wheel came off!"

"It still landed you in a ditch. And you were cross as a bear. But why should I help you continue being stupid? You are not likely to catch up to Ashlin."

"Well, I have to catch up with bloody Ashlin because he bloody thinks I shot his uncle!"

She drew back. "Really? But even he could not . . . unless . . . Terrance, what did you do to make him think such a thing?"

"I did nothing."

"He just took the notion into his head? Really now, Terrance, everyone knows Ashlin for the worst troublemaker, but he has no imagination. You must have done something."

"Nothing! I swear. I simply had the misfortune to find his uncle's lifeless body." He let go her skirts and sank back again. His head had started to pound to match the throbbing in his leg and a wave of exhaustion drained him.

She threw back the edge of her cloak, revealing a faded brown dress that clung tight to her slender form, and then she folded her arms. "I thought you would at least be honest with me."

He glanced at her, and she looked so mulish that a smile lifted his mouth. "Oh, for . . . well, he knew I was to have met his uncle to duel. And . . . and I was stupid enough to pick up a pistol to see if it had been fired."

Shaking her head, she knelt in the grass. "Which you no doubt waved at him."

Her assumption irritated him, both for its accuracy and for the tone of resigned certainty in her voice. "He'd started to yell bloody murder, so what else was I do to? Bow and politely thank him?"

Frowning, she stared at the dawn and ignored his question.

He resisted the urge to either continue protesting how none of this was his fault or to lie back on the grass with his eyes shut and wish this away. Instead, he watched her.

She was growing up. He could see that from the interesting curves now visible—the swell of breast and hip—which he could not remember from his last time home. What a pity that soon enough her blunt speech would be curbed into polite nothings and her direct stares would be trained into coy glances, and she'd no doubt become like every other lady he knew. Pure trouble.

"You know, anyone would think your family impoverished with how you dress."

She glanced at him. "Well, we aren't. Penelope even married a lord, you know."

His mouth twisted. "So I heard."

"And you are changing the subject." Her mouth flattened into a line as she frowned, and then she said, "If I were Ashlin, and if you showed yourself at Dunscombe Abbey, I would set every male servant in the place on you and get you tossed in the cellars until the constables came and dragged you off. He is Lord Dunscombe now, after all, which means it might not be wise to go anywhere near him just now. And you would do far better thinking about the entire matter after enough sleep to clear your head. You reek of brandy, you know."

He glared at her, but his head did ache, slowing his thoughts so that they tangled on one another. And he would give a good deal for a soft place to lie—blazes, but perhaps this whole disaster might blow away without his having to do anything. Perhaps Ashlin was already feeling foolish for his absurd leap in logic. Perhaps the truth indeed had come out already.

Or perhaps, even now, the law was being set on him.

Standing up, Sylvain held out her hands. "Give me your hands. And if you start to fall, do try to fall on your good side so you do not do any more harm."

He grinned at her, and Sylvain fought the urge to smile back. No man ought to own such charm. And she would not succumb to its potency. She frowned back at him, keeping her thoughts on his flaws, rather than his assets.

At the moment, pain dulled those amber eyes of his, and drink had left them red. Hard living had also started to coarsen his handsome, even features, blunting the edge to his jaw, leaving his face puffy. But in some ways that made his face more interesting—more masculine. He had been almost too beautiful as a boy, she knew.

She also knew from the gossip that reached her that women found him irresistible. What was it about him that made it so? Was it that grin of his, so light and boyish? Or that reckless edge of danger that somehow managed to cling to him. For herself, she suspected the truth of it was that his reputation got him more trouble than anything. He was just a man, like any, after all. But the reputation he was making for himself dangled like a lure to the ladies and a challenge to other gentlemen who wanted to be judged even more daring than the notorious Terrance Winslow.

Well, what others thought of him did not matter. She owed him a debt twice over. She would not forget that. And so she would do what she could for him. The trick would be to do so in a way that did not end with herself embroiled in his troubles.

He put his hands in hers and she noticed that he had lost one glove. So typical of him to be so careless, and not even to notice. Or course, she had forgotten to even wear gloves out this morning, and her face warmed that she had judged him before noticing the same fault in herself.

His grip engulfed hers, but with such a weak grasp that she knew he had injured himself worse than he had let on. Her irritation with him flared again—a grown man ought to be able to take better care of himself.

But it seemed he could not.

She allowed him to take his time to leverage himself up, keeping his weight on his right leg. And she had to brace herself to keep him from pulling her over. Gracious, but she had forgotten his size and the mass of him, and as he rose to tower over her, her mouth dried and her pulse lifted.

There was indeed more to his allure than just his reputation—there was a raw masculinity that left her feeling feminine and small. She never felt feminine or small anywhere else but with him—not when she stood taller than either of her sisters now, and had not a womanly grace to her name.

By the time he gained his feet, his face had gone pale again and sweat dampened his forehead, even in the chill of the morning.

He offered up another grin, this one forced, and said, "If you lead Drake into the ditch, I can swing a leg over him."

"And then you can slide off as he scrambles out again? That is not much of a plan."

"You have a better one?"

"Yes. If you have your horse on one side to lean on and me on the other, I think we can make Harwood."

"Harwood? Why the devil would I go there?"

She pressed her lips tight to keep from telling him that if she had him at Harwood she could look after him. He would not think he needed looking after, even though he obviously did. So she went for a more persuasive argument.

"Well, I suppose you could ride to Winslow Park. The argument with your father might last only a quarter of an hour, unless you lose your temper, too, and then it will no doubt end with you riding off in a huff. Or with the squire disowning you, which he has done now—what is it, three times?"

"Only twice."

"Ah, only twice."

"Mockery doesn't become you. Besides, I didn't intend to ride home. I can take a room in Halsage."

"That is five miles at the least, and Harwood is less than a field away. Besides, what if the constabulary has been set after you?"

"What if they have? I've done nothing."

"And you shall be doing more nothing if you end up in gaol while matters are sorted out. That will do your leg some good, will it not?"

"Damnit, I am not hiding away like a frightened rabbit."

"No one asked you to. But any animal has the sense to run to ground until the real danger is known. You need rest for a day or so until you actually know what is toward. And at Harwood, the entire east wing is closed—you could stay a fortnight and no one would even know you were there. But by tomorrow you may actually be able to think again, and start planning what you need to do."

Terrance shook his head. And then his mouth edged up— his practical-minded Sylvain seemed to have mistaken him for one of the creatures she found in these woods and nursed to health.

Which wasn't too far from the truth.

He also had to admit that she made several good points, but still it went against the grain to think of himself as hiding from anyone. The sooner he straightened out any misunderstanding, the better.

But his leg did ache, and the five miles to Halsage stretched out as an impossible distance, even assuming he could get on his horse and remain in the saddle. And he knew her to be right about Ashlin—he had lost his chance to muffle the man.

She leaned closer, tucking herself under his arm, taking his weight onto her slim shoulders as she said, voice dropping seductively low, "I can ask Mrs. Brown for some soup for you—she could do that without a word to anyone. And your horse can go down to the lower pasture—no one ever uses it."

He gave up. She had it all planned. A pasture for his horse, a heavenly soup from his father's cook, and no doubt her looking after him as if he were one of her rescues.

Well, he had also grown dizzy, standing up. His leg had settled into a continual ache. And if he did not get to a bed soon, he might well have to be hauled to one.

"And just what will your parents say when they learn I am their guest?"

Sylvain peered around the corner of the stables with Terrance's saddle braced against her hip and the bridle from his horse dangling over her shoulder.

The journey to Harwood House had not been as easy as she had expected. Terrance's horse had balked about having anyone lean on him—the big gray kept trying to move sideways. Eventually, Sylvain gave up trying to make that work, led the animal herself, and had Terrance lean on her. It said a good deal about his condition that he said nothing about her taking command.

He was leaning heavily on her by the time they reached the house, his hand gripping her shoulder almost painfully. However, he had not complained. But she had noted the tensing of his hand when he tried to take more weight on his bad leg than was wise. And she had heard the sharp intakes of breath when a rough patch of ground jarred his step.

No one, thankfully, had seen them enter, and no one seemed present now to see her slip back into the house through the side door—the one she used for her early morning excursions. A benefit, she supposed, to not having enough servants.

But watching eyes had not been her worry as she struggled with Terrance to the small room that had once served as her mother's study and which now lay in the neglected east wing. Terrance had collapsed onto the day-bed there without waiting for her to remove the dusty Holland coverings, and he lay there, eyes closed, mouth pressed tight.

Her heart tightened.

"I shall have to cut the boot off," she had said. "And you may need to have the bone set."

He waved away her words, his eyes still closed. "See to Drake first. I'll do well enough. The bone's not sticking out, so some strong linen will hold it together."

She had her doubts about that. But he had opened his eyes then, smiled at her, and told her, "Well—what about my blasted horse? You said you had a pasture for him."

Relieved, she had pulled off her cloak and draped it across him. He could not be that bad off if he could still curse and complain. That, at least, was her hope. So she had fetched his horse down to the far pasture, and left the animal content in the green field. She would leave the saddle and bridle with Terrance—he would eventually have need of them.

And she had already decided not to tell her parents that Terrance Winslow would be staying at Harwood.

The decision cost her a good deal, for she disliked deceiving either her mother or father. Everyone in the family, of course, practiced small omissions, particularly with her mother, for she had a weak heart and the doctor had warned them against any excitement or shock. And her father lived more in his own world of plans and investments that might regain the fortune he had lost.

Thankfully, he seemed to have at last given up such schemes—Penelope's doing, Sylvain thought. Even though she was now Lady Nevin, Penelope still acted as older sister, and sometimes even as mother to the family. And she still sought to turn their father's interests to things such as rebuilding the family fortunes in slow, measured steps rather than in rash ventures. Lord Nevin had been a help there, too, and with more than wise counsel, Sylvain suspected.

But none of them—not her parents, not her sister, and definitely not the rather starchy Lord Nevin—approved of Terrance.

Probably justly so, given his reputation for running off with ladies whom he did not marry.

With his injuries, however, she might coax her parents into granting him refuge. And that would then be the last she saw of him while he was in the house. He would be given over to the servants' care, and she would be kept under strict supervision—as if he might run off with her or otherwise compromise her.

A ridiculous idea, of course. Terrance had never shown an ounce of interest in her. Well, perhaps an ounce, but that had been a single event. And quite some time ago.

And if he had shown any more interest in her than that, she would have done something to make certain he lost it at once, she told herself. Ladies who earned Terrance's interest generally were not ladylike at all. No, it was a very, very good thing that he had always treated her more as a . . . well, as a sister, or a . . . a friend.

Except for that once.

But he had forgotten that—of course he had.

With a sigh, and her mind full of a summer long ago—the summer he had kissed her—she let herself into the house through the back door to the main hall, and collided with her father.

Three

For a moment, she feared she would topple over, saddle and all, but her father caught her arms and steadied her.

"What, daydreaming again?" he said with a smile. Then his stare sharpened as he glanced at the saddle in her arms and the bridle hanging from her shoulder. "Going for a ride inside the house today?"

She pushed her mouth into a smile and her hand tightened around the leather pommel of the saddle.

Her father started to frown. "Here now—you are not planning to take up riding astride, like some . . . some . . . some Amazon?"

"Father! Of course not! As if old Millie would allow me to fit her with anything but a side saddle!"

His frown cleared. His red-blond hair, so like her own, had gone far more silver this year and had thinned into fine wisps. He looked ready himself to go out riding in tan breeches, black boots, a buff waistcoat, and a loose-fitted brown riding jacket. And he must have tied his own neckcloth this morning, for he had it crooked and loose. Their butler, Bridges, who also acted as valet, would never have been so careless.

"Then what are you doing with that saddle? And here in the house, of all things?"

"I . . ." She hesitated, and then decided that the truth really would serve best—or at least as much as was wise. She was already blushing hot, and a lie would show too clearly on her face. "I am storing it."

"Storing? Why not do so in the stables?"

She wet her lips. "Because I . . . I did not want it confused with our tack."

He started to frown again. "But if that's not our saddle, why do you have it? Honestly, my dear Silly, I do wish you would not speak in puzzles and explain this."

"It is not a puzzle. I found it. Or rather, I came across a horse. A big gray. His rider must have fallen. So I brought it home. Horse and saddle and bridle. For I could not just leave them."

His eyes brightened with interest, and he stepped past her to glance out the door. "Really? A big gray? A mare by chance?"

"A gelding, but not one I know." And that she counted as another bit of luck. Terrance must have bought the horse in London, and fairly recently, so no one at Harwood was likely to recognize the animal. Now, if only she could slip away and hope that least said was soonest forgot.

Her father turned from the door with a sigh. "Only a gelding, eh? What bad luck."

Sylvain put on what she hoped was a sympathetic expression. "Still not found any mares for Willful?" she asked, hoping to distract him.

"No—not a one. Everyone who knows his pedigree, also knows he boasts an even more impressive temper. I thought Wilcox might breed his Firefly to him, but . . . well, I ought to have thought to buy my own mares before this. And when his get start winning—why even old Wilcox will be wanting his mare covered. But, here now, you had really best keep that tack in the stables. I shall ring for Bridges to take it out."

"But . . ."

"Oh, it's no trouble, my dear." Her father smiled as he strode to the bell-rope and tugged it.

Frustrated, Sylvain searched for some reason to hang on to the saddle and bridle. Terrance would need them when he left. However, she supposed she could always go and fetch them, as well as the horse—only what a great deal of bother! It meant more fuss than she had anticipated, and a greater danger of discovery.

However, she could think of no excuse to offer, so when Bridges arrived and her father explained the situation, she gave over the equipment with no word of complaint.

Then her father added, "Oh, and Bridges, do ask about if anyone is missing a big gray gelding—we must see him returned."

Sylvain's stomach tightened. But protesting such a reasonable course of action would only draw more attention, so she gave Bridges her thanks and then watched him and her father leave the house for the stables.

As she did, the suspicion twisted inside her that she ought to have known that anything to do with Terrance always did turn into far more of a tangle than anyone wanted. So she would just have to make certain that this particular tangle did not become more than she could manage.

Sunlight, bright and warm, woke Terrance.

It slanted across his face, streaming in with an indecent cheer, and for an instant he wondered why Burke, his manservant, had not left the curtains drawn.

Then he remembered he was not in London.

He put up a hand to rub his face as the memories of yesterday tumbled back in nightmarish succession. A misty dawn—too much brandy—that damn duel—Dunscombe's body—the relief—then a bone-cracking fall. Not one of his better days.

A day's stubble roughened his jaw and cheeks, and left him wishing for a razor, a hot bath, and a far softer bed than this lumpy sofa.

Sylvain had done her best to make him comfortable on the day-bed in this unused room. She had cut the boot off his injured leg—and a good thing, too, for the leg had swollen up like a tick. Fractured for a certainty. He'd broken enough bones to know it. At least it had not required resetting, so it ought to mend straight. He could only hope it mended fast as well.

Sylvain had also brought him pillows and blankets, musty from disuse but warm enough. He had actually dozed off under them, sleeping away most of the day. Later, she had slipped into the barren room with a lamb stew, smuggled in a thick pottery bowl from Mrs. Brown's kitchen at Winslow Park, along with crusty bread.

"She sent cheese, apples, and what she swears is the best cider in the county," Sylvain had told him, rummaging in the wicker basket she had brought with her.

He had almost felt guilty to have her waiting on him like an upstairs maid, but she seemed not to mind, and he had not the energy to protest.

Despite the tempting aroma of the stew, he found he had not the energy to do more than taste it and down a mug of cider.

The cotton taste in his mouth today stirred a suspicion that Sylvain had put something into the cider; he'd barely been able to stay awake after he drank the stuff.

At least he had slept sound last night.

His head also no longer pounded—only a dull throb was left, really. He could almost ignore the ache in his leg, and while his back muscles protested the abuse left by the fall he had taken, leaving him stiff as a Methodist preacher, he rather thought he would be able to manage well enough.

Slowly, he risked opening his eyes. The additional light did not increase the pounding in his head, so he attempted to rise.

He got no further than leaning on one elbow and just starting to shift his leg when a sharp twinge warned him against further movement.

So he lay back and closed his eyes again. It was not as if he had any appointments to demand his time.

Then he remembered bloody Perriman.

He really had to do something about Perriman.

Only what urgency was there now? Perriman had either stirred up a fuss, or had not. And perhaps the truth behind Dunscombe's death had already come out, which would make any such trip to see the man unnecessary.

Besides which, at the moment he was having a hard time doing much more than lying on this damn lumpy sofa.

The squeak of a hinge pulled his eyes open again. Tensing, he levered himself up on one elbow. But when Sylvain appeared, a silver tray weighing down one arm, he relaxed.

"You'll have to pardon me for not rising," he said, then ran a hand over his wrinkled clothes, as if that could make him any more presentable. He suspected he looked even more rumpled than he felt.

She glanced at him, her expression curious and not the least disapproving. "Could you?"

"Could I what?"

"Rise. I should think you are feeling today as if a horse fell on you—which it did."

A smiled tugged his mouth.

She looked away to concentrate on balancing the tray with one hand while she shut the door with the other.

Today she wore a faded blue gown instead of a brown one. A flounce had been added to the bottom, as if to lengthen the hem, but the dress showed more of her trim ankles than it ought. Blazes, but she had grown this past year.

And he was having a difficult time adjusting to this new version of the child he had known. Where was the lanky frame, thin and gawky? Where was the tousled hair and the face smudged with dirt, and the sharp chin? She had been an imp of a child, and he realized suddenly that some of the best memories of his younger years at Winslow Park had her in them. Most with him finding her in the woods, rescuing some animal, or on her back watching clouds, or knee-deep in the stream, catching fish with her father's pole.

She never had remembered to act the lady.

As she crossed the barren room, her slippers patting soft on the dusty wood floor, he knew that while she had changed in appearance, in so many other ways she was the same.

She had threaded a blue ribbon through her golden-red curls, which had been brushed free of twigs. That pointed chin had been washed clean, as had her cheeks, to show a scattering of freckles under sandy-lashed eyes. Wide and slightly tilted at the corners, those eyes had always seemed somber and far more knowing than appropriate for any child. She had at last grown into that look, and her figure had blossomed into attractive curves.

However, she had the same stubborn tilt to her chin, the same air of quiet reserve, the same streak of independence. What else, after all, would have made her think to bring him here to look after him?

She glanced up, as if sensing his stare, and offered a slight smile.

Battered as his body was, his blood quickened and his interest stirred at the warmth of that smile. He squashed those faint urges before they made more than a ripple on his awareness. Then he frowned.

She was a child still—blast it!

A girl who'd not had so much as a season in London, nor a proper court presentation, nor even been twenty miles from Somerset's border. What, she must be all of nineteen. Or perhaps twenty. He could not recall her exact age. But she was a good few years younger that he.

Blazes, why had he thought this idea of staying at Harwood, even for a night, a good one?

But he had not been thinking much yesterday. He had been too full of brandy, pain, and—if truth be told—the shock of finding Dunscombe dead.

Settling the tray on a side table—which she had brought into the barren room yesterday—she glanced at him. "I had cook send me a tray—hot chocolate and toast. Do you care for some? Or there is still cheese and cold stew from last night."

He struggled to a sitting position, careful not to jar his leg and wincing only slightly as he resettled himself. "You may keep your chocolate. Toast will do well enough."

She gave him the plate of toasted bread, then picked up a china cup into which she poured steaming brown liquid from a silver pot. Then she sank down with fluid grace to sit cross-legged on the floor.

The knot of awareness of her that had been forming inside him relaxed. A child. Just as he remembered. What lady would sit on the floor in such a casual fashion?

He bit into the toast, finding it thickly cut, richly buttered, and better than any he ever remembered having.

"Do you want the gossip as well?" she asked.

"What? Already?"

"There's been all of a night at the inn for talk. And a day. And Andrew—our stable lad—who was down at The Four Feathers, told Bridges who told Betty, who sometimes does as maid for me and for Mother, that you were all anyone spoke of."

He finished his toast, then put down the plate and dusted the crumbs from his fingers. Gingerly, he swung his legs off the day-bed to rest his stocking-clad feet on the floor.

The room around him looked much like he felt—hollowed out and dusty. Brown marks on the cream walls marked where paintings had once hung. The fireplace stood empty and black. A Holland cover draped some piece of furniture—a heavy desk, perhaps—against one wall, and the floor boards lay bare of any rug. None of it the least attractive.

Still, the sunlight streamed in bright through the windows, lighting up the dust in straight shafts, and warming the place. And he didn't have the prospect of a discussion with his father.

He only wished he had not slept in his jacket, for it looked wrinkled beyond salvation. At some point, Sylvain must have unbuttoned his waistcoat and taken off his cravat. He could not remember doing so—his uneasiness returned.

To cover it, he asked, "So does popular verdict have me guilty?"

Putting down her cup, she drew her knees to her chest and folded her hands around them. "I am afraid that Perriman has put it about that you shot his uncle."

Terrance dragged a hand through his hair. "Bloody idiot."

For a moment, Sylvain sat quiet, wondering if his curse was for Perriman or himself. She had intentionally stayed late in bed this morning, ringing for Betty, and offering up the excuse that she had started her time of the month as the reason she did not feel up to going downstairs for breakfast.

She squirmed now with guilt for the lie. And with even more guilt for having encouraged Betty to gossip.

Lifting his head from his hands, Terrance scowled at her, and Sylvain gripped one hand tighter with the other. He did not look happy at the news, and she had not expected him to. But, honestly, anyone seeing him just now might easily think him capable of any violence.

His black hair, cut short, stood up in spikes. Red rimmed his eyes, and the shadow of his beard darkened his jaw. With his disheveled state, he looked a dangerous enough rogue, and that angry glint in his tawny eyes even made her uneasy.

And she knew him well.

Which meant she must find some means to keep him from acting on that look in his eyes and getting himself into even deeper trouble.

"Is there more?" he asked, his words clipped.

"Just speculations as to why," she said, cautious with her words.

"And what is the top theory for that—other than utter stupidity?"

She hesitated, then said, "Are you certain you want to know?"

"I did not ask a rhetorical question—yes, I want to know."

"But if . . ."

"Sylvain!"

"Oh, very well, most seem to think it was so that Lady Dunscombe would then be free to marry you."

"What! Of all the utter nonsense!"

He gave a rude snort, and a tightness in Sylvain's chest loosened. "It is not that nonsensical—even I have heard the rumors linking your name with hers."

"You shouldn't listen to such gossip."

"I would hardly have any news for you today if I did not. Besides, I have met her, and she is rather pretty, in a rather overblown fashion."

"Overblown?"

"Yes, like a rose past its prime."

He grinned. "Jealous are you?"

"I am not. So many ladies' names have been linked with yours that I long ago stopped paying much attention to them. Now, as to the second theory, some think you must have simply been mad with drink. And, finally, a very few hold it had to be an accident."

"What sort of accident ends with a man shot in the back?"

"I am only repeating the rumors. And I will say that everyone does seem to agree that with Dunscombe having been the local justice, and him dead, that will make it an even greater tangle. And no one seems clear on whether or not Ashlin has actually laid charges against you."

Terrance rubbed the back of his neck, as if the muscles ached. Then he rubbed a hand over his jaw and glanced at his wrinkled clothes. "I need fresh clothes. And a shave."

She slanted a sideways look at him. "So you can go see him? We went though that, and you know you'll only end up locked in his cellar."

He glared at her. "What else am I to do? Hide myself away until he does act, or until everyone thinks I'm guilty?"

"What matters is if you have been charged. If you have not, Ashlin might be persuaded to reconsider taking such an action. And if you have, then any time with him is wasted, for it is the magistrate in Taunton whom you'll need to seek out."

Tapping his fingers on one leg, he seemed to consider the idea, and Sylvain held her breath.

Would this work?

She thought about how the plan had come to her last night, after the laudanum drops that she had put in his cider had taken effect. He had fallen asleep within a quarter hour.

As soon as he had, she had undone the buttons to his tight-fitting waistcoat and stripped the spotted neckcloth from his neck. He looked ridiculously young, asleep as he was, with the lines eased from his forehead, and his mouth relaxed. He had a beautiful mouth, curved and full—and it looked even better when not pulled into a grimace or a scowl. She had been unable to resist, and had smoothed a hand across his forehead.

Someone needed to look after him. Heavens knew he would not—he never did. And, if she left it to him, he would no doubt charge into this like a bull out to clear anyone from his pasture.

That was when she had decided that someone rational and calm needed to speak with Ashlin. Perhaps convince him how he might be liable for defaming Terrance's character if his accusations were not withdrawn.

The stumbling point had been how to approach Ashlin.

Then the plan formed all at once.

She leaned forward now, using Terrance's hesitation to give herself hope that he might agree with her. "You know, Father will have to go pay his condolences to the new Lord Dunscombe. I could easily go with him and speak to Ashlin, for I've known him since he was orphaned and came to live with his uncle."

One black eyebrow lifted with a sarcastic tilt. "So you'll go and talk of me, will you? That would earn you a fine welcome. And have you considered as well that one of the people you will be visiting must have shot Dunscombe?"

She frowned at him. "Nonsense. Almost anyone might have shot him."

He shook his head. "Only four people knew of that duel, and one of them is dead. We took care no one else should know of it—for pity's sake, it's not legal even!"

"Really? And Ashlin must have been one of the four, then? Is that how he happened across you?"

"Yes. I ended with him as my second—not that I had much choice, for he happened to be there when Dunscombe forced the argument. Cale was to second Dunscombe."

"Cale?"

"Lord Cale—no one you should know. In fact, Dunscombe's circle is not the sort you should know in the least! Gamblers and sportsmen, most of them—like himself. He despised those he could beat, and hated those who bested him, and while he was a bad sportsman, he was rich enough that he attracted all sorts of hangers-on."

"Then what were you doing in his circle?"

"I? Never you mind that!"

"Well, Father will still have to pay a call, and frankly, after all you have said, I would rather go with him than send him on his own. He would certainly be safer with my company."

Terrance scowled. He did not like this idea. And he had no reason for his dislike of it, other than it left his skin prickling to think of Sylvain anywhere near any of that lot.

Blazes, she was made for better than that riffraff.

Only he knew no way of talking her out of it. Nor was he in any position to be able to stop her from doing as she pleased. He was not her father, nor her guardian, nor even her brother—and he was rather thankful on all accounts.

Blast this damn leg of his!

If he was up and walking easily, this would not even be an issue.

She seemed to take his silence as agreement with her plan, for she stood, then smoothed her skirts.

"Honestly, Terrance, you know I am right. And besides, you need not worry. I was not certain I would take this with me, but with all you have said, I probably ought to."

"Take what?"

Stooping down, she reached under a cloth on the tray. When she straightened, a short-barreled pistol lay neatly in her palm.

Four

He reacted with instinct, reaching out to snatch the stubby-barrel pistol from her. Surprised by his abrupt movement, her hand jerked back, but he had already swept the weapon from her grip. Then he sat there, holding it and glaring at her.

She stared back, eyebrows raised, a touch of irritation in her eyes. "You need not worry. It is not even loaded."

"I should hope not—and don't you know better than to brandish a pistol about?"

Her mouth twisted, as if she thought his comment fatuous, and then she said, "Hardly brandishing. And I know enough to tell you that it is a muff pistol—my Aunt Emma sent it to Penelope for her to take to London, only Penelope would not. It's actually one of a pair, but I only need the one. And it has a safety latch on it, so that it cannot fire unless you shift the latch first."

He glanced down at the weapon. It did indeed have a latch that could be set to keep the trigger from being pulled—a useful enough feature if a lady were to carry this in a muff. Even with the stubby barrel, however, the pistol looked deadly enough to carve a wide hole in any target. Particularly in soft flesh.

Straightening, he cracked open the barrel, for he had seen the hinge and knew it must load from just in front of the striking pan rather than from the muzzle.

No ball. No powder. A clean bore down the barrel.

He glanced at her again.

Her chin had acquired a stubborn tilt. "There, you see. Un-loaded. But even without it, I should be far safer than ever you would be."

"Oh, I feel vastly reassured," he said, tone dry. "Have you ever actually fired this—or any other gun?"

Her chin lost some of its tilt, but her blue-green eyes still met his, her expression self-possessed as always. "Of course."

"I'll believe that when I see it." Slowly, he levered himself up to his feet, standing so that he kept his weight on his right leg. She frowned at him, but at least she knew better than to offer assistance, as if he were some gout-ridden ancient.

"I need a cane," he told her. And as her lips parted with the questions and protests he could already see forming in her eyes, he added, "Because, my dear Silly, before you go any-where, I am going to make utterly certain you do know how to shoot."

"This should do," Terrance said, stopping and leaning heavily on the cane that Sylvain had produced for him. The wind lifted the lapels of his brown riding coat and fluttered the spotted blue handkerchief he had pulled from his pocket and knotted around his neck in place of a neckcloth.

Sylvain had insisted that he was not well enough to walk—and he probably shouldn't be, for with each hob-bling step she saw how he grimaced. But he had sworn he would see firsthand if she could hit anything. And with his leg now splinted—his white neckcloth had served to wrap it tight, and she had brought him the two straight splints he had asked for from the woodpile—he seemed to think he could go anywhere.

He had tugged on his one good boot and what was left of his mangled one, the top clean cut away so that it did not flop. Looking at him, she thought she really would have to find him something else to wear. He looked rather too like a des-perate criminal just now.

He had been carrying his battered, muddy hat, and he gestured with it to the stone wall. "Here, put this on the top."

Lips pressed tight to keep back any further comment on his being out here—it would only set up his back more—she took his hat, strode to the wall, thunked down the hat, and strode back. Then she glanced at Harwood, measuring the distance to the house. She hoped it was far enough. Well, if the sound carried, at least it was shooting season, so a few shots should not warrant any great curiosity from her father and staff.

Then she looked at Terrance and asked, her tone kept casual, "Has anyone ever told you that you are mad?"

He grinned. "A hundred times. Now, let's see you load that toy of yours."

Toy, was it! Well, she might not possess any feminine skills, but she had a good aim with a bow and arrow, and a lethal one with a smooth, round stone in her hand. She would show him just what sort of toy she had! Of course, she had only fired this pistol once—and her father had loaded it for her. But she had watched him. And aiming anything was only a matter of judging distance and a steady hand.

Was it not?

Kneeling on the shaggy turf, she spread out the cloth that held pistol, powder flask, and a leather bag of lead ball shot. Thank heavens her father kept a well-stocked gun room.

They had gone to the east gardens, just beyond the hedge and stone wall that separated the expanse of green lawn from the main house. The gardens were actually more wild fields than tame lawn, with the vivid greens of grass and the dark hawthorn hedge blending together.

The wind whipped her skirt around her ankles, and she glanced up. Clouds banked thick overhead, piling into darkness. It was stupid for either of them to be out, actually, what with rain threatening. She glanced at Terrance—if only once he would listen to sensible advice. But she might as well wish for a treasure cave of riches for her family, and never to have to face the ordeal of a London Season for herself.

Things were what they were.

He stood with both hands grasping the cane. Twin white lines bracketed his lips, and a dull look glazed his eyes. Whatever would she do with him if he passed out?

Despite the lack of color in his face, he stood steady enough, balanced on the cane she had smuggled to him—the ebony one that her mother disliked, for she thought it too dark and grim. It quite suited Terrance.

And one good thing had come of this ill-judged idea—he now had proof just how much he needed rest, not rambling.

She turned back to her pistol—the sooner she had this over, the sooner he might be back inside and lying down.

It took a bit of a struggle to break open the pistol by its stiff hinge—and it annoyed her that Terrance had made it look so easy. Then she added shot and black powder as her father had done, closed the hinge, and stood. Had she put in enough powder? Or so much it would blow the barrel into shards? The aroma of sulfur clung to her hands, as did bits of charcoal. She turned to face the wall and clasped the pistol in both hands.

"You trying to choke the poor thing?"

She glanced at Terrance, then faced the wall again and pulled the trigger. Smoke and noise filled the air, and the ball ricocheted off the largest gray stone in a small puff. She had hit just left of the hat. A very near miss. She turned to Terrance, eyebrows arched with challenge—let him try to say that she could not hit anything now!

He glanced at her, one dark eyebrow cocked, his expression conceding nothing. "Load again."

She did, and when she straightened, he limped to her side. "Now hold it with one hand—it's a tiny thing, there's no need to throttle it. Turn to the side, and sight down the barrel. No, bend your arm a bit more—this ain't a bow you're pulling. That's too much. No, not that way. Oh, blast it . . ."

He had been gesturing with one hand, the cane in his other hand, as he confused her with his curt instructions. With a frustrated growl, he stepped behind her now, letting the cane drop to the ground and putting his arms around her.

As his right hand covered hers, she stiffened, her pulse skipping beats and her mouth drying. She had put on her blue riding coat against the cold of the day, but even through the thick wool, the heat of him washed over her. A scent—very masculine with a hint of cologne spice—came with the warmth, and even stronger was the wash of restless energy that emanated from him. It enveloped her like a heavy cloak.

He did not look at her, but she glanced up at him, her stare pulled by his nearness. He had bent down to put his face closer to hers so that he could sight down the barrel himself, and he seemed oblivious of her.

Every part of her screamed with awareness of him. Of his wide, muscular chest pressed against her back, of his long-fingered hand wrapped around hers, of his whiskers which scraped for a moment against her forehead when she turned and tried to concentrate on the pistol and the wall and his hat.

Her hands quivered, and she fought to focus her concentration—oh, why did he have to be so . . . so . . . so distracting! And why could she not keep her knees locked instead of softening, and her stomach from fluttering? And her head sensible? She ought to know better, for she knew him.

I will not become one of those weak-headed females who succumb to that too-potent charm of his! She repeated the vow again, as she had years ago. It really was the only way to deal with a rogue the likes of him.

"Steady your hand. Just let this arm hang down," Terrance said, then pushed down her empty left hand with his. "Loosely, my dear. Loosely. You want to absorb the kick of the gun, not brace against it," he said, and then he noticed how easily his fingers encircled her slender wrist.

Because he had hold of her, he felt the quiver go through her. He did not, however, mistake it for fear. He had too much experience with women for that. And suddenly his touch on her hand and on her wrist, his closeness to her, all took on a different meaning.

The swell of a soft hip brushed just below his hip, tempting with its curves. Her wrists and hands were still browned from summer, the skin kissed to a golden color. She had a fresh scent to her—or perhaps it was just the cold, crisp day? Or that she wore no perfume and so seemed more elementally female?

If he tugged a bit, she would fit nicely against him. A good height of a woman to hold—not so small that he had to stoop to kiss her, and not so large as to be cumbersome. An easy armful.

And what would she taste of?

Sweetness? Spice?

Then he remembered that he had kissed her once—or did his memory betray him? Ah, yes, now he remembered. Two years ago or so, when he had taken on a bet to kiss every female in the district. She had been one of the first to cross his path, and so he had kissed her—careless about it, a brush of his lips across hers.

She had tasted of peaches.

She had been eating one, he recalled. Sitting in a tree, and eating a peach and he had coaxed her down, telling her about his bet, and confessing that he was no doubt a fool to take on such a ridiculous wager.

And she had offered a shy smile, closed her eyes tight, and stood on tiptoes for him.

She had looked absurd. She had seemed such a child at the time.

And that all seemed a lifetime ago.

Half tempted to turn her about now to see if she still tasted of peaches, he glanced down at her, his blood heating as her hip brushed against him again.

His stare met eyes wide and huge with endless sea depths of blues and greens.

Blazes, but he really ought not take advantage of her in this fashion. But he would. He knew himself too well, and his own weakness for feminine charms.

He settled his arms closer about her. "Well, go ahead," he said, voice gruff. "Always aim to score a hit—no matter what the target."

She tensed under his hold, stiffening, hunching a shoulder, and he knew that she, too, must be aware of this sizzle of something between them. He grinned and leaned closer to her. Close enough to note the curve of her ear, close enough to smell the faintest aroma of soap on her skin, but still not close enough to satisfy.

Shrugging him off, she slipped away, took two steps, then turned to glare at him. "How can I hit anything with you holding me in that fashion? Really, Terrance—I am not one of your flirts!"

He straightened, a little disappointed, a touch relieved, and rather miffed by her assumption that she might be anything at all to him, particularly "one of his flirts." "And who said you were?"

"Your touch said quite enough, thank you!"

She glared at him, and he glared back. And then he grinned. "Oh, stubble it. I can't help it if you've become a damn attractive female."

Red flushed up her throat to flood her cheeks. "Well, I do not see why that must spoil our friendship."

Puzzled, he frowned. "Spoil? Why should it spoil anything?"

"Because it will—every female who has ever caught your interest soon loses it quick enough. Once you've done chasing her, and caught her. How often have I heard that story about you? Now, do you want that to happen between us? And for what—for a moment when you fancy me attractive!"

Scorn laced her tone and lashed into him.

For a moment, he wished he could pretend he did not understand. But he did. And she was right. Females—once they started clinging—very quickly lost his interest. Even the most attractive of them. Even the most seductive. Just as had the desirable Lady Dunscombe.

Whatever changed them, he had no idea. But change they did. And then his sentiments shifted as well. "It doesn't have to be that way?"

"Oh?"

"I have had a few passions that did not turn into obligations—and those ended very well, I'll have you know! Without the usual tears and demands and pouting sulks!"

He scowled at her, thinking of the hard jades who had been able to have such light affairs. Oh, hell! Why must women be such trouble! They all were—from his mother, who had left him and his brother—and whom his father had pretended had died—to every other woman he had known.

Except for Sylvain.

She had been a friend, really. An odd thing that, he realized, what with the differences between them. But she had always taken him for exactly what he was, with no fuss about it nor any attempt to mend his ways. And he knew with a flash of certainty that he did not want to lose such an uncomplicated relationship—he had too few of them in his life.

So what in blazes did he say to her?

He could think of nothing, so he continued to scowl.

Suddenly, she spun on her heel. Her hand jerked up and she squeezed off a shot. The ball hit the upper left corner of the hat, spinning it off the wall.

She looked over her shoulder at him, her stare defiant, her mouth set.

"A lucky shot," he muttered. But he couldn't suppress the smile that tugged at his mouth. Blazes, but with a few lessons she could be the best shot in the county. She had a good eye, and didn't flinch at the thunder of the pistol nor choke at the cloud of smoke left behind.

Her shoulders relaxed, and a smile lifted her mouth as well as she answered, "And when did you ever scorn luck being on your side?" She bent to gather up powder and shot.

Before she stood, she took up his cane, then she came to him. The color no longer rode high in her cheeks. "Do you have any more arguments as to why I cannot possibly look after myself?"

He took the cane, glad enough to have its support again. "I never argue with a woman who holds a pistol."

"You argue with everyone, Terrance."

"I do not!" he said, his expression harsh. But he could not maintain it, and soon grinned at her.

Shaking her head, Sylvain started for the house. Terrance fell into step with her, his stride pulled short and uneven by his limp.

At ease with him again—really, it must be a habit with him to start to flirt with any female in reach—she took his arm to help steady him. "Very well, you do not. And in such a case you will not argue if I now insist that you lie down again and stay down. For if you end in a ditch again today, I shall leave you there!"

"Heartless woman," he muttered, his tone filled with mock injury.

"Yes, I am," she agreed. And she only wished it were true, for it would make life far easier.

"Sylvain, my dear, a word if you please."

Holding herself still, Sylvain drew a breath as she counted to three and masked her feelings. She had learned the trick years ago, needing it any number of times over the years with Penelope, for heaven help anyone whom Ella decided needed cheering.

A pang of loss twisted inside her—she missed them so much. What she wouldn't give now for Ella's managing ways—and her advice. Or even for Cecila to confide in—though she would make it into a melodrama for certain.

But she had neither sister just now.

And she did have secrets to keep.

So she turned and pretended she had not been about to slip into the east wing to look in on Terrance before she went in to dinner. Only what would she say if Father asked?

She took another breath and hoped the poor light would hide any guilt that might color her cheeks or the tightness in her chest that might be mirrored on her face.

"Yes, sir?" Oh, that sounded weak, with her voice squeaking.

However, instead of any questions for her, he smiled and took her hand. "My dear—ah, but your hands are cold. Come with me to a fire."

Tucking her hand into the crook of his arm, he led her across the hall toward the library. She resisted glancing back over her shoulder at the door to the east wing.

Terrance would be fine. He must be. But was he staying off his leg, as she advised, or had he grown restless and started pacing? Or even wandering the house?

Well, she would have to hope he slept still. After their shooting practice, he had looked fatigued enough. Still, she had taken him some of her father's old sporting magazines for his amusement, and she had left him Trace—who had come home earlier this morning, tongue lolling, looking well pleased with his adventures, and ready to sleep off whatever excesses had kept him away.

Two of a kind, she thought, her mouth twisting. She had lectured Trace about his not disappearing again during fox hunting season—not that he paid any more heed to her than did Terrance. But the lecture had vented some of her frustration—both with Trace and Terrance.

Only still she worried.

Gracious, had a servant perhaps caught a glimpse of Terrance and mentioned it to her father? But if so, why no immediate word of it from him?

Forehead tight, she glanced at her father. Just why did he want a word with her? He never did, really. He was not the sort to have a word with anyone unless he absolutely had to, so this must be something unpleasant.

Trying not to betray her tumbling thoughts, she stepped into the library as her father held the door for her. Then she shivered. They never could heat the room well.

She glanced at the windows, but the velvet drapes were already drawn. Still, the cold seemed to seep through the stone walls. She knew it must have been even colder in the days when this had been part of the medieval hall, before the stairs and main entrance had been added.

The room still held Gothic touches in its huge hearth and tall ceiling. Oak paneling and shelving now covered the ancient stone walls. Velvet drapes of a deep burgundy swept from floor to ceiling on the deep-set windows that lined one side of the room, shutting out the cold and gathering dusk.

The bookshelves now held an odd assortment of magazines, bits of unmatched china—such as the trio of hideous porcelain Chinese lions—and only the occasional book remained as a reminder of the room's former use.

But four thick volumes—their ancient leather bindings blackened with age—did have places of honor at the front of the room, just left of the fireplace. Plain-bound, with holes punched into the spines for where they had once been chained in an ancient monastic library, they did not look valuable. Sylvain knew better. Those books—and a dozen or so more others—had been a treasure found in the house by her sisters. A much-needed treasure.

Her father was doing his best to keep these last four. They were all that was left of what had once been an astounding library built by one of the earliest Harwoods. The rest had been sold at auction to provide funds that might be invested and the interest used to restore the estate. Assuming, of course, that Father did not spend everything on breeding race horses.

But he could not possibly want a word with her about books or investments or anything like that. Perhaps it was something yet to do with the saddle and bridle and horse she had brought home?

A fire crackled, warm and bright in the huge ancient hearth, and beeswax candles gave the room a mellow glow—luxuries they had once been unable to afford. She took no comfort from them. Her hands remained cold. And stiff. She hated these sorts of talks as much as her father did.

Seating herself in the wine-brocade-covered chair a little ways from the fire, she tried to keep her expression empty. Her father remained standing, rocking forward and back on his black shoes. He had changed into evening clothes—black breeches and blue coat, a tidy gold brocade waistcoat and clean cravat—for dinner. He looked uncomfortable, and braced to bring up a disagreeable topic.

Well, if I must, I shall tell him the truth. He will not throw Terrance out.

"And have you been finding mischief to keep yourself amused?" Mr. Harwood asked.

Sylvain's eyes widened. She said nothing. Folding her hands tight in her lap, she sat still.

Mr. Harwood took a breath and dove deeper into a subject he knew would be tricky. However, he had promised Matilda he would speak to their daughter. He could not leave such a task to her, not when the doctors had warned against any strain to her heart.

So he smiled at his youngest, and searched for some sign that this would not prove as difficult as he feared. She sat very straight in her chair. Too straight.

She had on a pretty gown, something in pale green with darker flowery bits on it, which went well with her eyes, he thought. She looked lovely. Not as pretty as Cecila, of course, nor as striking as Penelope, who had such a dramatic height and dark coloring. But he had always had a special fondness for his youngest. She had been such a tiny baby, born early. So quiet, even as a child. Always amusing herself. So little, and so little trouble. Even her rambling about the woods, and bringing home the odd stray animal to tend, had never caused much fuss, other than the objections Penelope had always put forward.

Still, he had to speak to her now on about issue that he knew would not draw smiles from her. But he had hope that she would come around to it.

Yes, of course she would. How could she not?

"My dear—" he began again, then broke off as he realized he did not know what to say next. He cleared his voice, brought his hands from behind his back, and tucked his thumbs into his waistcoat pockets.

"With your sisters now living in London, you must be bored and looking for trouble to get into," he said, then smiled at his own small jest.

If anything, Sylvain's face paled until he could almost count her freckles. Her short red-gold curls glinted in the firelight as she shifted in her seat, and then she said, her tone as stiff as her back looked, "Not at all, Father."

He frowned. No, she would not be bored. His Sylvain loved the woods and the animals and Harwood. And he did not want to do this any more than she. He hated giving her up. She was his youngest, and he could almost wish she would be forever his baby. But he could not stop time—nor even slow its pace. And he must think of her future now.

Ah, he was not doing this well at all.

He glanced at her again, taking in her slim figure, her straight nose and pointed chin, and those large almond-shaped eyes. She reminded him so much of her mother.

With a sigh, he folded his hands behind his back again. Best get this over and done. She would not care for it, but she was a good girl. Always had been. She would see the wisdom, and would soon be happy about it. Of course, she would. How could a young lady such as she not be happy about such a thing?

Only he still had the gravest doubts. Sylvain really was not like other young ladies. His fault that—he ought to have been able to provide better for his daughters. Well, he could now, and he would! He forced a smile. His Sylvain deserved this treat. And she would indeed soon think it one. He would make certain of that. So he let the words tumble out.

"My dear, what do you think of going to London? To stay with your sisters?"

Five

Sylvain blinked with surprise. Then relief eased into her and she almost slumped against the cushions. All this fuss over a visit? What nonsense. And why should he be so uneasy about broaching such an idea to her? Then she frowned.

"Do you mean go to London now?" she asked.

"Well, not this utter moment. But what do you think, eh? You would like it, would you not? I mean, you do miss your sisters, after all. And what young lady does not want a bit of fun? You shall have all those shops to browse, and Penelope will enjoy taking you about and seeing that you meet all sorts of young gentlemen."

"So am I to go for her sake then?" she asked, a little amused.

"No, my dear. No, no. Though she and Cecila have each written to ask about your visiting—Cecila does so want to see you done up in the latest fashions. And, I daresay you might like to buy a few presents while you are there—your mother would be delighted if you were to send her a pretty shawl, or perhaps some of the latest novels. Cecila will send only those that that husband of hers publishes, not that Mother complains, mind, but she does get a bit tired of only poetry."

"So do I, but it is kind of Cecila to think of us," she said, the words an echo of what her mother had said. But, honestly, how could she deal with this when she had Terrance hidden in the house and with him facing a possible accusation of murder. So she said, certain that agreement would at least put this distraction to rest, "It sounds a delight, Father."

He stared at her. "Really? You would not mind? Of course, your mother and I have discussed it, and we both agree that it would be good for you to have some time in town before you are presented at court this spring."

Presented? An image of herself done up in some ghastly white gown and standing before the Queen rose in her mind—and she could just picture herself stepping on the hem of her gown as she curtsied, and then tripping and knocking into someone or something. She never did the right things, even at a country assembly. She forgot dance steps, for she never took time to learn them. And she was always the one who spilled the punch on herself. By ten of an evening she usually longed for home and her bed, for she liked best to be up with the dawn in the quiet of the day.

She swept those images from her mind. They had nothing to do with the moment, really. Instead, she simply smiled at her father and said, "Should we not go into dinner now? We ought not to keep Mother waiting."

He looked relieved—a sentiment she could echo—and as they strolled from the library, her mind shifted to the truly important topics. Such as how to make certain he took her tomorrow to Dunscombe Abbey.

By half past nine the next morning, Sylvain had washed, dressed, and waited only for the carriage to be brought round. It had proven ridiculously easy to arrange matters. Her mother had been the one to put forward the topic for her.

With her weak heart, Mrs. Harwood could no longer climb stairs, nor exert herself, but although her world was limited, she still managed to hear all the news. Over dinner, the three of them informally seated at the round rosewood table, she had asked about the news that had reached her that poor Lord Dunscombe had been shot to death.

Mr. Harwood had shifted in his chair, then glanced around at his wife's rooms. "Do you know, I think now that we take our meals here all the time, we ought to redo the room next to this to be a better dining room. What do you think, my dear? We might even put in a new hall to the kitchen so that the dishes might arrive a trifle warmer."

Moss green eyes bright, her cheeks pink, Mrs. Harwood regarded her husband. "For heaven's sake, Mr. Harwood, I am not like to have a seizure over a discussion of Lord Dunscombe's fate. And a new dining room would be lovely, but you must tell me now what exactly happened to the poor man."

Cautiously watching his wife for any adverse reaction, Mr. Harwood had given what details he knew. They were only the same ones Sylvain had heard.

Mrs. Harwood had not seemed the least upset at the news. Shaking her head, the ribbons to her lace cap moving softly as she did, she said, "Such a pity. And such absurdity to think that Terrance Winslow had anything to do with it. He may be quite wild, but he always had the strongest sense of fair play, even as a boy. Do you call on Lady Dunscombe tomorrow, dear? It would be kind of you."

From there, Sylvain had no difficulty in suggesting she might accompany her father on the visit, and he actually looked pleased that he would have her company.

"Mother always knows what to say in these circumstances, but they always seemed devilishly awkward to me," he later confessed to her.

She could understand why he might feel that way, for it was bound to be an awkward visit under the circumstances. However, she had a task to accomplish—she had to speak with Ashlin Perriman.

Glancing in the hall mirror now, she straightened her bonnet again, wondering if she ought to retie the ribbons more loosely. No matter how she put on any hat, they always gave her the headache. But she could not go calling on neighbors without one. Nor without proper gloves. She had chosen gray kid to match the velvet bonnet. They did not go with her

brown cloak, but they did match the black velvet muff she
carried.

The heavy weight from the pistol tucked in the satin pocket
sewn into the small muff made her think of Terrance. She
glanced toward the back of the hall, to the doorway that led
to the east wing, her lower lip caught between her teeth.
Should she just pop in for a quick word with him, to let him
know she had everything in hand?

But she had already been to see him. Both after dinner and
this morning.

Last night she had found him restless and irritable. So she
had found a deck of cards, and brought him a glass of brandy
from her father's study, and had stolen him some of the beef
from dinner, the aroma of which had pulled Trace out from
his hiding spot behind the window curtains. Then, by the light
of a single candle, they had played *vingt-et-un* and Macao and
talked about anything other than Dunscombe.

Terrance had laughed when she mentioned that she might
visit her sisters in London, saying with a grin, "You would be
as out of place as Trace here would be." And though she
agreed, she also found herself a touch affronted that he would
laugh at the notion of her in London.

By midnight, the candle had burnt to its socket, and she
had risen to go.

He had taken her hand before she left, his eyes the color of
the brandy left in his glass and his face shadowed in the flickering light. "There's not many as would do this for me."

Cheeks warm, she had intentionally misunderstood him.
"What—play cards with you most of the night? I should think
most any of your friends do that."

His mouth quirked. "You'll probably end up wishing you'd
left me in that ditch, but I'm glad you didn't. I'd be a sight
more glad, however, if you could find me something to wear
that's not this same shirt and breeches."

She had smiled then and relaxed. His other mood had been
something new to her, but this Terrance she knew very well.

So, this morning, before the rest of the house had woken, she had slipped into the old wing, carrying a pitcher of water and a pile of black clothing pulled from the servants' livery that had lain neglected and unused upstairs. She had taken a stiff white shirt, two cravats, a waistcoat, and the largest black jacket and breeches she could find. After all, if her father ever got around to replacing some of the staff, he would also need to buy new livery for them.

When she entered the unused study, she had found Terrance still asleep, the brown woolen blanket she had given him tossed aside, as if he slept restlessly. He lay sprawled on the daybed, his shirt rumpled and open at the neck, his torn breeches creased, his face darkened with a day's growth of beard.

Moving quietly, she had set down the pitcher and clothes, then pulled the blanket over him again. She had resisted touching a hand to his face. He did not look feverish. Instead, with his features relaxed by sleep, he looked devastatingly handsome.

The lines around his mouth and on his forehead had eased, taking years away, so that he looked ridiculously young and impossibly innocent. He stirred as she covered him, and under his shirt she noted the strong muscles, the chords to his neck.

And how his lips curved with a dream.

Something tightened in her throat. She wanted to smooth her fingers through his black hair, to touch her hand to his cheek, to just lean close.

Straightening, she had told herself not to be such a ninny. He might look a dark angel now, but awake he had far more to do with the devil.

The click of her father's boots on the floor and his voice pulled her back to the present.

"My, don't you look a treat," he said as he came to her, hat in hand, and with a greatcoat over his shoulders. Then he opened the front door for her.

Nervous now, she tucked her hands into the muff, and her fingers brushed the grip of her pistol. Gracious, was this a wise thing to do? But someone had to talk to Ashlin, after all. And she would just have to hope that he listened.

Terrance lay on the day-bed, his leg aching, one arm thrown over his eyes, and the vaguest memory of a dream clinging. The details had slipped away, but the feelings from it remained—pleasant feelings. Of being safe. Of being loved.

Blazes, what rubbish!

Scrubbing a hand over his face, he pushed away the last tendrils of illusion. Soft emotions such as these had about as much substance as dreams. They were the stuff of novels and girlish fantasy. And his body let him know the truth of the moment: he needed a piss, coffee, and to get into clothes that did not smell of stale sweat and dirt.

Slowly, he eased himself up. His leg hurt less than it had yesterday—meaning that today he only had to grit his teeth, and that he was only half-stiff. Still, he would take any progress he could.

Then he saw the neat pile of clothes and the blue-patterned pitcher beside them.

He grinned.

So that's where his dreams had come from.

Pushing himself off the day-bed, he hobbled to the window. Sylvain had brought him a chamber pot yesterday, but he'd just as soon water the garden as have a pot to empty.

The windows he had discovered yesterday opened with only a bit of muscle put into it, and looked out onto a half-wild garden, well screened with a bramble of wild roses and shaggy hedges. A sharp breeze swept in as he lifted the window sash, but the cold slap of it swept away the last bits of sleepiness.

A moment later, fully awake—and feeling it in every

muscle—he closed the window again, then hobbled back to the pitcher and the clothes.

He found a sponge in the pitcher, so he stripped and washed, working quick, for the chill did not encourage lingering. His old shirt served well enough to dry himself. Rubbing a hand over his face, he decided his beard would have to wait one more day. Then he turned to the clothes Sylvain had left. The quality of them—rough cotton and wool—left him half ready to throw them aside. Only then he glanced at the door. What in blazes would he do if Sylvain were to slip into the room just now, with him stripped bare?

He grinned. He'd give much to see her reaction, but at least she would not be likely to shriek and run.

A snuffling sound drew his attention and he found Sylvain's three-legged fox nosing the basket that had been sent over by Mrs. Brown. Searching for crumbs, like a sensible beast. Terrance's stomach rumbled as well. It seemed a long time since last night's beef.

"I suppose we'll have to make do with what's to hand," he told the fox.

The animal crouched low as he spoke, its dark eyes cautious and its nose twitching. He could remember offering to shoot the poor beast when Sylvain had come to him to help her free it from a steel trap. Instead, she had insisted that he sever the mangled leg and had told him she would see to the rest.

He had not thought the poor thing would live. Blood and dirt had matted its coat. Shock had glazed its eyes. No telling how long it had lain there, gnawing on its own limb in an attempt to free itself. But the animal had never once snapped at Sylvain, and once freed, went limp in the blanket that she wrapped around it, as she cooed soft words to it and held it close.

She had a touch about her. A way with mending creatures. He had lost count of all the animals he had seen in her care over the years. Well, he would have to hope that touch might work with his leg as well. He didn't have as many to spare as did her fox.

Glancing again at the clothes, Terrance began to dress.

He never wore drawers, or an undershirt. But his shirts were of fine lawn, not this coarse cotton, and he could wish he had something between him and these garments. They fit, but he liked his jackets cut so close that they formed a second skin—not tight in the shoulders and loose at the waist. And he usually wore buckskins or wool knit pantaloons, not old-fashioned breeches so loose that they stayed up only because of the braces attached to the waistband.

But they were clean, so they would do.

So would his leg, he decided, testing it gingerly.

Sylvain had not brought him stockings or shoes, so he used his own. He cut the top off his one good boot, so that it matched the other, making what looked like a ragged pair of shoes. A pity that, for he liked these boots. Then he wrapped his broken leg tight with a cravat to give it support and pulled up his long white stocking over the top.

Staring down at it, he thought he looked like a gout-ridden old man, what with his leg wrapped and bulky under the stocking. He grinned—with that, these ill-fit clothes and his stubble, he almost had himself a decent disguise, for he doubted any friend of his would recognize him—or at least want to acknowledge that they knew him.

He took a few steps—wincing as he did—but managed to walk. Damned if he would stay another hour cooped up in this room.

Rather than go through the house, he went back to the window and opened it. It was only a long step down to the garden, and if he went around the back of the house, he might easily come up to the stables as if he had crossed the pasture, rather than as if he had come from the house.

The only trick would be to see if he might then borrow a horse and some sort of carriage, for he was not fit to ride just yet.

Sliding open the window, he stepped out. Then he glanced back into the room.

"Well, are you coming?" he asked, feeling foolish to be talking to a fox.

Seated on its haunches, the animal stared at him, its eyes glimmering with whatever calculations foxes made. The animal glanced at the empty basket once more, then rose up and padded across the bare floor, head bobbing. For only having three legs—two in back, and one in front—it moved with more speed and ease than Terrance would have ever credited.

It popped over the windowsill, then streaked for the hedge, head bobbing, obviously out to hunt its own breakfast.

Terrance watched the glimmer of red disappear into the greenery. Then he turned, on the hunt to make do for himself.

Dunscombe Abbey looked nothing like a monastic retreat, Sylvain decided. The ruins of the original abbey could be seen from the graveled drive, off to the right, nestled in a well-tended parkland. Stone windows shaped like praying hands edged the roofless structure, and other gray stones lay tumbled in the grass. The ruin looked a suitable place for rest and contemplation.

The main house, however, looked more like an overgrown hunting lodge. The half-timbered Elizabethan structure rambled into a peaked roof, and stones from the abbey had been used to add a wing to one side, leaving the structure unbalanced.

With its small windows and sagging timbers, it did not look a happy house. But perhaps her opinion of its owners colored her view of the house, Sylvain decided.

The carriage that stood in the drive, however, could be viewed as nothing but luxurious.

Four gleaming chestnuts stood in black harness, each horse matched with the same white blaze on its face, and the same ankle-high white socks. Two purple-and-gold-liveried grooms

stood beside the leaders. Behind the team, a closed carriage
waited, doors open on one side. Painted in purple and picked
out in black, with its high wheels and well-sprung body, it
looked done up in the height of style, and left Sylvain aware
of her father's coach with its old-fashioned body and its faded
brown paint, a pair attached, and no footman.

But who was arriving—or leaving?

The drive was wide enough that the Harwood carriage
could be halted next to the other, and then Sylvain's father
stepped out ahead of her and turned to hand her down.

There was no crest on the door of the carriage, so Sylvain
leaned toward her father. "Whose do you think it is?"

As she asked, a lady swept from the house, the skirt of her
tan traveling dress billowing, her dark brown jacket tight and
short, cut like a man's jacket, but fit to display a lush figure.
Her hat, set at a rakish angle and lavishly trimmed with white
feathers, curved around her face, obscuring her features but
it was tilted enough to reveal a glimpse of deep gold curls.

A tall, fashionably dressed gentleman followed her from
the house, a black cloak thrown over a dark green coat and
black trousers. He carried his hat in his hand, and his high
shirt points and starched cravat left him carrying his head
high and proud. The sun glinted from his bright, straight
blond hair. He had a slight build and stood only as tall as the
lady. However, he carried himself with masculine arrogance.

The lady half turned to speak to him; her voice carrying an
impatient edge to it. "I don't care. With Cale gone, there is no
one amusing here anymore. Let Ashlin manage the rest!"

Frowning, the gentleman caught the lady's arm as she
started to turn, stopping her on the top step and pulling her
close as he spoke to her, his voice only a low rumble.

The feathers on her hat quivered as she answered. "I told
you—I don't care what anyone whispers! I won't be buried
here another minute!"

The man's voice rose. "Bad choice of words, sister."

Her head jerked, but the lady spun on her heel, skirt

swirling as she pulled away from the man. As she turned, her stare locked with Sylvain's.

No one could fail to recognize that face—a flawless oval, red pouting lips, dark brown eyes framed by thick, inky lashes and arched sable brows that rose against a complexion of pure cream. For a moment, Lady Dunscombe froze, a bright flush staining her cheek and a flash of something in her eyes.

Annoyed to be overheard, Sylvain wondered, her own face warm at having to witness such a scene? Or honestly embarrassed?

The emotion vanished before Sylvain could decide, and Lady Dunscombe came toward them, her steps light and her hands outstretched. "Mr. Harwood—How kind of you to call. And is this little Sylvain all grown-up?"

Six

Ellena watched the girl stiffen. *I've said the wrong thing.* But what else could she do? Tell them the truth—that she was in a panic to leave? That would go well. Instead, she widened her smile and caught the girl's hands. The girl drew back as if shocked or unwilling for such familiarity, but Ellena ignored that. She would smooth things over—she would smile and be kind, and then she and Edwin could leave this wretched place.

"My dear, you have grown so much since I last saw you. Mr. Harwood, what do you do to produce such lovely girls? I vow you and your wife have a secret to it—and have certainly perfected it by now. You must be so pleased with them—two married now, I understand, is it not? What a delight and comfort they must all be to you."

She knew herself to be chattering, but if she did not, she might give in to the scream lodged in her chest and she could not do that. Lady Dunscombe never screams. And never frowns. And never makes a scene. Myles had taught her that within a year of their marriage.

But if she did not soon get away from this house she would do all those things.

Instead, she smiled tighter.

Edwin's boots scuffed on the stone steps behind her. That steadied her. She had Edwin. Yes, they had each other still. They had always had each other. Two orphans who had done well for themselves. Or at least she had done well enough to help Edwin along. And she would lean on him to get her through this, as she had with so much else.

She let go Miss Harwood's hands, but then hers tightened again on nothing but the thin kid of her gloves. *Oh, but, what had Terrance done—oh, the fool! Why had he left her in such a fix?*

She realized that Mr. Harwood had tipped his hat and said something—some polite nothing, she hoped. Only now he looked expectantly at her. His daughter stared at her as well, with an unnerving gaze, her eyebrows almost flat lines, and the most unflattering bonnet on her head.

Pulling herself together, Ellena did what she knew how to do—all she knew how to do, really. She performed the social niceties; she made introductions. "Mr. Harwood, my brother, Mr. Edwin Hayland. And this is Miss Harwood."

Edwin stepped forward, taking his hat off to Miss Harwood, then taking Mr. Harwood's hand. Ellena watched, nerves tight and her skin prickling with the desire to be gone.

She could be proud of her brother at least—there was little enough else in her past to bear. Two years younger than she, he had just turned twenty-eight, but he might be taken for thirty-five, and not just because of the gray that had lightened his hair to nearly silver, for he had a quiet manner, and a serious expression that gave nothing away.

There were times she wanted to pummel him because of that. Because he would stare at her, his slate eyes unreadable, his face as handsome—and as cold—as any Greek statue. Yes, that was him. A statue. Handsome, but hard. She never knew if he pitied her, or just put up with her because she was the one who had married money.

She would rather the latter. She did not want any man's pity. Not even her brother's. She had known what Dunscombe was—or most of it—before she had married him. Now he was gone. And she would not regret any of it. But, oh, she wanted this part of it done. She wanted gaiety, laughter— life again. Where had Terrance gone?

The panic bubbled, so she smiled more, and then the smile cracked as Mr. Harwood turned to her. "We were so sorry to hear of your loss, Lady Dunscombe. It must have been such a shock."

"Shock? Oh, yes. Dreadfully so." The words came out as if rehearsed, and she knew they must sound so, for Mr. Harwood frowned at her lack of feeling, and his daughter stared at her, and now she felt the weight of Edwin's warning.

He had not wanted them to leave today, but she could not stand with any more of Ashlin's ridiculous posturing. Nor the emptiness of the house. Every time she heard a door slam, or a window rattle, she jumped. She had the most absurd feeling it was Myles returning. But he was dead. Everyone said so.

Only she wished she had seen the body. She ought to have insisted on that, but they had taken him to the chapel for burial. And instead of looking at him, she had manufactured a credible faint when they told her the news, and she had been taken to her room. Then she had buried her face in her pillow so they would not hear her laughter.

Myles dead. Only where was Terrance now that they could be together? He could not have meant those things he had said to her—could he?

The tightness rose in her chest, nearly choking her. She needed London. Needed creatures such as Cale who would tell her again and again of her beauty, and declare their devotion. It would not mend what Terrance had done to her heart, but it might make her forget him. Just a little.

Edwin was saying something, smoothing things over, muttering about accidents. She heard mention of Terrance's name and her interest sharpened.

"Terrance didn't shoot Myles—he could not have. Why, he had left the abbey the day before, right after . . . right after dinner."

Again, everyone stared at her, and she knew her too-quick tongue had blundered. Ashlin could be blamed for that—oh, she could not bear his rantings another day.

Edwin smoothed the moment, his voice calm. "No one here has accused Mr. Winslow of anything, Lena. That, I hope, will be left to the magistrates."

"Do you know when the inquest will be?" Mr. Harwood asked.

Before Edwin could answer, she put her hand on his arm. "Dearest, we simply cannot keep the horses standing in this cold."

He glanced at her, face passive, but a muscle twitched at the back of his cheek. She had no idea what that meant. She shivered and drew up the collar of her coat. Then she turned to the Harwoods, giving Mr. Harwood the brilliant smile that always melted any man. "You must forgive us for running away in this hectic fashion. I do so regret not having more time. And thank you so much for your kindness."

His cheeks reddened as she offered her hand, and he swept her a gallant bow.

She started for the carriage, then stopped next to Miss Harwood. Such an innocent. Not a pretty girl, with her height and that uncompromising stare. Had she ever been so wide-eyed as this?

Voice soft, the girl said, "Thank you for thinking Mr. Winslow innocent."

Ellena drew back. For a moment, she stared harder at her. Then she smiled and answered, her own voice pitched just for the two of them. "Oh, he's no innocent, my dear. But he would have waited for the duel to start before he shot Myles."

She started to turn away, but paused, uncertain where the impulse rose from, but curious now about this girl. "My dear, if you ever come to London, you must call. We'll be staying at the Pultney—won't that be charming? I've never stayed at a hotel before, but dear Edwin swears it is utterly respectable, and I couldn't bear to stay at Duns—"

She broke off. She was saying too much again. And Edwin looked ready to leave.

With another forced smile and a nod to Mr. Harwood, she

let Edwin guide her to the carriage. He stopped to say something to Miss Harwood, and a sudden pang of jealousy shot through Ellena. She would never be so young again.

Why had she made that comment about Terrance? What was he to her anyway?

Leaning back against the deep leather cushions, she turned her face away from Miss Harwood and Dunscombe Abbey. She had her money—she had made certain that Myles would leave her well settled. She needed nothing from any man now.

Still, her hands twisted the strings to her reticule. As the carriage rocked with Edwin's weight, she turned and glanced at him. He had taken off his hat and sat opposite her, his back to the horses. The footman shut the door.

"We look guilty running away like this," he said, his voice rough.

She thought she heard censure, but with him it could as easily be a distaste for such hurried decisions. He always had to calculate everything. She lifted her chin. "You mean *I* look guilty."

For an answer, he only stared at her, his face unreadable as always.

Frowning, Sylvain watched the carriage start forward, the chestnuts high-stepping away in a brisk trot.

Mr. Harwood voiced her sentiments. "My—an odd visit to be sure."

She tilted her head. Odd, but revealing. Lady Dunscombe had known of the duel—had someone told her after, as part of the explanation for her husband's death? And Mr. Hayland—she had watched him listening to what his sister said. He had not shown any surprise. But then he had revealed little of his feelings—unlike his sister.

She was infatuated with Terrance—Sylvain knew it. She knew it from the way the woman had said his name, from the words that had staked possession of an intimate knowledge of him.

He is no innocent.

Sylvain scowled.

She still found it difficult to think well of any lady who had so little regard for the sacred vows given in marriage—a lady's word ought to bind her every bit as much as did a gentleman. And yet there had been something desperate in Lady Dunscombe's eyes. Something that almost left Sylvain wondering if Lord Dunscombe had given his wife good reason to look elsewhere to meet her needs.

"Shall we go in now?" her father asked.

Sylvain turned and started up the shallow stone steps to the front door. Would Ashlin also be packing? Why were those connected to Lord Dunscombe so eager to leave before he could be buried or mourned?

She remembered meeting him—briefly at a hunt meet, and once at the local fair. A large man, with bright, quick eyes and big hands, and expensive, well-made clothes. She did not remember much else of him, other than a loud voice and a booming laugh. And that he smelled of the stables, and of tobacco.

The footman held the front door for them. Black crepe had been tied to the knocker and wrapped around the servant's upper arm, denoting the house's official mourning status.

While the servant took their hats and gloves, Sylvain kept her muff, with the excuse of having cold hands. She wished she had thought to put the pistol elsewhere, for it seemed absurd to carry it now with so many gone from the house. But there was still Ashlin here to see—only she could not imagine him shooting his uncle. Let alone him shooting the man, then leaving, waiting for Terrance to arrive, and coming back so that Terrance could be blamed. That seemed far too complicated—and far beyond the Ashlin she knew.

The footman led them to a paneled drawing room, lit by candles and a fire, both of which were needed, for only faint sunlight fell in through the mullioned windows that over-looked a south lawn.

Standing before the fire, Mr. Harwood folded his hands be-hind his back. Sylvain seated herself near a window and glanced around the room, though she kept thinking of Lady Dunscombe.

The room looked nothing like her ladyship.

Hunting prints hunt on the walls, along with a stuffed deer head and what looked like an elk. A pair of sabers with red tasseled hilts hung over the fireplace. She had seen no feminine touches in the hall, either, with its suits of armor and displays of halberds, pikes, broadswords, axes, and other ancient weapons. Had Lady Dunscombe not cared to make an influence in her husband's life, or had she been unable to?

Sylvain thought again of that booming voice and those bright eyes, and she shifted in her seat. How difficult might that have been to live with every day? Even so, that did not quite excuse the lady's utterly abandoning her final duties to her husband. Why had she left so quickly?

A drawling voice, touched with the faintest lisp, drew her attention. "Mr. Harwood, how good of you to come. And Miss Harwood."

Rising, she made her curtsy, and while her father strode forward, offering his hand, she had the chance to study Ashlin Perriman and to see if her memories of him from a year ago still matched.

He looked as if he had dressed to spite his uncle. Instead of breeches, or even pantaloons, he wore trousers that bagged around his hips and ankles, and black shoes. Cecila had written her of the fashion—Russian trousers, they were called. They were of a pale lemon and matched the lemon vertical stripes on his waistcoat. His coat was of deep purple, tight fit at the waist, buttoning there above his waistcoat, and puffed at the shoulders as if to make them seem larger. Instead of a cravat, he wore what looked a gold silk scarf loosely knotted.

With his narrow face and thin body, he could not be called

a handsome man—his eyes were too pale a blue and too close-set, the jaw too long. But he had thick golden hair that curled in lush waves.

The only scrap of mourning about him was the band of black crepe about his arm.

She had felt sorry for him when she had first met him. He had been twelve and it had been the summer before he was to go to Winchester. His parents had died in a boating accident, and so Ashlin had come to live with his uncle, now his guardian. Her pity had not lasted. He had done nothing but complain about everything.

Then she had seen him at Squire Winslow's hunt meet— and had watched his uncle belittle everything about him. Ashlin could not mount properly, nor hold the reins well, nor sit correct. Every criticism came with a joke made at Ashlin's expense—and she had watched him shrink and fumble even worse. Others laughed. And as Ashlin cringed, it became worse.

Thereafter, she had tried to be friendly to him.

But Ashlin made it difficult, for it wore dreadfully to listen to the complaints, which only became larger over the years.

He came forward now, a small smile in place, as if he wanted to appear happy to see them, yet not so happy as would be out of place given the circumstances.

"My boy, so sorry to hear the news," Mr. Harwood said.

Ashlin gave a deep sigh. "Yes, it has been almost un-bearable—and the weight of responsibility that now bears on me . . . I do not know how I shall endure. But, pray sit down. I have ordered tea, or would you take some wine, Mr. Harwood?"

"Oh, we shall not stay so long as that, sir."

Ashlin's thin lips curved into a smile. "But I insist. The least I may do is offer you some hospitality. Do, pray, sit near the fire. This house is nothing but drafts." He waved a hand. "I suppose I shall have to bear the expense of having it all done over, now that I am come into the title and its duties—

the seat of the Baron of Dunscombe ought to command some respect, do you not think?"

Mr. Harwood's eyebrows rose as if he did not know what to think, or say, and so Sylvain changed the topic. "My mother sent you her regards, though she is not well enough to visit. She was saying just last night what a shock it was— and how she cannot believe that Terrance Winslow is at all involved."

Ashlin's eyebrows rose. "Not—oh, but he is. I swear, in fact, that I'll not feel safe until that man is in Newgate. He is a dangerous fellow!"

"Really, sir, those seem strong words," Mr. Harwood said.

"Strong?" Ashlin pulled out a handkerchief, pressed it to his lips, then took it away. "Strong is what I had to be when I found Mr. Winslow standing over my uncle, the pistol still in his hand!"

Ignoring his theatrical tone, Sylvain leaned forward in her chair. "So you admit that you did not see him shoot Lord Dunscombe."

Both men turned to stare at her. Cheeks warm, she knew she had put herself forward more than she ought, but she kept her gaze on Ashlin. There was too much at stake not to press him. "Did you check to see if your uncle's body was still warm?"

He drew back, looking appalled. "Warm? I did not stay for anything. I had to ride for my life, what with that madman threatening to kill me."

"But if the pistol had already been fired, then Terrance could not have shot you with it for it would have been empty."

Ashlin blinked at her logic and said nothing. But his mouth tightened as if he was irritated.

Mr. Harwood cleared his voice, then leaned toward her. "My dear, we should not dwell on a topic that must distress our host."

She turned to him, ready to argue this, but two footman in blue-and-silver livery and wearing powdered wigs arrived with a silver tea service. Accepting a cup of tea with milk, she declined anything to eat and waited as her father discussed the weather with Ashlin.

When the servants left, Sylvain put down her tea, then, in the next lull in the conversation, she turned to Ashlin again. "Did you find it distressing relaying your harrowing story to the authorities?"

He stared at her, mouth pulled down and a look in his eyes that reminded her a good deal of him as a petulant boy.

"Authorities?" He made the word a distasteful drawl. "As if I would trust my well-being to a bumpkin of a constable who spends his days at The Four Feathers and a magistrate who is never in residence! I think not."

Ignoring her father's frown, Sylvain asked, "Then you have not had Ter—Mr. Winslow charged?"

Ashlin's mouth twisted at one side into something like a smile. "Oh, I've done better than that. I've put up a reward for Bow Street Runners to apprehend the man."

By the time Terrance reached the back of the stables, his leg ached and his temper had soured into a foul mood. It worsened as he limped through the stables, noting the empty stalls and the lack of so much as a decent pony cart or shooting gig in the carriage house.

Not a single groom to be seen, either.

At Winslow Park, there would have been heads knocked together and a peel rung over the entire staff at such neglect.

Blazes, but he had had no idea just how bad matters must have been for the Harwoods. He could quite see closing a wing to a house to save money, but to have to reduce the stable to what looked to be two ancient hacks seemed shocking. He had, of course, glimpsed the stallion in the paddock. But he had no intention of going near that animal. The beast had once belonged to his father, and had just about killed one of the grooms at Winslow Park.

No, what he needed was a decent driving horse and a tidy gig—and he could not find either of those here.

Glancing down the tidy brick aisle, he shook his head. Two of the stalls had their doors open, and straw spilled onto the bricks—a pair of horses had gone out, he guessed. With Mr. Harwood and Sylvain? Blazes, were the two of them even now at Dunscombe Abbey?

He frowned at the thought, still uncomfortable with the notion of Sylvain being there. However, if she had her father—and that pistol of hers—close by, he could not see how she could come to any grief.

And she had a sensible head on her—not like some females. She would manage well enough.

But that left him without the means to go anywhere.

Limping from the empty stables, he looked around the stable yard once more, assessing what to do. The wind tugged at his coat collar, sharp and cold, and the need to do something danced along his skin, a prickling, as if a storm were brewing. He looked up at the sky and judged rain by nightfall, if not sooner, for the clouds were gathering in dark clumps.

Blazes, but he had to do something. He could not just sit in that room another day.

Only he could not see a clear path of action, either. He could, of course, saddle Drake and ride to Dunscombe Abbey to confront Perriman. The idea tempted.

But he was already limping again, and if he were to be honest about it, he was not quite certain he could mount a horse. Why did he have to break his left leg? He could try mounting from the right, but he'd never trained Drake for that, and the gelding had enough of an obstinate streak that Terrance could just see the horse putting up a fuss about someone getting on from the "wrong" side.

Digging his hands into the pockets of his loose breeches, he started back to the house.

Blast, but his leg did ache again. As did his stiff shoulders, and his side, and his head again. Perhaps he would just sit

down for a time. That would leave him in better fettle for
when Sylvain returned. Then he could question her about
what she had learned, and make some plans.

The corner of his mouth twitched—was this not exactly
what she had said he ought to do. Impertinent girl! And too
smart by half. Well, he would not tell her how right she was—
no sense inflating her opinion of herself.

But he would be interested to see just what she had to say
about her visit to Dunscombe Abbey.

"I thought I raised you with more manners than to put me
to the blush with questions that could only be considered pre-
sumptuously rude."

Swaying with the carriage, Sylvain stared at the tips of her
gloves. Her ears burned, but she risked a glance up at her father. He sat with his profile to her, looking out the carriage
window, one hand holding the leather strap that hung next to
the door. His face sagged with disappointment.

Sylvain glanced away. That hurt more than his anger.

"To quiz Ashlin—Lord Dunscombe—in such a manner . . ."
Mr. Harwood broke off, shaking his head. Then he added, "I
can only be glad your mother was not there to witness such
brazen behavior!"

Sylvain pressed her lips tight to hold back the explanation of why she had not acted as a young lady should at a
social call—meaning, smiling and only answering questions put to her. Any excuse would involve mention of
Terrance—and that would put her father into an even worse
mood with her.

Almost as if reading her thoughts, her father sighed, then
said, "I know Terrance is . . . well, something of a friend to
you. But he is well able to account for his own actions. He
does not need your defense."

"But, Father, Ashlin is telling lies about him!"

Mr. Harwood shook his head. "My dear, you cannot call a man a liar when you do not know the facts yourself."

Sylvain scowled, and knew herself trapped. If she said anything about Terrance having told her the facts, she would then have to explain how he had done so. She gave a small nod. "I do beg your pardon for doing anything to shame you—and I am sorry to be so difficult."

Mr. Harwood reached out to pat her hands, then he settled back against the worn velvet of the carriage cushions. "Well, now you see, my dear, why your mother and I wish for you to go to London—you'll learn soon enough there how to go on much better than you did today."

She offered back an absent smile, relieved that he no longer seemed so distressed, but with her thoughts turning back to their visit. "Father, why do you think Ashlin is so adamant that Terrance Winslow must have shot his uncle? I mean, did it not strike you as a rather extreme measure for him to be hiring Bow Street Runners?"

"Well . . . actually, it might be quite sensible. That is what Bow Street is for—to get the facts straight. I would expect that he wishes what we all hope—that they will uncover the real killer."

Sylvain nodded, but wondered if he was right about this. Would Bow Street be a help—or did they wish only to collect any reward that Ashlin might have offered? And why had Ashlin thought to hire them, instead of simply reporting the matter to the local authorities? Did guilt drive him—not for causing his uncle's death, for how could he have . . .

And then the thought of how he might have murdered his uncle leapt into her mind. Her skin tingled. It seemed so obvious that she wondered how she had missed it. Ashlin had always had the means to hire people to do things for him. He had hired the Runner. He could as easily have hired someone to shoot his uncle.

But how could such a thing be proven?

By the Runners? After all, if Ashlin could hire them, why

could Terrance not employ them to get to the truth? They certainly could not want to apprehend an innocent man, for it would do their reputations no good.

Sitting up straighter, she shifted on her seat. She had to talk to Terrance about this idea, and about the Runners.

Leaning forward, she glanced out the window. They had turned down the drive to Harwood House already. In just a few moments she would be home and she would have to find an excuse to slip away and see Terrance.

But as she looked out the window, she saw two black enclosed carriages pulled up before Harwood—impressive vehicles, each with a team of horses, grooms tending them.

She turned to her father. "Are we expecting visitors?"

Seven

"Visitors?" he asked, then leaned across her to glance out the carriage window. "Well, now, I wonder . . ."

His words trailed off for as he spoke their carriage slowed, then rocked to a halt. Sylvain did not wait for a footman, but opened the door nearest her and jumped out.

The grooms—post boys, she saw now, for the near horses of each team were saddled to be ridden rather than driven—glanced toward her with polite nods, then looked at her father as he came forward to speak with them. He spoke low, so that she could not hear, but one of the postilions, a dark, wiry fellow, jerked a thumb to the house.

With a tip of his hat, her father turned away. As he came back to her, she glanced at him, curious, but he only said, "Shall we go in, my dear?"

Forced cheer lay underneath his words and he avoided meeting her gaze. She frowned, not trusting this. What was it that he would rather avoid? A half-dozen questions formed, but, conscience still smarting from the lecture he had just given her on putting herself too far forward, she pressed her lips tight.

She really could act a lady if she must.

Only that left her fidgeting with her muff, and wondering if she might use the excuse of visitors to slip away—but she did rather wish she knew who had called on them.

As soon as they entered the house, her father suggested she

leave off her cloak and bonnet in the hall. "Your mother must be expecting us."

She did as he asked, but she kept her muff with her, explaining when her father looked at it, "My hands are still cold."

The excuse sounded thin to her, for she had used it once already. But he only gave her a distracted smile, and her shoulders relaxed. It would not do to have Bridges or another servant come across her pistol. Then she went with her father.

While in the hall, she heard the voices—her mother's melodic tones, and an answering voice, a woman's, pitched too low to recognize. As they entered, the lady who had been sitting with her mother on a green damask-covered couch broke off her words and rose.

Tall, sharp-featured, and somberly dressed, she presented almost a masculine figure. Her dark blue traveling gown imitated a gentlemen's clothes, with a short coat buttoned across her small chest and a narrow skirt. A hat, rather like a man's top hat only flatter, covered black hair that had been pulled back and up. She held tan gloves in one slender, long-fingered hand. A small, plain gold watch lay pinned to the bodice of her dress—a useful, not ornamental, decoration Sylvain judged.

As she followed her father across the room, their steps muffled by the rose-patterned carpet, Mrs. Harwood made the introduction, saying, "This is Mrs. Godwin."

The name meant nothing to Sylvain, but shrewd black eyes swept over her, inspecting, assessing, and—Sylvain felt certain—judging her barely adequate.

Sylvain's chin lifted at the critical measuring, and she stared back, determined not to be intimidated.

At first she had thought the lady to be near her mother's age, but she could see no gray in the wings of black hair that showed from under the hat, and no lines on the sharp-edged face. The woman held herself with authority, and while slender, her height gave her a presence that Sylvain almost envied.

The lady's smile—slight, with just the right degree of polite interest—never faltered, but Sylvain noticed her glance once at the gold watch pin as if she were impatient to leave.

But why was she here?

A suspicion began to form and she glanced at her father, who avoided her gaze, and then at her mother, who smiled back at her, but with her eyes misting. "Oh, my dear, you must be so excited!"

The suspicion became a chill that shimmered along her skin. "Why must I?" she asked.

Mrs. Harwood blinked in surprise, then glanced at her husband. "Why—did you not talk to her?"

Mr. Harwood cleared his throat, tugged at his watch chain and then straightened. "Talk to her—of course I did. We spoke last night, did we not, of your visit to London."

He smiled, but Mrs. Harwood glanced from him to her youngest child, a frown tight on her forehead. She knew that she ought not to have left it to Stephen. He always meant well, but he could be maddeningly vague. And now, here was Sylvain, pale-faced and with a faint touch of panic in here eyes. She ought to have been prepared with all the particulars, and instead, she probably had only been told vague terms.

She had wanted this to be an easy parting, with Sylvain delighted to go—gracious, the house would seem so empty without her. But she had made up her mind—she and Stephen had agreed, after all. And it was not as if they were sending her away to strangers—she would have Penelope and Cecila to help her with her first steps into society.

Her throat tightened at the thought that she could not do this—but she forced a smile. She would not have Sylvain thinking this anything but a treat—for everyone. And she would not allow the girl to become a crutch for herself and Stephen. It would be too easy to keep Sylvain here with them, and allow the years to slip pleasantly past.

If would be a different matter if she came home again. Then, at least if she chose to remain at home, she would do so after having had the chance to meet some eligible young gentlemen and see a little of the world.

Watching her daughter now, Matilda patted the cushions beside her. Sylvain came forward and sat, eyes downcast, her muff tucked next to her and her hands folded in her lap, a perfect, demure young lady—only, of course, she was no such thing. Well, she would learn to be one. Or at least she would have the chance to learn.

"Penelope has sent Mrs. Godwin to be your escort to London—and your companion once you are in town. Isn't that thoughtful of her, dear?" she said.

Sylvain glanced briefly at Mrs. Godwin, and then she looked at her mother again.

The color had faded from her mother's face. And the hand that now lay over Sylvain's trembled slightly. She knew the signs of strain. Her mother should not be taxed any more today. So she forced a smile. "Yes. Quite. I—well, I had not thought . . . I had imagined the visit not yet planned. Are we to depart soon then?"

Mrs. Godwin answered, her voice brisk, "Lady Nevin did not want to burden your family with the care of grooms and horses, so I was instructed to arrive early enough with fresh teams so we could depart at once. I allowed a quarter hour in the schedule for packing, and another quarter to say adieu to your parents."

Stunned, Sylvain stared at her. "A quarter hour!"

"It may seem little time, but Lady Nevin said you were to bring only the essentials for the road. All else you may require shall be purchased for you in London. And I shall be happy to assist you now for I am a practiced and efficient packer."

Panic sizzling through her, Sylvain started to protest, but Mrs. Harwood laid her fingers across Sylvain's lips. "I know, my dear—but best fast and away, or we shall both be in floods of tears. I expect you to write to me daily, however, as I shall write you."

Desperation welled in Sylvain. What of Terrance? And

Trace? And Mr. Feathers? She almost blurted out that she could not go. She had responsibilities here. And who would read aloud to Mother in the evenings? Or find Father's glasses when he misplaced them?

She could not do this!

Her mother's hand tightened on hers, and suddenly Sylvain wanted to grip it hard and plead with her not to send her away. Only that would not do—not with Mrs. Godwin's black eyes on her so hard, and not with her father looking guilty for not having told her everything last night, and not with her mother looking pale-faced and already too tired from this.

Hands icy, she rose, remembering at the last moment to take up her muff. She glanced at Mrs. Godwin. "I can pack my own things, thank you."

With a short curtsy, she fled.

She went at once to see Terrance. What did she tell him? *I'm going away, you'll have to fend for yourself?* Face hot, she rejected that unfeeling comment. It was the raw truth, but there had to be something more she could do for him. But what, if she was to depart in less than an hour?

Lips tight, she wished Penelope had come—with her own sister she would have had no trouble giving arguments. Which was probably why Penelope had sent Mrs. Godwin in her stead. She would have a few things to say to her sister about that.

Only just now she had to face Terrance.

Putting back her shoulders, she opened the door into the study. And then stared into an empty room.

Fingers clenching on the doorknob, her nerves strung as tight as a poacher's snare, she blinked. Gone? How could he be gone!

Oh, bother the man—could he not stay put and out of trouble for even an hour?

The tidy pile of clothes she had left had been replaced by his rumpled breeches and shirt.

Coming into the room, she gathered up the clothes and put them into the basket, then she went to the window.

Perhaps this was for the best. If he was well enough to take himself off, then she would not have to worry over him. He would not even know that she had left for London.

But if he came back . . .

She glanced around the room again, then went to her mother's old bureau cabinet, which had been too heavy to move from the room for use elsewhere. Dragging off the Holland cover, she sneezed at the dust. Then she opened cabinet doors and rummaged in the various compartments. She found a stub of pencil and the back of an old household linen inventory, which did well enough for a note.

Conscious of the seconds ticking away, she scribbled a message, mentioning both Bow Street Runners and her departure for London.

She left the note on the basket of clothes.

He had, she noticed, left behind his blue spotted handkerchief. The one he had wrapped around his neck yesterday—heavens, had it only been a day ago that they had gone out to see if she could shoot?

Hesitating, she ran her hand over the silky material. Then she snatched it up and tucked it into her sleeve. Stupid sentimentality to take it, of course. He would probably not come back to even notice it was gone. He would not care, either.

Just as he would not notice her departure either.

Mrs. Godwin waited ten minutes. She judged the time, needing no more than one glance at her watch to start her calculations. Time was a precious commodity, not to be wasted.

She used the time to offer the Harwoods every reassurance as to their daughter's well-being—yes, they would stop for regular meals, and no, they would not stay at any inn that looked the least bit disreputable. Then she suggested that perhaps she might indeed assist Miss Harwood with her packing after all.

"If she has not traveled much, she may not realize what is most suitable for the road," she said. They could hardly argue with such logic, she knew.

Mrs. Harwood offered a tired smile. "Actually, Sylvain never gives much thought to what is suitable for anything."

Allowing her smile to widen a fraction, Mrs. Godwin said, "That is why I am here." She rose and went to the door, with Mr. Harwood rising as well and offering to show her to Sylvain's room. But she had seen the daughter with the parents. She now wanted a glimpse of the girl on her own. Always best to have the full measure of one's charge.

At the door, she turned to him and said, her voice low, "Please, sir. Do tend to your wife. This parting must be a strain on her, and we should do all we can to ease any distress she might feel."

Frowning, he glanced at his wife, his forehead bunching with worry and his eyes clouded. She saw at once how much he must care for her, and an unexpected sympathy welled inside her. She knew the difficulty of caring for a loved one—it could be dreadfully hard to see the person one knew become crippled and changed by illness. Her respect for him grew. She could not think of another gentleman she knew who would regard his wife with such love—or such concern. But perhaps that was the fault of the world she moved in.

She did not care to touch others, or to be touched, but she laid one hand on his sleeve. "Please, sir. I shall ask your butler to take me."

He turned to her, gratitude warm in his eyes, and she found herself offering a genuine smile before she turned and left.

She had herself back under control by the time she reached the hall, her half-smile in place, her emotions tidied away.

The butler took an inexcusable four minutes to meet her, and so she gave him a frosty glance and told him, "You are to take me to Miss Harwood's room."

His neck reddened at the rebuke in her stare, but he only offered a curt bow and then led the way up the stairs and down a hall. At the first door on the right, he hesitated—deplorable that the butler of the house should act so indecisive. She dismissed him, then waited for him to leave.

Lady Nevin—Miss Harwood's sister—had led her to expect rather more of a child than she had glimpsed in the young lady downstairs. A much-indulged girl who could be shy in company. That might indeed be the case. However, she had learned years ago, when she had first taken up her profession of chaperoning young ladies, not to judge character from a relative's point of view. Emotions biased such opinions.

The Miss Harwood she had met downstairs looked to have a stubborn, independent streak that would be bound to lead her into disaster in a world which expected ladies to be biddable conformists. Had her own family underestimated Miss Harwood?

Turning to the door, she knocked softly then entered, hoping she might surprise the truth into the open.

She at least managed a surprise.

Miss Harwood glanced up from where she knelt beside her wardrobe, a pair of boots in one hand and one green glove in the other. A maid stood in the room, three dresses piled in her arms. More dresses covered the bed in a tangle of pastel colors. An open portmanteau, the bag only a quarter packed with white undergarments, lay on the floor next to three bandboxes, their tops off and nothing inside them.

"I see we do need a bit of organization," Mrs. Godwin said, stepping into the room and pushing up her sleeves.

In the end, it took most of an hour to get Miss Harwood packed—and Mrs. Godwin did not know whether she wanted to sit down and give in to laughter or strangle the girl. Neither could be considered part of her duties, however, so she rejected both options.

The girl had managed to decide not once, but twice, that

she could not leave without a book she had left downstairs. After the second time she came back empty-handed, Mrs. Godwin told her flatly, "There are very good bookshops in London and I've no doubt your sister will allow you to visit them."

Miss Harwood then debated which of her shawls to take, so Mrs. Godwin packed them both, but then Miss Harwood said she thought she might take one other besides. She left and came back with a plain wool shawl from her sister's room, as well as yet another portmanteau.

Mrs. Godwin eyed this, but Miss Harwood merely smiled and said, "It's not to pack, but to bring home gifts I might buy."

Taking the bag, Mrs. Godwin put it aside. "One does not take empty bags on a trip. As to what you might buy, Lord Nevin will no doubt see to its arriving here."

Finally, Mrs. Godwin closed the last bandbox with a slap of the lid into place and said, her voice firm, "We must not keep the horses standing any longer."

Miss Harwood had glanced around the room, a hint of tears welling in her eyes, and Mrs. Godwin knew that if she did not soon pry her from this house, she never would.

One would think Miss Harwood to be leaving something far more than her room at Harwood behind.

"Come along, Miss Harwood. To be late is to show disdain for the value that others might put on their time."

With that she handed the bandbox to the maid, and took Miss Harwood's arm to lead her downstairs. The girl's steps dragged, but she seemed to have run out of excuses to slip away—whatever was the girl running off to check on?

Mr. Harwood met them in the hall, his eyes brimming with tears as Miss Harwood gave in to a restrained sniffle.

Uncomfortable at the thought of the emotional farewell this foretold, Mrs. Godwin leaned closer to Miss Harwood and said, her tone intentionally sharp, "Come now, you cannot want to make your parents unhappy with an outburst of childish feeling."

Miss Harwood shook her head, her red-gold curls glinting as she did. And Mrs. Godwin nodded with satisfaction—she would do well enough. She might lack polish, but she had sense and intelligence. The rest could be learned.

"I shall wait for you in the coach. I recommend you take no more than five minutes—long farewells only prolong the pain of parting."

Miss Harwood glanced at her, a distressed look in her eyes, and Mrs. Godwin made up her mind to give the girl every distraction possible for the rest of their journey to London. She would need it, for her homesickness would be hard.

As she walked out the door, she gave one glance back. Father and daughter stood together, their coloring so alike in their sandy hair, their blue-green eyes. They stood with hands clasped, neither one saying anything, the girl looking stricken but trying to smile, the father looking pale-faced and unhappy. This parting affected them deeply.

She turned away, her steps quick. She must be losing her touch to be so easily affected.

It actually took Miss Harwood eight minutes to appear in the carriage. She arrived with her face flushed, and eyes watery, but without the tears Mrs. Godwin had expected. Her bonnet sat askew on her curls as if she had just slapped it on, and she dragged the extra portmanteau that Mrs. Godwin had set aside into the coach. It now looked heavy with something.

Mrs. Godwin frowned.

Miss Harwood bundled herself into the opposite seat— Mrs. Godwin had placed herself with her back to the horses, as suited her position as an employee—then settled the portmanteau snug against her legs.

She said nothing—offered not even a single excuse for the bag she had dragged with her. Instead, she turned in her seat to let down the carriage window. She did not wave and shout her good-byes, but sat still, staring at her home, eyes enormous in that narrow, pointed face of hers.

Mrs. Godwin said nothing. Better to allow the girl time to

master her feelings. But as she waved her handkerchief out the window—the signal she had arranged for the postboys to drive on—she wished she knew what Miss Harwood had decided she could not leave behind.

When the carriage turned from the drive onto the lane that would take them to the main post road, Miss Harwood sat back against the cushions. She fixed her stare on her hands, now folded in her lap.

The girl looked calm, but Mrs. Godwin fancied she detected a maelstrom of emotions churning beneath the surface—or was that only her own imagination?

She leaned forward to put up the window again with the side latches, and then she turned to Miss Harwood—her charge now. For a moment, she studied the girl, her head tilted and considering. Then she said, "You are an interesting young lady. I expect you shall have to be an original in London. It is the only hope."

The comment pulled Miss Harwood's attention away from herself, as Mrs. Godwin had hoped. She had lovely eyes, Mrs. Godwin decided. The color changed from blue to green as her mood shifted, and they were well shaped and framed by dark, red-gold lashes. Now if only something could be done to dress her to advantage. And to tame that stride of hers and that too-direct stare, and my but did the list not seem daunting.

"Hope for what?" Miss Harwood asked.

Mrs. Godwin shook her head at such an indelicately blunt question, but she answered, "For you, Miss Harwood. For your success. A young lady does not scramble into a carriage with her bonnet askew, carrying her own luggage. Since you have brought him, you ought to have had that disreputable-looking footman of yours carry it for you, instead."

Eight

The back of her neck prickled, but Sylvain resisted the urge to repeat the word "footman" as if she were an idiot, or had no idea of having brought one with her. A footman? A disreputable-looking footman? One, perhaps, who had a bad leg?

It had to be.

Terrance.

Who else would be so mad? Harwood certainly had but one footman—Peter, their cook's youngest, an earnest sixteen and far from disreputable-looking.

Turning to stare out the window, she bit her lower lip and frowned. What was he thinking? He could no more pass for a servant than she could—his arrogance alone would betray him, even if her sisters did not at once recognize him.

Part of the blame must fall on her. She must have given him the notion when she left him a change of clothing from the servants' livery. And she had left him that note, with mention of London and the Bow Street Runners. He had read it—she knew he had. The second time she had slipped down to the study to see if he might have returned, she had seen the scrap of paper gone. But he ought to be resting that leg of his, not jostling it about in a carriage!

Scowling, she squirmed in her seat.

The man had to be more than mad—and he was going to drag her into the worst trouble with this masquerade, unless . . .

Might his arrival in London with her make Penelope angry enough to pack her back home in disgrace? A smile curled inside her. Such a lovely notion. However, not something she ought to rely on. Far more likely was that she would earn endless unpleasant lectures and a mortifying letter posted home, which would only upset mother. And she could not allow that. Not with her mother's health.

Well, perhaps Terrance had a plan—she wanted to hope so, but she had her doubts, and if he did not, they would simply have to improvise.

The soft-sided bag at her feet squirmed, and Sylvain adjusted her cloak to cover it, then she glanced at Mrs. Godwin.

The other woman seemed not to notice. She had taken out a small book bound in brown leather and was making notes with a stub of a pencil.

Leaning back in her seat, Sylvain let out a breath, but she did not relax. One never ought to, really, with Terrance Winslow close by.

By midday, tired of swaying in a coach, bored with doing nothing more than watching endless greenery, Sylvain begged Mrs. Goodwin to make a proper stop and take a meal.

Mrs. Godwin had arranged for frequent changes of horses every fifteen miles, but they never stopped for longer than it took to unharness one team and buckle the next into place. Sylvain had not had time to do more than either swallow a mouthful of hot tea or step out of the coach and back in again before the postilions sounded the coaching horn and urged the team forward.

She had seen nothing of Terrance. And, as she told Mrs. Godwin, "I at least need to use a privy!"

The woman's perpetual half smile faltered at this blunt mention of bodily needs, but Sylvain did not care if she shocked the woman.

With a glancing at her watch pin, Mrs. Godwin allowed as how they might stop for three-quarters of an hour in Chippenham. That seemed an inadequate amount of time to do

anything, but Sylvain did not argue. She did not want to waste
the time. Instead, she stepped from the carriage, taking her
portmanteau with her.

Mrs. Godwin followed her out and then glanced at the bag,
"And you may give that over to your footman. There is a
rather musty odor coming from it and I would just as soon not
travel with it in our carriage."

Sylvain said nothing, but Mrs. Godwin needed no answer.
She had already turned away to talk to the innkeeper about a
private parlor and to order a meal of cold meats and pies.

With excuse enough to seek out Terrance, Sylvain walked
to the other coach, the bag dragging at her arm and shoulder.

The luggage coach had arrived before theirs and the horses
had already been led away. Glancing through the open door,
she saw only brown leather seats with baggage piled high on
one side and just room enough for one passenger to stretch
his legs.

Turning, she looked around the stable yard.

Another carriage—a yellow-bodied, two-wheeled gig
drawn by a pair of grays—stood in the yard, its driver standing idle with a tankard in one hand, his slouch hat and
old-fashioned frock coat proclaiming him local gentry. Stable boys held the heads of the horses while another man, a
blacksmith to judge by his leather apron and his thick arms,
picked up the nearest horse's hind leg. With horses being led
to the stables, and the milling postboys, and the clutter of
vehicles, the yard seemed a place of noise and bustle.

A sense of being misplaced swept over her, tightening
her throat and chest. They never had such fuss as this in
Harwood's stable yards.

She pushed aside the comparison. It only made her think
of home, and that only started the ache again.

Switching the heavy bag to her other hand, she made her
way to the stables, which lay in another square of buildings
and were connected to this one by an archway. Once through
the wide arch, she stepped from clatter into quiet.

Stalls lined the square; some with doors open—the stall empty—some with horses hanging their heads out, the top half of the stall door opened back for them. Bucket handles rattled and the indistinct murmur of grooms came from the stalls, but the brick yard stood empty, and Sylvain's half boots echoed as she strode to the first open stall. With a glance over her shoulder, she slipped into it, then shut the bottom half of the door behind her. Kneeling in the straw, sweetly pungent under her boots, she opened her bag.

Trace stared up at her for a moment from where he lay curled tight, his eyes dark and wide, his thick red tail curled around him like a blanket over his paws. Then he lifted his head, stretched upward, and poked his nose out, black whiskers twitching.

"Take advantage while you may," she told him, standing again before the open bag. "I have no idea how long she will keep us on the road today."

"Hours most like."

The deep voice startled her and she twisted around, straw crunching underfoot, but even as she did, she recognized that deep, careless drawl. Annoying how her pulse lifted, she thought, scowling at Terrance. He must have followed her, and why could he have not called to her in the yard, rather than surprising her in this fashion?

As if oblivious to her frown, he lounged over the half-door, a brown pottery mug in one hand. He wore no hat and with his black coat and waistcoat stark against white linen, and his unshaven face, he did look a disreputable servant of sorts.

Or like a gentleman slumming.

His mouth crooked with a smile. "However, at this pace, we ought to make London tomorrow, so I suppose we ought to count that fortunate."

Folding her arms, Sylvain tilted her head and stared at him. "How did you ever think you could pass for a servant?"

He straightened. "What? Don't I look the part?"

"And what of a demeanor to match? And a respectable face?"

Mouth twisting down, he rubbed a hand over his jaw. "Oh, I've orders from your dragon to remedy that—at once if possible."

"She is not my anything. And I think you need more than a clean-shaven face."

Tawny eyes glittering with amusement, he leaned over the door again and gestured to the fox with his mug. "Seems you are in a bit of a glass house yourself to be tossing such stones. How respectable is it to bring a fox to London?"

Sylvain looked away. It had been an unwise impulse, but when she had seen Trace at the window downstairs as she was leaving Harwood she had been caught by a desperate need. One she did not want to admit. Wrinkling her nose, she struggled to make up an excuse. "I . . . I . . ."

"You what? Wanted company?"

Face warm, she glanced at him. How did he know? Or was he guessing. In either case, she did not want to have this conversation, so she said, "We were speaking of you, not him or myself. And this ridiculous pretense. What of when my sisters see you?"

He gave a shrug. "They won't. I'll be away before then. I don't plan to be seen by anyone in these clothes."

"And how do I then explain that I had a footman and lost him? Mrs. Godwin is bound to say something, you know."

Terrance frowned. He paused to drink from his mug, and then he said, "Why not say you dismissed me?"

There, that should do her. In truth, he had not thought of what she might have to do once they parted company. He had thought only that he had found a convenient means to get to his rooms in London, and from there he could both see to his own needs and make plans. It had seemed ideal—particularly with his pockets near empty and his leg aching and stiff.

Sylvain stared at him, her expression still disapproving.

"So I am supposed to be presumptuous enough to turn off one of my father's servant then? And what if Penelope asks me for a name and writes home to ask of you, and my father writes back that. . . ."

"Enough!" He held up a hand, almost ready to laugh at the troubles she had started to list. Blazes, but she worried too much. "If that won't do for you, say I came with you only to visit a sick relative, which I left to do—or better yet, don't tell them anything. Leave it a mystery and pretend ignorance."

Sylvain glared at him. "I am not that good a liar."

"Oh, you'll learn soon enough in society," he muttered, an odd look in his eyes.

She studied him a moment, puzzled by the cynical bite to his tone. Chewing her lower lip, she tried to hold back her curiosity, but the question burst out anyway. "What do you mean, I shall learn? Do you plan to give me excuses to practice? Besides, it is not as if I can keep my ears from turning red when I lie, you know!"

His face relaxed again into a smile that softened the hard edges around his mouth and eyes. "Do they? I'll have to watch for that. Now fetch your fox. The least I can do for you, if I am putting you to all this bother with tales you must invent, is take him with me to the kitchen and see if I can manage some scraps and water. I don't think your dragon will care for him begging at table from you."

She started to tell him that she could look after Trace, but that would be a stretch of the truth and she could already feel her ears tingling. Besides, she was supposed to give her bag over to him.

Bending down, she called Trace to her. He had been sitting in a corner of the stall, ears and eyes intent on the wooden slats of the wall—hunting mice, she assumed. As she snapped her fingers, her gloves muffling the sound, he glanced at her. Then, with a last reluctant glance at the corner, he turned and hopped to her, bobbing his way through the straw on his three legs. She gathered him up and pressed her face to his wiry fur, taking comfort from his familiar strong, musky smell and his warmth.

She had not been wrong to bring him.

He needed her. He did.

Setting him into the bag, she soothed him with soft strokes and muttered promises that it would not be long. He seemed not to mind the small space—a good thing that foxes liked burrows. At least Trace had always preferred to keep himself under her bed or tucked into a corner of her wardrobe.

But Terrance's words dug at her. Perhaps she ought to have left him at Harwood. What would she do with him once she reached London? However, if she had left him, who would have looked after him? And what if he had gotten into a fight with her father's dogs again?

Still, her heart twisted as she closed the bag on his dark, liquid eyes. Before she could feel worse about it, she rose, opened the stall door, and stepped out.

Reluctance dragged at her as she gave the bag over to Terrance. "He is partial to lamb. And he will drink your ale if you are not careful."

Amused, Terrance glanced down at Sylvain, his mug in one hand and the bag with her fox in the other. The bag squirmed and Sylvain glanced at it, her hands clasped tight before her, as if she was trying to keep herself from reaching out to take back her bag—and her fox.

Unable to resist teasing, he asked, "Shall I see if they have a chicken coop that I can loose him into?"

She looked at him, the worry now gone from her eyes, replaced by sharp indignation. "No, but you may at least look after him with rather more care than you give yourself."

With that, she turned and strode away, her skirts snapping around her ankles. Her step really was far too long for a lady.

He watched her, eyebrows lifted, enjoying the view but smarting from her last comment. What the blazes did she care how he looked after himself? And he did a perfectly good job of it, thank you very much!

But then he frowned.

Limping, his leg offering stabs of pain at each step, he started back to the inn.

Well, perhaps not a perfectly good job, as his leg reminded him. There had been that duel. And this blasted tangle to which it had led. And that disaster of an affair with Lady Dunscombe. And before that . . .

Irritated now, he scowled at himself as made his way to the inn's kitchen.

What the devil was it to Sylvain, anyway, if he did not look after himself all that well?

The question lodged like a rose thorn under his skin. He set is aside long enough to charm a tavern maid into a fresh mug of ale for himself and some roast beef and bread, which did well enough for him and his charge.

And then the coachman came to find him, with curt orders for him to drink up. "We're to be at The Pelican in Speenhamland afore yer ladies. An' that means leaving now."

The fellow had a surly manner and Terrance thought of telling him what he could do with his ideas of leaving on the instant. Then Sylvain's criticism nudged him.

He still had not shaved, but if he got to Speenhamland well beforehand, he could tidy himself and have dinner and rooms ordered for her—just as if he were a proper manservant. That would show her that he could not only look after himself, but her as well, and that dragon her sisters had sent. He almost grinned. His own man, Burke, would fall down in a faint to see him taking orders, instead of giving them.

However, Burke himself always managed an air as haughty as a duke's. So Terrance gave the coachman a cold glance, told him he'd be along presently, and turned back to his ale.

With a huff and muttered complaints, the coachman left. Not certain the fellow would wait, Terrance drained his ale, slipped the last slice of meat into the portmanteau, gave the tavern maid a wink and a quick slip of his arm about her waist. Then he rose to follow the coachman out.

The coachman had already mounted to his seat when Terrance limped into the yard.

"Come on," the fellow yelled at him. "I'm hired to drive, not nursemaid the likes of you!"

Jaw tight, Terrance thought of striding across the yard to drag the fellow down by his coattails for such insolence. But he clenched his fist tight on his anger and merely limped across the yard and pulled himself into the coach. Footmen, after all, weren't supposed to go about pummeling coachmen. And if he ever again thought to present himself as anything but a gentleman—even a disreputable one—he promised himself that he would lay down until the notion passed.

Even Mrs. Godwin looked fatigued by the time they stopped for the night. Their coach rumbled into the yard of The Pelican with a clatter of wheels and steel horseshoes on cobblestone and the harness jingling. Now that the sun had set, flambeaus lit the archway into the yard of the half-timbered Elizabethan inn. A half-moon gave fitful light, sliding out and then disappearing behind clouds that surged black across the sky. The wind had come up ten miles back, slipping in under the carriage door, and Sylvain wondered if her numb, cold feet would hold her upright.

She climbed stiff and shivering from the coach, following Mrs. Godwin into the warmth of the inn—and then she stopped in the narrow hall, her eyes widening with surprise.

Terrance gave a short bow to her. Then he turned to ask Mrs. Godwin if he might help her with her outergarments. In the yellow glow of lamplight, clean-shaven, his black coat brushed, a white clean stock tied neat around his neck, he looked darkly handsome. And almost a perfect footman.

Except for the look of devilment that lit those tawny eyes.

She glanced down at his legs. Somehow he had found proper shoes to go with his white stockings and black breeches, but she noted that one stocking bulged a little, as if he had wrapped his leg. She was impressed.

He was saying something about rooms, a private parlor, and dinner, and asking if Mrs. Godwin would care to sample his recipe for hot punch.

Sylvain stared at him, her jaw now slack. Had she ever seen him so civil? Then she glanced at Mrs. Godwin to gauge that lady's reaction.

Instead of her usual polite half smile, a warm expression actually softened the lady's mouth and lightened her eyes. As Terrance helped her with her coat, color even flushed her cheeks. *My goodness, she is really rather an attractive woman!*

Then her face warmed as she realized that she had thought of Mrs. Godwin as a sharp-faced dragon—just as Terrance had called her.

He leaned closer to Mrs. Godwin and said something that had her smile widening, and a sharp twist tightened around Sylvain's heart. She looked away. Absurd to be jealous. Terrance did not even care about the woman. But he could still charm her it seemed. Not even Mrs. Godwin could resist him. Which really ought not to be a surprise.

When he came to her, Sylvain glanced up at him, then said as he reached to take her gloves, "You need not bother."

Mischief glinted brighter in his eyes. "It's no bother, Miss. I assure you."

His hands brushed hers, a touch of warmth and vitality, and he winked at her. She pressed her lips tight to keep herself from reminding him that such behavior hardly suited any proper footman.

"Will you take tea or punch, Miss Harwood? I know how partial you are to my recipes."

"For disaster," she muttered, staring at him and trying to will him to take himself off before he did something to give himself away as an utter fraud.

"What was that?" Mrs. Godwin asked, turning around to look at Sylvain.

Sylvain straightened. "I was just saying that I ought to ask you if I may have some punch."

"You may. But do try to speak up in future. Precise enunciation indicates good breeding and eliminates the need to repeat yourself."

Sylvain saw Terrance's lips twitch. She looked away before he provoked her into either saying something or laughing at this farce. She vowed not to look at him again.

That proved impossible.

He went with them to the private parlor he had bespoken, and stayed to make up his hot punch—a heady mixture of rum, water, sugar, and spices, warmed with a hot poker in a pewter jug. Again he had impressed her—she would not have thought he would know how to make much more than a glass of brandy by pouring it from a bottle.

Two sips, however, decided her that she had best not take more. Someone ought to be sober and sensible—besides Mrs. Godwin, that was.

Mrs. Godwin drank her glass, accepted a second, and seemed unaffected by either. However, the punch did seem to put her in a mood to be pleased, for she smiled more easily now and began a steady conversation about the points of interest they had passed that day, and notable houses they would travel near tomorrow.

Having Terrance hover over them during the meal kept Sylvain on the edge of her chair as she waited for him to make some ghastly mistake. Twice she had to bite her lower lip to keep from saying anything as he limped around the room.

He really ought to be off that leg.

But he seemed determined to act the model servant. And he did, except that when he spoke to the staff of the inn he sounded far too cultured, his tone too commanding.

If anyone else noticed, they said nothing. And the deep bows he made forced Sylvain to turn away, the insides of her cheeks caught in her teeth, for she really did want to give in to the giggles that ticked inside.

When the second course ended, she decided she could stand no more. "Thank you, Terrance. Now I do insist that you rest your leg."

"Very good, miss. Are you certain there is nothing else you wish for tonight, miss?"

His tone could not have been more servile, but the wicked gleam in his eyes left her wishing she could box his ears for trying to provoke her. Instead, she stared at him, and said, her tone firm, "Thank you. But, no, thank you."

With a low bow, he turned to go. At the door, he gave one more bow, and Sylvain pressed her lips even tighter. She did not relax her hold on herself until the door shut on him.

Mrs. Godwin turned to her then. "What a useful fellow. I see now why you brought him. But whatever is wrong with his leg?"

Ears tingling, Sylvain met Mrs. Godwin's inquiring gaze. Then she stared into the fire. "Uh, that . . . that is . . . actually, that is why my father sent him to London. He has family there, and he is supposed to see a doctor. At once, in fact. Right as soon as he arrives. He is not even to stay to help us unpack."

Her ears now burned and she thought she must sound addled, but she managed to meet Mrs. Godwin's puzzled stare with a smile and only her heart pounding loud in her ears.

After a moment, Mrs. Godwin gave a nod and rose from the table. "I think I must have had too much punch. I shall retire now. Good night, Miss Harwood."

Smile fixed, Sylvain waited while Mrs. Godwin took up a candle and left. She sat in her chair a few moments longer to make certain Mrs. Godwin would not return. Then she rose, took up a single candle from the sideboard, and stepped into the hall in search of Terrance—he really had to be told not to put her through this again.

Finding one of the maids from the inn, she asked where she might find her footman. The girl, young with dull brown eyes, asked if Miss wanted him fetched.

"No, please do not trouble yourself. I only wish to know where he might be."

"He's got t'room just t'other side of hall, miss. He asked to be close so as if he was needed."

With a muttered thanks, Sylvain ran up the stairs. She hesitated only a moment to be certain of the room. Unwilling to make too much noise, she scratched on the door and then slipped in.

Terrance glanced up at once. A candle burned on a dresser near the door and another gleamed yellow on a table beside the bed. He half lay and half sat on the narrow bed, his bad leg propped up and a pillow between his back and the wall.

With his coat off and his waistcoat unbuttoned, he no longer looked much of a footman. He looked far more like the rogue she knew. His shirt lay open at the throat, displaying a muscular neck and framing a glimpse of his broad chest. Beside him on the bed, Trace lolled, upside-down and getting his belly scratched by graceful, long-fingered hands.

Mind blanking, Sylvain watched those hands and struggled to remember why it was she had come here.

Then he said, his voice so low that it vibrated in Sylvain's chest, "Ah, so perhaps there is something else you wish for tonight?"

Nine

He had said it to tease. Because she looked so prim as she stood there, her back pressed to the door, a candle held by quivering hands, and her eyes wide with only an edge of blue-green around the black pupils. He said it because he could not remember having enjoyed himself more of late, even with the ache in his leg and despite the problems that loomed before him.

He had set himself to act as a superior manservant, thinking only of seeing to her comfort as he ordered rooms and chose the dinner and saw to arrangements.

But then she had arrived with her warning frowns and he had remembered his desire to prove just how wrong she was about him.

And he had.

Blazes, no wonder Burke stayed with him. Who would expect there could be such satisfaction in anything so menial as looking after another person. But perhaps the appeal really lay in the novelty of it. Or perhaps the pleasure came more from watching Sylvain's reactions—he could swear she had come closer than he tonight to giving them both away by laughing out loud, or making some comment.

But she had said nothing.

So he still wanted to see if he could goad her into blurting out her thoughts. He did not think it her nature to keep anything back—and he liked to believe that, with him at least, she would always remain so open and guileless.

His words did pull a response, but not anything he had expected. Candlelight flickered over her pointed chin and sharp cheekbones as she spoke, her breath making the flame flutter. "I told Mrs. Godwin you had family in London and that Father had sent you there to see a doctor."

His hand stilled on the fox's rough coat and smooth skin. How in blazes was a family connected with seeing a doctor, of all things?

The beast's wiggling called him back to his task and he started to rub again. But the animal had done with him, it seemed. It righted itself and jumped from the bed to go to its mistress.

Terrance watched as she leaned down to rub her hand over the fox's head, cooing to it. A trace of envy rippled through him. Of course, he did not care to be fussed over and cosseted. But Sylvain had a touch about her. A rather nice one, he recalled, from the other day when she had been seeing to him.

And it seemed, as well, that she was indeed learning to lie. He didn't know whether to laugh or frown, however, at the story she had invented—it sounded lamer than his bad leg.

Easing himself off the bed, he limped to her. She straightened as he approached, and her fox slipped into the shadows of the room.

"You really should not get up," she said, frowning at his leg. Then she glanced up, a wary look in her eyes. "And why are you staring at me like that?"

Reaching up, he took her chin between his finger and thumb, then turned her head a little to the side. "I want to see if your ears do turn red."

She pulled his hand away with hers. "They were earlier, but I am not lying now."

"No, but you are blushing."

Her chin lifted. "I have nothing to blush over!"

He grinned. "Ah, your ears actually do redden—only it's more of a rose-pink on the tips rather than a red."

She wrinkled her nose as if she did not care for his study of her or such descriptions. "That is not the topic at hand—I came here to tell you that I would rather you not wait on myself and Mrs. Godwin tomorrow."

Putting one hand on the door, he leaned closer. "Why? Did I not give excellent service? Don't you like how I look after you?"

Looking down, she fussed with her candle, then she glanced up at him again, her expression cross. "Must you loom? I cannot talk with you looming."

Pushing off from the door, he took her candle and set it on the dresser. Then he took her hand and led her to his bed. Seating himself, he had to tug on her hand to pull her down so that she sat next to him. "Better?"

Chin down, hands in her lap, she glanced around. She looked more nervous than her fox had been when he had loosed the creature from its bag.

"For pity's sake, what's got you so flustered?" he asked.

"You have! And you know very well that you have, for you set out to do just that."

Pretending innocence, he made his face go as blank as he could. "What—me? I have acted exemplary this evening, I'll have you know. If we'd struck a wager on it, I would now be collecting my winnings."

"You may do this for a gamble when I am not there to watch—and agonize. I was certain Mrs. Godwin would catch you winking at me!"

He grinned now. " 'Least you weren't falling asleep by the fire with boredom."

The slightest smile betrayed her, and he pounced on it. "Ah, you see. Admit it—there's nothing like going against all the odds and beating them."

She stared at him, eyes still huge, her expression intent. "Is that why you do it? Why you take on every mad challenge? Even if it ends in trouble, or worse?"

Suddenly restless, he rose and glanced into the dark corner

of the room. "I supposed I should take your fox to the barn tonight and let him answer nature's call in the straw, not here."

Sylvain, it seemed, was not about to allow him to change the topic. "I thought that feeling you described to be more relief rushing in after excessive anxiety."

Terrance glanced at her, one eyebrow lifted and a blank expression on his face.

Wetting her lips with the tip of her tongue, Sylvain waited, her hands folded on her lap. His waistcoat hung open to show the braces that kept up his breeches—they really were too large for him. They hung loose on his narrow hips.

Digging his hands into his pockets, he at last offered a crooked smile. "Well, better to feel relief than feel nothing."

She thought about this for a moment, then asked, even though she knew she ought not to pry, "When did you stop feeling things? When your mother died?"

For an instant, he held still and a touch of anxiety washed over her. Had she gone too far? She had often wondered about this part of his past, but she had never had the opportunity to ask him. The memory lay sharp in her still of how her own mother had nearly died seven years ago. That near brush had shaken her, more than she had ever told anyone. Had he gone through the same tilting of his world?

It no longer seemed such a good idea to have brought this up to find out.

His eyes had darkened to the color of old brandy. His jaw tightened, and she saw now the resemblance to his father. She had seen just that narrowing to Squire Winslow's eyes, and the same pulse beating near his temples, before the squire erupted with anger.

However, a heartbeat later, Terrance grinned. "Trying to make me into some poetically tragic figure, are you? Sorry, but you're out on that one. That was only a story my father put out to save face that she left him."

She stared at him. Then the full impact of his words struck her.

To have a parent die, she thought a tragedy for any child. But to have one's mother leave? She could not imagine.

"Left?" she repeated. Entirely new questions bubbled up. "But why? Where did she go? I know your father is not the easiest of men, but how could she leave you and your brother?"

He gave a shrug and looked away again, into the darkness of his room. "How should I know? It was not as if she left a letter to explain anything. How in blazes do you ever find that fox of yours—ah, there. I see him. It's the gleaming eyes that give him away. Should I take out a soup bone to lure him back, do you think?"

Sylvain heard the warning in his too-casual tone. She really ought to let it go now, but she wanted at least one answer or she would not sleep for thinking on it. "If she left no note, then how did you know that she did not die? I mean, unless your father . . ."

She let her words trail off as he turned to stare at her, his face half shadowed, his eyes so hot that she almost flinched from that stare. The look passed in an instant, but it had left her shy of him.

Limping to her side, he sat on the bed again next to her. Then he said, his tone heavy with mockery, "My father . . . not much he ever told me, or Theo, for that matter. We got the same story as the rest of the world—she had gone to Tunbridge Wells to take the waters for her headaches, and contracted a chill and died."

Sylvain pressed her hands against her thighs. She dared not move. She could not remember Terrance ever speaking of his brother—or his father, for that matter. He had always avoided the topic of his family, she realized now. Just as he had avoided his home, once he had grown old enough to leave it.

She watched him, her forehead tight, wondering if she ought to say or do something. Would he welcome her sympathy, or scorn it as pity? With a touch of disgust at herself, she decided she could be quite as bad as Penelope at meddling. She ought to know better than to do that, but she seemed unable to help herself with him.

Staring at him, she studied his expression, searching for some clue as to his real feelings. But he had his careless manner back in place, with his mouth crooked into a cynical half smile. His eyes gleamed a little too brightly, but that could be nothing more than irritation at her prying.

When she said nothing, he added, his tone casual, "If you must know how I found out—well, I looked in her coffin. Simple enough to do. And I must have been a goulish child to even think of it."

"No," she said, drawing the word out with care. "I understand wishing to see her again—to say good-bye."

He grinned and shook his head. "That was not what I wanted. I seem to remember being furious that she'd gone off and left us with my father—not, as you say, the easiest of men. He hadn't even put in rocks to weight it. 'Course I don't recall her being anything but a slip of a thing—and always sick with her headaches after my father's yelling started."

Looking away, he shrugged. "How can I blame her now for leaving when I did the same myself as soon I could."

Sylvain swallowed hard, but the knot that had lodged in her throat remained. He might pretend to others—and even to himself—but she saw the pattern clear now. It had mattered to him. And it had left a scar.

How many women's names had she heard linked to his? Ladies who had run off with him—only to be left by him? Dalliances with women whose married status put a distance between him and any lover. And the risks he took—what a very good way to forget the past by burying it with too many troubles today.

He might deny all he wished that he did not care that his mother had left—but his actions were those of a man who did his best to make certain no other woman would ever have the power to hurt him. Heavens, any woman who cared for him would be doomed to heartache. So the trick with him would be not to care at all. To be as heartless as he was.

Or at least pretend.

So she tilted her head, and said, her tone brisk, "I think I had best take Trace to the stables—I can manage him far better than you can with that leg of yours."

"Nonsense—it's well enough."

"Yes, I saw that from your limping."

Terrance grinned, the slight tension eased fully from his eyes and face, and she knew she had done right not to press him just now. Perhaps there would be a time later—or perhaps not.

"Very well, then I'll admit it's aching like blazes, and I'd just as soon not go down steep stairs and up again. There is one thing you may do for me, however."

She had risen to find Trace and scoop him into her arms. Now she turned back to Terrance, Trace panting happily in her hold.

Terrance had lain down on the narrow bed again, his bad leg propped up. Lounging there, his undone shirt pulled lower by his weight and his eyes half closed, veiling the wicked glint, he looked sinfully decadent. She could almost imagine that the conversation of the last few minutes had not taken place. That it could be forgotten.

Only she doubted if it would be. By either of them.

Cuddling Trace in her arms, she asked, her tone deliberate, "Yes, what is it?"

Terrance stretched backward to lock his hands behind his head. "Be a dear and bring me back some horse liniment, will you?"

The request, so prosaic after everything that had just gone before, struck her as absurd. He was a man suspected of murder who had disguised himself as a footman. A man whose mother had run away and whose father had pretended she was dead. A man who had fought a duel, and gotten into who knew what other scrapes. A man who had run off with women and left them, brokenhearted, no doubt.

And what he wanted of her was horse liniment.

With a small shake of her head she promised, "I shall see what I can manage."

He closed his eyes. "Oh, I've no doubt you'll manage very well. You're a resourceful lot, you Harwood girls."

She glanced at him again, trying to see if he was teasing with such a comment. But he only lay upon his bed—an utter rogue to do so in a lady's presence really.

He was asleep when she returned, with the candle guttering in its holder, casting fitful flickering light over his face and his chest, which rose and fell with a steady rhythm.

Loosing Trace again, who had thankfully not wanted to linger in the stall she had found for him, she went to Terrance.

Even with his features relaxed, he looked exhausted. Dark smudges shadowed his eyes. The events of the past few days had carved new lines in his forehead, and around his mouth—small lines, but she could see them. Tempted as she was to pull a blanket over him, or touch her hand to his face to ease those lines, she did not want to wake him.

She left the glass bottle of liniment that she had been given by one of the stable boys on the dresser. After hesitating, she left Trace with him, too. Perhaps he had no need of a mother. Perhaps losing her as a boy really had not mattered to him and she was making more out of it than existed. Perhaps he got himself into trouble for no other reason than that he liked being a rogue. No matter. Just now he had need of friends. And Trace could be good at that. Far better, she suspected, than ever she could be.

Then she blew out the candle and returned to her own room.

Undressing quickly, for the night had taken on a sharp autumn bite, she slipped into her nightclothes and then into bed. The sheets had been warmed earlier by a brick, but had since cooled and so she tucked her feet up close to herself. The bedding at least smelled of lavender, not mildew. But it seemed odd not to be in her own room—she could count her times away from Harwood on one hand.

Still, it was not the cold or home or her bed that she thought of as she lay in the darkness.

Instead, she remembered the first time she had gone wandering in the woods. And had lost her way. She had been terrified. She could still remember sitting down to cry, and looking up to see him towering over her, a gun in one hand, a dark hat pulled low over long black hair that had been tied back, and his shoulders broad even back then. He had frightened her more than anything else she had seen.

She remembered the terror even now—one that sat heavy on her chest, suffocating. And the hard ground under her, her face burning with tears and her chest aching with sobs. Pulling off his hat, he had sat down next to her, despite her howling. Then he had pulled her—stiff with fear—onto his lap and told her that the rabbits would not come out to see her if she did not stop making such noise.

Something in his voice had calmed her. She smiled in the darkness, remembering. It still could, actually.

And as her sobs quieted, the rabbits had come out—timid at first, then more brazen as they foraged. He had started to whisper to her then, telling her about the woods, and how to find her way home in them by following the stream that ran from them to just behind Harwood House.

At last, with her cheeks left sticky by her tears, he had stood up, put her on her feet, brushed the leaves from her skirts, then held her hand as they walked back to Harwood.

She frowned, trying to remember more of it, but the images blurred, though the feelings remained. How old had she been? Four? Six? He must have been a boy himself at the time. Had her parents thanked him? She could only remember watching him walk away, his gun slung over those broad shoulders as he whistled something.

With a sigh, she turned on her side.

What a treacherous thing memory was—almost as much so as a heart. Putting herself on guard against both, she tried to find sleep. But it took hours before the memories finally faded and left her to even more teasing dreams.

They departed Spleenhamland early, with the sun barely up on what promised to be a bright, if crisp, autumn day, and Mrs. Godwin telling Sylvain that she really had time only for one cup of tea, not two, and that they would have cold meat later while on the road.

"That will put us in London a quarter after two this afternoon," she said.

"But my stomach is empty now," Sylvain complained as Mrs. Godwin bustled her to the coach.

Mrs. Godwin's ever-present smile faded. "A lady does not speak of her body parts. That betrays an indelicate turn of mind."

"What does it betray when she faints from hunger?" Sylvain muttered.

Hearing the remark, Mrs. Godwin glanced at her. "Fainting is a suitable feminine weakness—however, I would recommend you do so only when there is a gentleman close at hand to catch you, or if a soft surface is nearby."

Sylvain's stomach growled, which earned her a sharp glance from Mrs. Godwin, but Sylvain merely stared back defiantly.

Before she stepped into the carriage, she glanced around for Terrance. However, the luggage coach had either left before this, or would leave afterward, for she saw no sign of it, nor of him.

Which is, she told herself, what she had asked of him last night. So why should she feel so disappointed?

Taking hold of herself, she focused more on watching the scenery. She had, after all, never been so far from home. However, she really did think that this part of the road looked a good deal like the roads in Somerset.

As they neared London, she edged forward in her seat and

stared out the window, trying to see the road ahead or behind them. Other carriages passed them, but none of them
looked like the luggage coach.

Would she be able to see Terrance before he left them in
London? She must, for how else would she get Trace from
him? And that was an excellent reason why she so very much
did want to see Terrance again.

He had told her once that he had rooms at the Albany, some
sort of gentleman's club. How would he get there without aid?
Would he try to walk on that leg of his? Had that liniment
helped him at all?

Mrs. Godwin seemed to mistake her anxiety as interest and
began to point out notable sights: Lord Grenville's seat at
Dropmore Hill, a view of Windsor Castle—actually, a quick
glimpse of the towers above the trees—the seat of the Earl
of Sefton, and Earl Harcourt's at S. Leonard's Hill. Repress-
ing a yawn, Sylvain had to struggle to think of something
polite to say when Mrs. Godwin pointed out the woods be-
longing to the Countess of Orkney.

As they reached what seemed to be the edges of London—
to judge by the traffic and dense houses—the road narrowed,
the buildings rose taller and Sylvain forgot about Mrs. Godwin. What she had taken for London seemed to have been
another village, she realized. This—with its street vendors
crying their wares, its crowd of carts and wagons and carriages, its smells of soot and horse dung, its hurrying
pedestrians and boys leaning on their brooms at street cross-
ings, its ever-rising buildings that loomed above the road so
that she had to crane to see the soot-stained chimneys—had
to be London.

She wished suddenly that Terrance was not to leave them
at once. Or that she had not had to come here. Or that . . .
oh, the city seemed immense. Far larger than she had ever
imagined, for she had thought it would be like Bath—all
well-ordered streets and not this clamor and vast hodge-
podge of crowded buildings.

When their carriage turned from the main road, however, the streets widened and also became less crowded. Sylvain glimpsed discreet squares, with white stone houses that faced into green parks. Gentlemen in tall hats, form-fitted coats, and pantaloons strolled with stylish ladies. Elegant horses trotted past, some ridden and some harnessed to stylish carriages.

Their coach turned yet again, this time into one of the squares, and then stopped before one of the stone buildings.

Sylvain stared up at the structure, her heart beating fast and a sick tightness in her stomach. It looked rather daunting. However, her sister was Lady Nevin now, after all. But somehow she had never quite pictured Penelope in such a grand house.

"Ah, a quarter past exact," Mrs. Godwin announced, glancing at the watch pinned to her bodice.

Stepping from the carriage, Sylvain saw the luggage coach in the street just ahead of them and her heart lifted. She moved to it at once.

The sight of the empty seat stopped her at once. Her portmanteau sat on the floor. But Terrance had already gone.

She glanced in both directions, hoping for at least a glimpse of him. Nothing. He had said he would vanish before Penelope could recognize him, and he had.

She tried to smile. To be grateful. She would not have to worry about him now, or fear that her hiding him might be discovered. He would no doubt visit the Bow Street Runners and sort out any misunderstanding about the duel, and that would be that.

So why this wretched, aching hollowness inside?

It must be no more than hunger.

She rubbed at her temples, then reached into the coach and took up her portmanteau—comfortingly heavy and squirming. At least she had Trace.

Mrs. Godwin frowned at the bag, but Sylvain ignored her and stepped ahead.

A footman—one utterly unlike Terrance, for he wore his livery with discrete style—held open the front door for them.

Pulling in a breath, Sylvain stepped into the hall, and tried to remember that she was visiting her sister, not some utter stranger. Mrs. Godwin at once spoke to the waiting servant. "Please take Miss Harwood's things."

The man stepped forward and his gloved hand closed over Sylvian's as he took the leather handles of her bag. She pulled back at the same instant. And then a female voice shrieked her name.

Startled, Sylvain half turned, almost dropping the bag, but the footman had hold of the other handle so that he pulled open the bag. Panicked, Sylvain only had the chance to glance back at him before chaos exploded.

Hand pressed against his bad leg, Terrance limped up the last few steps to his rooms in the Albany. He had not had funds enough for a hackney, but after making his way to Piccadilly he had managed to beg a ride on the back of wagon carrying lumber. The wagon had taken him near enough to the short street that led to the Albany, and all he could think of now was how good it would be to sink into a comfortable chair with a brandy.

As he had hoped, the door opened under his touch, and he called out, "Burke, I need a bath, clean clothes and a—"

He broke off his orders at the sight of a stranger lounging in one of the two leather-covered wing chairs next to the fire. Wiry of build and in his late thirties, Terrance judged, his gaze sweeping over the fellow even as his temper fired and he took a measure of the man. Light brown hair cut short, receding from a high forehead. A shabby brown frock coat that had seen better years, as had the gray breeches and worn riding boots, which sagged at the ankles. The fellow's nose had been broken several times—and might be in for yet another breaking, Terrance decided. Over its crooked length, shrewd gray eyes regarded Terrance through the smoke from a long, white meerschaum pipe. The fellow had a face like a terrier—sharp, pointed, and a little too keen for comfort.

Terrance shut the door behind him, and then turned to face the fellow again. He knew as well as anyone in London the scarlet waistcoat worn by most Bow Street Runners. However, he had no intention of being hauled off by a bloody thief-taker. Nor of entertaining such a man.

Folding his arms, he glanced at the gilt-edged clock on the mantel, then said, his tone flat. "You have exactly one minute to explain how you come to be so at home in my rooms—and if I don't like what I hear, I'm chucking you out the door myself."

Ten

For a moment the man's eyes narrowed and his mouth thinned. He looked as if he might be weighing the odds of force actually being applied, and Terrance almost hoped the fellow would hesitate longer than one minute.

Instead of waiting the time out in silence, however, the fellow spoke up in a reedy voice touched by Cockney. "Mr. Winslow is it? There's a few as wants a word with you about Lord Dunscombe's untimely end."

Terrance glanced at the clock again, with its dial facing held by a pair of Nubians. The minute hand had not yet clicked, but it would soon. He looked back at the Runner.

Smoke curling before his face, the fellow glanced once at the clock and seemed to rethink his tactics, for he reached into one coat pocket and pulled out a silver ring with four long keys that looked as if they might fit most any lock, and probably did. "Might say as I invited myself. Never was one for dashin' about if I didn't have to."

Terrance glanced around the room. It looked its usual disorder of books left open on side tables and sporting magazines abandoned on the carpet—he had forbidden Burke any senseless tidying that left him unable to find things. A large vase by the door held a collection of walking sticks, umbrellas, and riding crops. Hunting prints hung on the dark green walls, and thick gold velvet drapes obscured what little noise from London drifted to the Albany's windows. Several snuffboxes—two of them silver—lay on the mantel. A brass tray held decanters of port and brandy. Everything seemed normal—except for the Runner.

Still, he could not but wonder, so he asked, "And what else did you invite yourself to?"

"Now, sir, I'm an officer of the law, I am. Wouldn't do for me to go helpin' myself to anythin' more than a comfortable place to sit, though I wouldn't say no to an offer to wet my throat. Been quite a wait for you, it has. An' you might be interested as to what else I have to say. It ain't just questions I came about."

Still tempted to toss the fellow out, Terrance checked the impulse. He had not believed that Perriman had involved the Runners, but he had underestimated the man's idiocy. And if now he tossed this fellow out, that would result also in his having to quit his rooms. At least until he had this damn disaster started by Perriman ended.

Limping to the sideboard, Terrance eyed the crystal decanter. Why not a drink? He wanted one himself. He took up the heavy leaded decanter, pulled out the stopper, and splashed the amber liquid into one cut-crystal tumbler, and then another. After putting the decanter back on its brass tray, he took up the glasses, limped back to the fire, and handed one to the Runner.

The fellow had cheek enough to raise his with a toast and a smile that looked only a touch cynical. "To your health, sir."

Terrance sat down in the chair opposite and stretched his feet to the fire. "Seems an odd toast for the likes of you— seeing as it's not my interests you've come about."

"Not a bit of it, sir. The way I see it, we have a good deal in common, we do."

"What? That you're here to see about claiming the reward Perriman's posted for me, and I'm to oblige with my cooperation? How much did he offer, by the by?"

"Three hundred pounds, sir. For your apprehension for questioning. There's not yet been an inquest an' charge brought upon anyone. Not just yet at least."

Pausing with his brandy halfway to his mouth, Terrance frowned. "Three hundred! Is that all?"

"That's a fortune to some, sir."

Terrance glanced at the Runner's faded coat and his scuffed low-heeled boots. "Not to you?"

"Well, now, can't say as I wouldn't be pleased to pocket such a tidy sum. Only I'm aimin' a might higher."

Eyebrow quirking, his disdain for the fellow deepened. "So you expect me to best the amount, eh?"

The man smiled, thin lips curving, but with his gray eyes as sharp-edged as ever and giving nothing away of his feelings. "Runner's got two things of value, sir. The reward money as ends in his pocket and the name he makes earnin' it. One, you might say, rather goes to make t'other. Ever heard tell of a John Townsend?"

Frowning, Terrance shook his head. His leg ached and the ill-fitting clothes chaffed his skin. He knew he must stink of his own sweat. However, as he sipped his brandy, the name slipped into place. "There was a Townsend at some ball or other once. Heavy-set fellow, dressed on the florid side. Someone remarked that he acted as personal guard to the Regent on occasion."

"He does that, right 'nuff, sir. Right friendly he is with the Prince. Goes to the swell parties, he does, looking after the ladies' sparkles and the gents' finery. Three hundred's a night's work to him. And why? 'Cause he has himself a reputation, he does. There's a dozen of us at Bow Street, but it's Townsend the thief-taker—Townsend the Bow Street Runner of the *ton,* Townsend the great man. He's made himself stand above the rest of us, an' that's where I'm headed."

Sipping his brandy, Terrance let the burn of it relax into him. He studied the man intently now. An ambitious fellow, it seemed. Not the most ethical of men, or he would have seen it as his duty to bring Terrance to justice instead of using this to further his own interests. Still, that suited Terrance well enough. Only it left him wondering just how much he could trust the fellow. The only thing he had found to be more dangerous than ambition was desire. Together, they could bring down nations.

"And what's the name you're going to make famous?" Terrance asked, deciding he had best know all he could about this fellow. "And what do you want from me, if not a reward for my skin?"

Standing, the Runner tapped the tobacco from his pipe into his palm and tossed the shreds of burnt leaf into the fire. It sputtered and crackled, and the aroma of tobacco grew stronger. At least he smoked a good mix, something woody and not perfumed.

"Waddington. Reggie Waddington. As to what I want . . . well, takin' the wrong man for a crime ain't what Townsend done to be remarked."

"You think I'm the wrong man then?"

The man tucked his pipe into his right coat pocket and then smoothed his vest. "I ain't sayin' you are. But I looked at this six ways from Sunday, an' what keeps comin' back is there ain't much you stood to gain by having done that fellow in. Now, it might've been a crime of passion by what I hear about her ladyship as were married to the blighter."

"Who in blazes told you that?"

Waddington's smile widened, and he looked pleased to have startled Terrance. "Well, now, servants do talk. Only what I heard is that any passion there cooled off some time ago—least on your side of things. 'Course there's other reasons I'd rather not stake my future on you being the man as is wanted here—and there's others who come off well for the fellow being dead."

"Perriman you mean?"

"It ain't that nob as has my interest, sir. Only I ain't a Townsend as can go waltzing into fine drawing rooms askin' questions to find out for a certainty if what I do think may be true."

Wary, Terrance glared at the man. "So you want me to turn informer for you?"

"That's a harsh word for it. But then it's a harsh world, ain't it? An' I'll warn you straight now, sir. If you're charged and I have to bring you up before the magistrate, it'll be in my interest then to see you dangle from the nubbin' cheat. I ain't goin' to be known as the Runner who brought in an innocent man. But I'd rather look a right hero by provin' this ain't no simple case of hauling a known villain into the courts."

Terrance sat still, his empty brandy glass in his hand. He could see how Waddington saw to profit from this. He could also imagine Waddington saying nothing of his suspicions against another if that was what suited the man best—he would let him hang.

But whom did Waddington suspect?

He disliked the idea of prying into the affairs of others. However, he had had his curiosity stirred. And his anger. Whoever had shot Dunscombe might be quite willing to let him hang for it. His hand clenched around his glass, and the crystal edges dug into his palm. Bloody all—he'd not sit idle and act as some pawn for another.

Staring at Waddington, he asked, "While I'm making these inquiries, what's to keep another of you fellows from arriving on the scene? You can't be the only one looking for me."

Rocking back on his heels, Waddington tucked his thumbs into his waistcoat pockets. "Well, now, common thought just now is that you're either still in Somerset layin' low, or must be dashing for the nearest port—Bristol or Plymouth. That's good for a fortnight at least. An' I've a few tricks myself. So as long as you're not standin' in Hyde Park to tell the world who you are and where you are, I reckon we've the better part of a month, and maybe a bit more. But it ain't the slow ones as gets hired at Bow Street. An' when word gets out, you can be certain it'll be me as brings you to Bow Street."

Waddington's eyes never changed from flat gray as he spoke. *Cold-blooded bastard,* Terrance thought, not the least

surprised. He nodded. And then found himself startled to realize that a trickle of fear shivered in him. Murder charges.
That lay far beyond any sin he had ever committed. And he
wondered just how he had become the sort of man whom others could believe had shot a man in the back.

Scowling, he brushed away his uneasiness. He had not yet
been charged, nor taken. And he would not be. Blazes, he had
never thought of his name before, but he knew now that he
was not about to become the Winslow who dragged the family name into the gutter.

Tone blunt, he demanded, "Just where would you have me
start?"

Waddington unhooked his thumbs from his vest and
straightened. "Well, now, I been wonderin' just how familiar
you still are with that newly made widow?"

As soon as Trace slipped from the open bag, Sylvain
dropped her hold on the handle and grabbed for him, barely
brushing his fur. The footman jumped back, dropping the bag
so that its bone handles clattered on the marble floor. Mrs.
Godwin muttered something that sounded rather like a muffled curse, and the female—Cecila, of course—who had
shrieked Sylvain's name, let out a startled laugh. The maid
who stood just behind her on the stairs let out an earnest cry
of pure horror.

Eyes wide and dark, Trace streaked for the nearest hiding hole, or what resembled one—just under the flat base
of the round table that stood in the center of the hall. As he
did, Sylvain heard the front door latch click open behind
her.

Spinning around, she ran to the door and slammed it
closed, then leaned against it and begged, "Please—please be
quiet everyone."

Only Cecila seemed to hear her, for she had descended the
stairs to come to Sylvain's side. She clasped her sister's hand,

her blue-green eyes brimming with both amusement and ex-
asperation. "You idiot—how good to see you! Whatever were
you thinking to bring Trace with you? Penelope will have a
fit! Good day, Mrs. Godwin. I hope you did not have too
bothersome a trip from Somerset."

She said the last as Mrs. Godwin, face red, turned to her,
eyebrows flat and her expression thunderous, as if she had
something blistering to say. Cecila's calm words seemed to
check her temper, however, so Sylvain turned her attention
back to Trace. The footman had knelt on the floor to stare
under the table base, and the maid was still shrieking about a
beast loose in the house.

Face tight, Sylvain glanced at her sister. "Do you think
Penelope must really find out?"

A knock sounded on the front door and then the knob
twisted and the door slid open an inch, but Sylvain braced her
weight against it again. The image of Trace slipping out into
London streets—and the press of wagons, carts, and carriages
she had seen—shuddered into her. He would know nothing of
how to avoid so many wheels. She swallowed hard. She could
not bear it if anything happened to him.

A sharp voice cut into the commotion, stilling the maid's
cries and bringing the footman to his feet. Even Mrs. Godwin
turned.

"That is a sufficient fuss, thank you, Doris. Jefferies, do
please brush the dust from your breeches."

Lady Nevin came into the room, and Sylvain almost did
not recognize her own sister. Her hair had been cut to draw
out the red glints in the soft, brown curls, piled with what
looked lush careless abandon. Her skin glowed, and the long-
sleeved peach gown suited her complexion. High-necked, the
gown emphasized her figure. It also, as she came forward,
showed the soft swell to her belly.

Well, no wonder her sister had not come to Somerset to
fetch her. Sylvain at once demanded, "Why did you not write
that you are to have a baby?"

Penelope started to answer, but Cecila cut in, sounding both smug at the news and determined as ever not to be overlooked, "I am to have one as well!"

Frowning at this, Penelope caught Sylvain's hand away from Cecila and pressed a kiss to her youngest sister's cheek. Then she frowned as a muffled voice drifted through the door. She glanced at Sylvain—leave it to her sister to bring such disorder with her. Gracious, how she had missed her!

"Dear, I think you have shut Nevin out—that really will not do, you know."

"She's got her fox with her," Cecila explained. "Under the table."

"I cannot let him slip out, Ella," Sylvain said, her tone desperate.

Penelope glanced from one sister to the other. "Sylvain, go and stand between the door and your fox. Jefferies, do let his lordship in—if he catches me so much as opening a door, it will be another lecture about my delicate condition. You will not believe how I am fussed over," she told Sylvain.

Shoulders relaxing, Sylvain moved at once to obey her older sister's orders and sat on the floor beside the round table. A reddish nose poked out and black whiskers quivered.

An agitated movement from Cecila drew Penelope's eye—she noted at once her sister's sudden pallor and the sheen to her skin. She leaned closer to her at once. "There is an extra basin in the armor in the drawing room, dear."

With a nod and a hand her to her mouth, Cecila excused herself and hurried from the room.

Then Jefferies opened the door, and Penelope turned to her husband, who stood on the doorstep, hat in hand and dark eyes flashing.

Scenting freedom, the fox bolted, slipping through Sylvain's grasp, darting past the footman. Even with three legs, he was fast. Sylvain gave a cry, but Nevin bent, scooping up the animal by the scruff of its neck. He frowned at it a moment, then glanced at Sylvain and, with a lopsided smile cradled the animal into his arms.

"What, no owl as well? Or does Mr. Feathers await in the carriage?" he asked.

Penelope smiled at him, and pressed a hand to her stomach. When she saw his dark eyes follow the gesture, she took her hand away. He saw too much. The Gypsy part of him, she assumed. And the legacy of his early years, when he had survived by living on the road like a vagabond. He had even been the first one to notice her pregnancy. He stroked the fox's head now, and the animal panted nervously in his arms, but did not struggle. She smiled at that—would he teach their child his Gypsy ways?

Striding to Sylvain, he gave her care of her fox, then touched a hand to her cheek. "He will be happier in the garden, little one. Jefferies will show you. And after you settle him, come in for something to eat. You must be famished."

"Yes, dear, do please," Penelope said, and then she turned to Mrs. Godwin. "And could I trouble you to take Doris to the kitchen for something restorative? I should not impose on you, but she looks as if she's had a shock. And I expect you might care to rest then yourself?"

Smiling, Mrs. Godwin curtsied and moved at once to do as was asked of her. She stopped only to give Lord Nevin a good day, and Penelope resisted the urge to shake her head. Her Gypsy lord had but to smile, and flash those dark eyes and most women melted to his whims. Not all, of course. A few high-sticklers of London society had closed their doors, despite the fact that he had inherited a title that went back centuries.

Let them, she thought, chin lifting. Others called on them— bankers, and men of new wealth, inventors, and politicians who liked Lord Nevin's speeches of progressive reform. Change seemed in the air in London these days, although for every step forward there too often came a backlash of laws from the elite, as they sought to keep their power.

Still, they had found friends at Holland House, and in other places. Enough so that she did not fear that Sylvain might be shunned. She would not have brought her to London otherwise—and what was Sylvain thinking to bring her fox with her? Gracious, but perhaps she had left this too late?

As the room cleared and peace settled again, Nevin came to her. "I step out for an hour and find you on your feet and in the middle of excitement—do you listen to nothing the doctors say?"

His black eyes snapped, but Penelope smiled at him. His fussing would have driven her mad if she did not know its source. But his sister had confided to Penelope about her miscarriage. Her hand drifted to her stomach as she thought of Glynis, Lady St. Albans', strained words. She had been obviously reluctant to disclose such a personal grief—and one that still seemed to haunt her.

And then Glynis added, "He won't admit to you that he is worried, but I know him. And while we can do nothing about what God wills, if you want to bring him comfort, then let him fuss. St. Albans has vowed to take me to the most boring of his estates next time I lie in, and I expect he'll be having me carried about by a litter and I will grow miserably fat."

She had spoken with a smile, but Penelope had seen the shadows that haunted the back of her eyes. To miscarry a baby, even one not yet three months grown inside you . . .

She shut off the images and fears. She would be healthy. And so would her child. And she would not tempt fate by either being too careful, or not being careful at all. After all, Lady St. Albans had done nothing more than trip on a step and fall.

Well, she would be careful of her steps. And Nevin, she knew, would be even more careful for her.

Giving him her hand, she smiled at him. "I listen very well. And Cecila can tell you we did nothing more than lie about, with her reading to me from the fashion magazines—which entertained Cecila and left me bored to somnolence."

He glanced around. "Where is she? Has she left? I thought Cecila was to stay, and that Bryn would join us for dinner?"

"Your cousin has promised he will be here. But Cecila is otherwise occupied just now. It is not just morning sickness for her, but morning, afternoon, and evening."

Nevin kissed her hand. "You were the same the first month. Now tell me why Sylvain brought her fox with her—and how? I thought you judged Mrs. Godwin up to the task of only bringing your sister, not her pets."

Leaning on his arm, Penelope walked with him as he led the way to the square of garden at the back of the house. "I suppose I ought to have warned her about the foxes and owls and hedgehogs and all else, but it actually did not occur to me that she might bring one of them. I ought to have known better. And I ought to have brought her to London last spring."

Pausing in the hall, he turned to her and pulled her close. "We were, as I recall, doing other things, such as taking a honeymoon. And you might think you need to know everything, and anticipate even more, but I assure you that would make you the most tiresome companion."

She pushed against him, but only lightly. "Nevin, you cannot kiss me in the hall. What if a servant sees us? I, at least, know what is due your rank."

"I'd rather have what is due me as your husband—so kiss me fast and hard before we are caught out."

Sylvain stepped into the house from the back garden to see Nevin's arms tighten around Penelope, his touch both protective and possessive. Cheeks hot, she watched them, half embarrassed to have glimpsed this moment of intimacy and yet also delighted that her sister had found such happiness. Stepping quiet, she backed out again, nearly colliding with the footman who had started to follow her inside.

"I think I ought to spend a few more moments with Trace

to make utterly certain he is over his fright," she said, her ears
tingling.

The footman said nothing, and his expression betrayed
nothing as he bowed and then stood back to await her pleasure. In truth, she found him a bit daunting, and he kept
reminding her in odd ways of Terrance.

And that made her think of Nevin and Penelope kissing.

Sitting down on a stone bench, she watched Trace. Or
watched the hole he had dug for himself and in which he now
lay hidden amid a bed of thyme, rosemary, and lavender.

Odd, how her sister's happiness should also bring this unsettled yearning. Ridiculous, in fact. Terrance mattered no
more to her than did this fellow Jefferies, and she was well
out of it now that he had taken himself off.

But she did start to wonder just where the Albany lay situ-
ated in London? And what sort of trouble was Terrance
getting himself into now?

The next few days gave Sylvain little time to think of Terrance, for her sisters seemed bent on remaking her.

Penelope had in a hairdresser, who lamented Sylvain's
short curls in a flow of rapid French, then cut her hair and
two days later returned with two artful hair arrangements
that could be pinned into place to give the illusion of longer
curls. She thought it odd to wear someone else's hair to
augment her own, but as the maid—Doris—told her,
"'Least you won't be wearing any improvers."

At Sylvain's questioning glance, Doris gestured to her own
ample breasts. "Wax ones as give you a figure a wet nurse
would envy. Only I heard tell Lady Morton had hers found
out when she stood too near the fire, and one melted."

Sylvain's giggles over this encouraged Doris to confide
other social disasters, from drooping pantaloons that came
untied and fell onto the street from under a lady's dress, to a
too-full skirt whisked up over another lady's head by a strong

wind. While amusing, the gossip convinced Sylvain that her false curls would no doubt fall off at some critical social moment—such as when making her first curtsy to a royal prince.

Every other morning the dancing master came to instruct her, and in the afternoons Mrs. Godwin sat with her to list the endless rules of conduct, from how she must never decline a gentleman's request for a dance, to how deep a curtsy she must make to a duchess.

Then came the dressmaker, and shoemaker, and corset maker, and glove makers, and the milliners with their ribbons and bonnets. Everything required fittings, materials chosen, styles selected. Penelope argued for conservative choices in pastels, while Cecila pushed for the latest trends in lower waists and billowing sleeves. Penelope won most disagreements, but mostly due to Cecila's having to often quit the room, her face pale and her fingers pressed to her lips.

And Sylvain could almost wonder if such misery was worth enduring just to have a child.

She also decided she would rather fuss with the dolls brought by the dressmaker to display the latest styles than bother with her own wardrobe.

In truth, she felt almost as if she still occupied the nursery, with Penelope and Cecila dressing her and arranging her schedule, and with Mrs. Godwin correcting her posture if she slumped and forever telling her what a lady did or did not do. Yet the staff at Nevin House treated her with respect. Doris consulted her as to what Sylvain would wear for day or dinner, and how she wished to have her hair arranged. And while Bryn teased her that she would become too stylish for his company, Nevin treated her as he always had—as if she were his blood sister. He took her to see some of London, and not the unusual locations, but to tour the stately Burlington House, to visit the architect Sir John Soane in Lincoln's Inn Fields, and to see the Harwood Arcade—the glass-covered street of shops built as an investment by her father and Nevin.

At the end of four days, with new clothes arriving daily,

Penelope announced that Sylvain could attend Lady Omsbury's social evening. "It is nothing formal, and will be just enough company to entertain without there being so many faces that you become lost."

Wrinkling her nose, Sylvain tried to slip out of the evening by reminding Penelope of her delicate condition, but her sister only smiled. So she protested that she had not had enough dancing lessons. With a shake of her head, Penelope came over to Sylvain and put a hand on her shoulder. "Silly, I know it can be frightening to step out of one's own cozy world, but it is the only way to grow, you know."

That silenced Sylvain. She had not thought of this.

She was still mulling over Penelope's words as she stepped from the carriage at a quarter past seven that evening and entered Lady Omsbury's elegant town house in Half Moon Street.

She stopped in the hall to allow a porter in deep blue livery to take her evening cloak, and to tug up her long yellow kid gloves which matched her gown, and which felt as if they were slipping down her arms every time she moved.

Then another lady stepped into the hall and Sylvain forgot about her gloves.

Lady Dunscombe stood in the doorway, a black velvet cloak over her gown and her brother beside her, also in black evening clothes, his tall beaver hat and ebony walking stick in his hand. She did not expect to be remembered, but Lady Dunscombe, who had been glancing around almost nervously, smiled and came forward. "Why, if it is not Miss Harwood! How charming you look—as bright as a spring daffodil. Edwin, you remember Miss Harwood, do you not?"

Eleven

With an automatic smile, Edwin Hayland stepped forward to assure his sister that of course he remembered Miss Harwood. But his glance moved away and up the stairs, as if he sought someone else, and his words were too smooth for Sylvain to believe.

Taking off her cloak, Lady Dunscombe gave it to the porter with careless grace, and envy shot through Sylvain. Her throat ached with it.

Above the lady's dark, low-cut gown, diamonds glittered. Perfect matched round gems that flashed in the candlelight at the lady's every movement and breath. Drop earrings gleamed and swung from her ears, glimmering as they peaked out from her careless tumble of golden curls. And from the bodice of her deep purple gown a bow-shaped diamond broach, with another drop dangling, flashed fire.

Sylvain's mouth dried. Heavens, if she had such magnificent gems to draw the eye, she would never worry again about being such a drab slip of a thing.

She caught hold of herself at once. Where would she ever wear such things if she owned them? How absurd.

Half ashamed of her own greed, she glanced away. But when she glanced back, the glittering stones still drew a wistful longing from her that she might wear such jewelry.

Lady Dunscombe and her brother finished exchanging polite nothings with Penelope and Mrs. Godwin, and turned to mount the stairs. Sylvain watched, envy still stirring. Heads turned as the couple moved into the room with their match-ing grace, fair coloring, and dramatically dark attire. She noted the condemning expressions on other ladies' faces, but Lady Dunscombe kept her head high. Only her flashing diamonds betrayed a slight, nervous quiver.

With a jolt of insight, Sylvain knew that Lady Dunscombe had worn the diamonds just as she would have—to act as a shield, to give herself a reason why others might stare.

A sensation of kinship with Lady Dunscombe startled Sylvain, making her frown. Before she knew what to make of the feeling, Penelope leaned close to whisper, "You must be polite, of course, but that is not a connection to en-courage."

Surprised, Sylvain turned to her sister. Penelope never spoke ill of anyone. "Why ever not?" she asked.

Arching her eyebrows, Penelope stared at her as if she should not have to explain, then said, "Mr. Hayland is a gamester, and his sister runs with a fast set. Arabella's will be far too tame for their tastes, so they must be putting in an appearance to quell the gossip."

"What gossip?"

"Gossip that is not suitable for your ears—that's what." With a frown, Penelope moved off to greet their hostess, a handsome, dark-haired woman who smiled at Sylvain and began to introduce her around.

Sylvain soon had more names in her head than she could fit to the faces present. She smiled at everyone until her cheeks ached, and bobbed curtsies that several times threat-ened the threads in her hem. However, no one seemed to expect more from her—even Mrs. Godwin's smile widened at such a proper reserve in a young lady. If they only knew how she longed to go home and put on a comfortable dress, not this one with a new, biting corset and stiff bodice and itchy lace at the neckline.

She noticed that Lady Dunscombe and her brother took seats near the window, but few approached them. As Sylvain glanced around the room, she heard the whispers and saw the glances sent in their direction.

Neither Lady Dunscombe nor her brother seemed to notice, however. Their attention seemed focused on the entrance. It seemed they did not care to even speak with each other, for only once did Sylvain see the two golden heads bend close.

So why had they come?

Half an hour later, Sylvain wondered why anyone stayed. The evening seemed to be only talk, although as the drawing room filled, doors were opened into two other rooms and four tables arranged for cards.

Penelope sat talking with Lady Omsbury, and Mrs. Godwin, encouraged by Sylvain, had gone to one of the card tables to make up a fourth for whist.

Wandering back into the other room, Sylvain noticed how crowded it still seemed—ladies in bright evening dresses and pastel gowns mingled with gentlemen in blue or black coats and dark breeches or pale pantaloons. Other ladies had worn their jewelry, but she saw nothing else that sparked the desire that Lady Dunscombe's set had stirred in her.

She looked over at them again, and shock tingled on her skin.

The man stood with his back to her, but she could not mistake those broad shoulders so beautifully framed by a black evening coat, nor the short-cropped black hair, nor the height of him. He bent to say something to Lady Dunscombe—his dark looks contrasting with her golden ones, and Sylvain's eyes narrowed. The lady glanced up at him, eyes luminous with tears, full lower lip trembling. After a glance around the room, she put her gloved hand on his arm. He turned and started to leave.

Even if his profile had not given him away, his limp would have. As Sylvain watched, one hand clenched tight on her fan and her heart thudding, Terrance left the house with Lady Dunscombe on his arm.

She turned away, a sick tightness in her stomach, to walk

back into the room where Penelope sat and Mrs. Godwin played cards. A straight-backed chair stood alone against the wall, so she claimed it, then stared at her gloved hands.

How could she have been so wrong?

She had thought it had ended between them. She had been convinced by how he had spoken. She put a hand to her stomach, feeling as ill as Cecila. And then she remembered his story about his mother.

She wanted to die.

How affecting she had thought it! How she had invented feelings for him, making it so dreadful that he would be unable to commit to any woman.

Fool. Fool. Fool!

He had shrugged off any such notion. But she had not wanted to think him callous. And then he had wasted little time in finding his way back to the beautiful Lady Dunscombe.

She had made him into what she wanted to think him.

Then she frowned.

How had he known to find her here?

Looking up, she stared at the strangers around her. A black-haired young woman in white to her left laughed at something the gentleman next to her said. An elderly, hook-nosed woman with ostrich plumes in her hair and an ancient brocade gown entered the room supported by a gentleman in knee breeches who looked enough like her that he must be her son.

How had he known?

Penelope had said this was not the sort of gathering that Hayland and Lady Dunscombe frequented. So why would Terrance come here to find them?

Edwin Hayland came into the room, moving as gracefully as his sister had. He glanced around, ignoring the few smiles sent his direction by some of the women. With a frown, he strode to Sylvain's side, and asked, his voice clipped by tension, "I beg your pardon, but have you seen my sister? I stepped out for a moment and seem to have misplaced her."

He smiled as if making a jest, but his slate gray eyes remained flat and cold. The aroma of tobacco clung to his clothes. Sylvain could imagine he had stepped out to smoke either a cheroot or one of the small cigarillos, such as Frank Silk had taken up as the latest thing.

Parting her lips, she started to tell him that his sister had left with Terrance, but as his gaze swung back from searching the room to fasten on her again, it struck her that earlier Mr. Hayland and his sister had appeared to be waiting for something—or someone.

Had they known Terrance would be here? Perhaps he had an assignation to meet them—or just to meet Lady Dunscombe—and Mr. Hayland had invited himself?

Everything shifted.

This must have something to do with Lord Dunscombe's death. Yes, that made sense. Her heart lifted, but she tried to be honest—was she grasping for the hope that Terrance had no real interest in Lady Dunscombe beyond clearing his name? Oh, why must he make everything so difficult with a reputation that made it dangerous to trust him!

Still, she would trust at least that she was not being stupid about this. Too much lay at stake for her to do otherwise—he still stood suspected of murder, after all.

Forcing a smile, she said, "She was here but a moment ago. Would you care for me to go with you to see if she might have gone into the lady's retiring room?" Her ears burned at that, but she wanted time enough with him to ask a few questions.

Mr. Hayland at once offered his arm. "That would be kind. Thank you."

She had to ask the directions for the room set aside for the ladies to attend their personal needs. As they mounted the stairs, she glanced at him and asked, her tone casual, "Did you have business in town?"

"No. Only a desire to be away from the countryside."

"Oh? It seemed so urgent that you leave Somerset when I saw you last."

He glanced at her. "My sister's idea. Her husband's death left her—distraught."

"Because he was murdered, or because she believes Terrance Winslow responsible?"

His step hesitated, then he continued up the carpeted stair. "That is blunt speaking."

"Well, how could anyone who really knows Mr. Winslow think he would shoot any man in the back?"

He lifted one narrow white hand. "My late brother-in-law was a deadly marksman—I should not have cared to face him in a duel."

She glanced at him. His mouth had tightened and something dark flashed in his eyes. "You did not like your sister's husband?"

The barest smile softened his mouth, almost making him handsome. "Did anyone, Miss Harwood?"

She had more questions, but they had arrived at the room and he turned to her. "If you do not find my sister within, please let me know at once."

His abrupt tone invited no further questions, and his cold stare left her uncomfortable. So she turned and let herself into the room, disappointed to have learned so little from him other than that he disliked Lord Dunscombe.

Guilty for having lied to him, she at least went through the pretense of a search. When she stepped out again, her hands lifted in a helpless gesture, Mr. Hayland gave her a short bow, then turned and left, his movements agitated and quick.

Why was he so upset to find his sister gone? Did he seek to keep her under his watch? Perhaps so that she might not incriminate herself in her husband's death?

I should not have cared to face him.

A chill tingled on her skin, making the fine hairs stand up on the back of her arms. Perhaps she actually had learned something. But could it help Terrance?

* * *

Temper barely in check, Terrance glared into the darkness of the hired hack and wondered if this would go any easier if he just throttled her. She had yet to give a direct answer to any question. "Ellena, if you ever actually cared anything for me . . ."

"How can you say that?" Lady Dunscombe turned her face away to stare out the carriage window, melodramatic hurt trembling in her voice.

Overplaying it as usual, Terrance judged with a scowl. Blazes, but did the woman love her theatrics!

He had ordered the driver twice round Green Park and had tossed a guinea up to the man. At this rate, it would take a dozen turns to drag anything from her other than recriminations.

Drawing in his breath, he opted for his last resort—raw truth. "You're only angry that I ended it before you could. You'd already started eyeing Cale as your next conquest."

She twisted around to glare at him, eyes glimmering and jewels flashing in the dim moonlight that slanted through the carriage window. "I loved you!"

"Very Drury Lane. But inaccurate. You loved what you thought I could give you—your youth back! You even told me so once."

The sniffles stopped. She sat still, but the glimmer of jewels revealed quick, shallow, angry breaths. Finally, voice low, she said, "You're horrible! How can you be so cold when we once meant everything to each other?"

Once. Past tense. Some progress at least.

"Rubbish! You used me to get back at a husband who neglected you." His mouth twisted. "If you honestly cared for me you would hardly have thrown our infatuation in front of your husband's face just so he could call me out!"

Hate dripped from her voice. "I'm sorry Myles didn't shoot you!"

Terrance smiled and folded his arms. "He might have if someone else hadn't taken his chance from him."

"Someone? I thought you . . . ?"

Her words drifted off and he stared at her, appalled. "Thought I shot him? In the back! And even so, you'd swear you loved me! Well, that shows how well you think of me!"

Her tone shifted to the petulant tones he knew too well. "If you had shot him for me—"

"For you! Oh, that makes any dishonorable behavior acceptable, if I did it for you! Of all the conceited—"

"It is not conceit! That is the depth to which I believed your passions ran. I thought you did it to free me! So we could be together. And what right do you have to speak of honor—you have barely a scrap of it to your name!"

Glaring at her, Terrance almost wished he could stop the carriage, open the door, and put her out on the street. However, even he had his limits. He also had to admit she was right. His face burned with that.

But what right had she to throw stones at him. She had broken her marriage vows—he at least had never made promises that he later broke. He never pretended to be other than what he was.

And while he might have abandoned more than a few females—four actually—he never left them in anything but comfortable circumstances. Usually ones they preferred. That had certainly been his experience with the vicar's daughter, who had run off with him—and then taken a stronger fancy to a fellow with a bright uniform.

He also did not go about shooting anyone in the back— blazes, but he at least knew how to be a good sportsman!

Eyes narrowed, he glared at her. "I did not shoot your blasted husband, not for you, nor for anyone else. But you and your nephew certainly seem bent on making the blame stick with me!"

"Ashlin? Don't even speak to me of him! It's all his fault anyway. He put it about that you had shot Myles. And he's become so unbearably pompous since the title came to him that I actually found myself sympathizing with Myles's loathing for him."

She sat quiet a moment. The steady clop of hooves against the street carried to them. Then she asked, "Do you believe he . . ."

Again her words trailed away. Terrance's mouth twisted down. Why must she be so damnably vague! "What? Did in his uncle? Your husband went out of his way to torture the poor bugger for every lack he has—that could drive any man to murder."

"But how could he have when he . . ."

"He what?"

"Well, I had breakfast with Ashlin that morning. Neither of us had slept well. And Myles left the house while we ate. We glimpsed him from the breakfast room as he strode out."

"So you knew about the duel then?"

Bitterness laced her words. "No, I did not. I knew Myles had argued with you the night before, but no one said anything to me of a duel. Not Ashlin, and not even Edwin, though he tried to swear he knew nothing of it beforehand."

"He did?"

"Well, yes. Only my maid had seen him on the stairs that night, listening to something Ashlin and Lord Cale were saying. She thought nothing of it until after that morning, and then she knew they must have been speaking of the duel, for she had heard mention of pistols."

"Have you told anyone of this?" he demanded.

"Why should I? It hardly matters."

"My hanging for murder matters—thank you very much!"

Harness jingling, the carriage rocked as the hired hack trotted along nearly empty streets. Light and shadow flickered into the carriage as they passed great houses with doors lit by flambeaus and link-boys who guided their patrons home with lanterns hung from tall poles.

Voice timid, she asked, "You won't really hang . . . will you?"

"Not if I can help it. But I'm going to need more to slip the noose than my sayin' I didn't shoot him."

Terrance leaned against the stiff leather seat, his arms crossed and senses alert. He had a lover's knowledge of this woman, and though they had both once cherished illusions of each other, they had done with that, he hoped. He could hear her thoughts turning now. And some flicker of genuine feeling for him must have remained in her, for she reached out her hand to touch his.

"Perhaps Ashlin did do it?"

"What—he broke his fast with you, galloped madly over to shoot your husband, hid away, and then cantered up again after I had arrived? That don't work."

"Well, then, a highwayman! Or perhaps Cale shot him—he had lost considerably to Myles a few months . . ." Her words drifted away again, this time catching on a tight edge in her voice.

He stared at her. "What is it? What are you not telling me?"

"Nothing. I . . . It must be nothing."

He leaned forward and snared her hand in a hard grip. "Tell me, Ellena. Or you can tell the Bow Street magistrate."

In the near darkness, her eyes widened. "You wouldn't."

"Wouldn't do all I can to save myself? Or do you now hate me enough to want me tried for a murder I didn't commit?"

Her chin lifted. "Ashlin wrote to Bow Street to send Runners to find you. You cannot simply walk in there now."

Letting go of her hand, he twisted and then pulled down the carriage window to yell out, "Driver, take us to Bow—"

"No!" She grabbed his arm, dragging him back.

"Tell me, Ellena. You were speaking of Cale and his gambling with your husband. Is it Cale you seek to protect?"

"Do not be absurd!"

"Then who is it? Someone else who lost a good deal to your husband? I knew how blasted competitive he was. Who else did he skin at the tables?"

She shook her head and he could swear her face had gone pale as death in the moonlight.

His eyes narrowed. "You'd never fight so fierce for yourself—or a lover, I think. But you would for one other. It's your brother, isn't it? How much did he lose? Five thousand? Ten?"

She let go of him. "I hate you!"

"Very well. I'll ask Edwin."

"No! He . . . he did not even know of the duel until after."

"You just told me he did."

"I was wrong—my maid got it wrong. She did not hear what Edwin overheard really. And Myles lured him into that card game! You know how he would sneer at another man to goad him into taking up one of his stupid challenges."

"Oh, I know," he said, thinking of how Dunscombe had forced a duel on him, keeping at him with sly insults. He had borne with most of them until Dunscombe had started in on the ancient rumors about his mother not being able to bear his father's temper. Accurate rumors, but ones Terrance had not been able to endure hearing come from Dunscombe.

"How much did he lose?" he asked.

She shook her head, then said, voice quiet, defeated, "A hundred thousand."

Numb, Terrance sat back against the seat. A hundred thousand! Even he could not imagine such a loss—and he had had many a bad night at the tables.

Dunscombe's death voided such a debt of honor.

"He didn't shoot Myles," she insisted. "He didn't rise until late that morning. He would never hurt anyone!"

Pity welled inside him for her. It would injure her a good deal more to lose her brother than it had her husband. "For your sake, I hope you may be right. Now, where are you staying?"

Reluctant and pouting now, she gave him the name of the Pultney Hotel. The hack took them there, and Terrance stepped out, favoring his bad leg, then turned to give her his hand. Pulling her skirts up with both hands, she stepped from the carriage, shunning his touch. She did not even glance at him, but swept into the hotel, head high.

Relief eased into him, and a smile edged his mouth. His

suspicions of her brother had seemed to put the final end to her infatuation. Thank God. What in blazes had ever interested him beyond that pretty face and figure?

His mouth crooked at a sudden memory of Sylvain once remarking, as they sat in the woods near Winslow Park, that choosing the wrong person had to be worse than choosing no one at all.

"It's better than being alone," he'd shot back, smarting at the truth in her words.

She had glanced around them, pointedly staring at a nest of starlings, then at a squirrel chattering at them, and then at Terrance again. Then she had asked, "How is anyone ever really alone?"

He had grinned at her, thinking her a child to classify animals as being anywhere near a companion, but perhaps she had more wisdom than he had credited. It certainly gave her an easier life.

With a word to the driver to take him to the Albany, he swung himself back into the hack, then put his bad leg up on the seat.

And how was her life now? Had she managed to keep her fox with her, or had that half-Gypsy husband of her sister's killed the beast for its pelt? He scowled at the thought, but then decided Sylvain would not allow that.

So what was she doing? Going to balls? Decking herself out in silks? He smiled. More likely her sisters had her done up to suit a respectable young lady—in shapeless white.

Regret feathered in him again at her future. Would she become like Ellena—a woman who married badly and then spent her years seeking relief from her life? Then he remembered her scorn for a "wrong" choice. Would she marry instead some upright, earnest young fellow?

He tried to picture the sort of young swell who might be right for a girl who kept a fox and an owl for pets, and who tanned herself brown in summer, ran loose in the woods, and had no love for dancing or dresses.

No images came to mind. But he doubted she would mind having to go back to Harwood to look after her parents.

The hack arrived at the Albany. Getting out, Terrance tipped the driver, then he limped to his rooms.

Opening his door, he called out, "Burke! Bring paper, ink and pen. You're to take a note to Bow Street."

Grumbling, Burke moved to obey his order. Ten minutes later he left with a note for Waddington and instructions to put the note directly into Waddington's hands.

"You'd think me a ruddy pageboy," Burke complained.

Terrance grinned. "You've the height—or lack of it. Just see that you wait for an answer from him."

"You want me to polish his ruddy boots while I do?"

"Don't expect him to tip you for it, if you do. Those boots of his don't have enough leather left to take a shine. Now, off with you."

Still grumbling, Burke left. An hour later he returned and thrust Terrance's note back at him. "He weren't there. A fellow said he's been called off to Richmond for two days."

Terrance swore.

Sylvain waited a day before she found an excuse to stroll along Piccadilly, past the Albany. She had learned from Nevin that the building stood at the end of a small street, just off Piccadilly and next to Burlington House. When he asked about her interest, she remarked it was actually the great Burlington House and its gardens she wanted to see.

His dark eyes glittered with skepticism, but he offered to drive her past it if she wished it. She thanked him, saying she would rather do some exploring on her own.

To allay any suspicions, she took Doris with her. Piccadilly boasted sufficient shops to justify strolling along the street, and she even stopped at Swain, Adeny, Brigs and Son to buy a riding whip she did not really need.

The excuse of disliking the whip served as reason enough

to take it back the following day, even though Doris suggested a footman return it instead.

With a sharp wind blowing, bringing dark clouds, she decided to wear her new wool pelisse and velvet bonnet. The long fitted coat was her favorite of anything in her new wardrobe, for she loved the deep russet color and the black braid trim across the bodice.

She also took her muff, but she only remembered the pistol tucked in the inner satin pocket when she stood in the hall and put her hand inside. Brushing the cold, hard lump, she at first frowned at it. Then she remembered. She glanced at Doris, who stood ready, tidy in her blue-gray maid's uniform and her black cloak. Then Sylvain looked at the porter beside the door. If she took the time to run upstairs and hide the pistol, that would give others in the house time to notice her actions. Mrs. Godwin might invite herself along, or Penelope might insist that the footman take her whip back to Swain, Adeny, Brigs and Son. She could not risk losing her opportunity.

With a word to the porter to say she had gone shopping should anyone ask, she strode out, Doris two steps behind her.

Her steps dragged as they walked past the Albany, but she saw no sign of Terrance. How could she get word to him? She did not trust any of Penelope's servants enough for them to take him a note. And she could not go to his rooms without stirring up a fuss—an unmarried lady could not visit a gentleman. So what next?

She returned the whip, debated over gloves, looked at bridles and side saddles, and finally left. They walked back on the opposite side of the street from the Albany. Again, she slowed her pace, but no one stepped from the narrow entrance with its flanking columns.

With a sigh, she turned, ready to tell Doris that they would go back to Nevin House now.

And then she glimpsed him.

He strode down the opposite side of Piccadilly, top hat at a rakish angle and favoring his left leg, but his stride still long. She could see the back of his close-fitted blue coat and his buff pantaloons, tight around his legs.

She started to follow, lengthening her step so that her skirts and coat hem snapped around her ankles.

"Where're we going, miss?" Doris called out.

She paused, glancing back. "Hurry. This is important."

The maid's eyes seemed to brighten with interest at that.

But when Sylvain turned back, Terrance had vanished.

Breathless, Sylvain reached the spot where she had last seen him—no tall gentleman with a rakish hat caught her eye. Only wagons and servants out to shop for their households for the day.

"Did you want to take a stroll in the park?" Doris asked. Sylvain glanced at her and the maid gestured. "Green Park. There's milkmaids as will sell you a glass straight from their cows."

Turning, Sylvain stared into the unexpected expanse of green that lay just ahead. "Yes. The park. Come along, Doris."

The maid nodded, her steps lagging, but she pointed out the path that ran beside the reservoir to Constitution Hill. Sylvain walked faster, using the long stride she had acquired from roaming the countryside. She glanced around, and then she saw him, half hidden by the shade of a large oak.

Smiling, she stared forward again. But then she checked her step. A gentleman had approached Terrance and now stood talking to him, and a shiver that had little to do with the cold wind chased along her back. Even from this distance she recognized Edwin Hayland.

Twelve

What had Ellena told her brother of the other night's conversation? The question troubled Terrance, and Waddington had advised caution because of this.

"He's bound to suspect somethin'," Waddington had said when Terrance had at last gotten hold of the man yesterday. "That might work for us. You just keep him curious. Write sayin' as there's somethin' you must see about. An' I'll be back tomorrow."

"Tomorrow for what?" Terrance had asked, but Waddington only offered a sly wink and departed.

It grated still that Waddington had done no more than shake his head over mention of Hayland's gambling debt and say that it was not enough. "Not when it sounds as if that sister'll act the innocent for him as to what he knew. That ain't somethin' I can take to a magistrate."

Not enough. Terrance's mouth tightened and he forced it to relax. If he had not agreed to this blasted scheme, he would have grabbed the man by the lapels and simply shaken the fellow until he said if he had shot Dunscombe.

Looking at Hayland, however, he found it difficult to believe he might have. He looked the proper gentleman, done up in tasteful, understated clothes—blue coat, white starched cravat, gold and blue brocade waistcoat, buff breeches. The only touch of vanity showed in his gleaming Hessians, with their gold tassels dangling from the low-cut boots.

The man also seemed to have an uncanny control of himself.

He ought to have shown some emotion—surprise, even disapproval. But Hayland's gray eyes—like the choppy waters of the reservoir under the overcast sky—reflected nothing.

Propping his gloved hands on the gold top of his bamboo walking stick, Hayland stared at the trees around them, whose color had started to turn. A scattering of dead leaves brushed past their feet.

"If you're expecting me to intercede on your behalf with Ellena, I should say I never did care for her connection with you," Hayland said, his tone indifferent.

"It's not that," Terrance said, trying to sound as desperate as Waddington had said he should. He glanced around him. "I'm in the devil of a fix and I've run out of options for help."

Eyebrow lifted, Hayland looked at Terrance. "Why turn to me?"

Terrance's mouth quirked and a reckless gleam came into his eyes. "Because Ellena told me about your debt to Dunscombe—seems you had little reason to love him. I thought you might sympathize. And I've got to quit the country before I'm hung for a murder I didn't commit."

He went on to explain what had happened on the morning of the duel.

Edwin held still. He had not thought of Winslow as a quitter—not of any battle. As he listened, he stared at the man who had so infatuated his sister. A hard man. Rather like Dunscombe in that, but with real strength underneath, he sensed. Dunscombe had lacked that. Dunscombe had suspected his own weaknesses, Edwin knew, and forever sought to disprove them—to the world, and himself—by being more of a man than any other around him.

His mouth twisted. Knowledge of his brother-in-law had not left him immune, however, to the man's manipulations. He ought to have kept himself in better control, but Dunscombe had known his weaknesses, too. He'd offered a chance to win his own fortune. God, how he had wanted to be free of needing Ellena's generosity! Instead, he had lost. And then

Dunscombe had toyed with him, telling him he had six weeks to come up with the funds or face ruin.

"Not debtors' prison," Dunscombe had said, flashing his white teeth in a quick, mirthless smile. "Can't have my brother-in-law there. But unless you leave the county, I'll have to tell my friends not to play with a man who cannot pay."

Ruin. Utter social ruin. A gentleman could do many things, but he could not lose a bet and then not pay—not and be called anything but a liar and a cheat.

He knew why Dunscombe had wanted him gone—knew because they had shared that one drunken night during which they had revealed their real desires to each other. Dunscombe had not been able bear that someone else had glimpsed the truth about him. He had hated that.

Edwin's hands tightened. He relaxed them again and smoothed the leather of the back of one glove. Then he focused his stare on Winslow, away from the past. Best not go there.

Terrance finished his story and stood silent now, his weight on his right leg as he braced himself with a brass-headed walking stick.

"What, exactly, do you need?" Hayland asked.

"I'm not going to waste my time in prison, not even for a day. 'Course it might be different if I had something to keep me here. But I don't, so why not leave? Only it's a risk for me to try the main roads or the docks. And this bad leg of mine means I can't ride cross-country. So I need someone to cash a draft on my bank and purchase my passage. I'd send my man, but I can't trust he'll not betray me for that blasted reward."

All lies, Terrance knew. Most of them invented by Waddington. *Put his mind on your bein' in trouble—you want him feelin' smug an' easy that it ain't him.*

Terrance had thought the plan absurd, but now as he saw Hayland nodding and his shoulders relax, he realized that Waddington had been right. Hayland now seemed to feel unthreatened, and as if he had some control over Terrance's fate.

Eyes narrowing, Terrance struggled to hold his impatience

in check. A governess strolled in the park with her charge—
a young boy. A lady stood not far off with her back to them
and what looked to be her maid next to her. And in the distance, milkmaids watched their grazing dairy cows, whose
bells clattered when they moved to fresh grass.

"Why not ask Ellena?" Hayland asked at last.

"Do you want her insisting that I take her with, or cutting
up at me for leaving?"

"No. No." Hayland faced him and something flickered in
his eyes. It might have been relief. Or real sympathy. "And I
don't want any man to swing for Dunscombe's death. The
man deserved his fate."

Terrance nodded. He reached into his waistcoat pocket and
pulled out a draft on his bank. "So you'll do it?"

Taking the bank draft, Hayland studied it. Then he glanced
at Terrance. "What makes you think I would not give information at Bow Street for your apprehension?" He sounded
genuinely curious.

Reaching again into his waistcoat pocket, Terrance pulled
out a gold cravat pin engraved with the ornate intertwined letters "EH." "Yours, isn't it? I found it that morning."

Hayland pulled back. "Mine? But I wasn't wearing it that
morning when I . . ."

Eyes widening, and sweat now glistening on his upper lip,
he broke off his words and stared at Terrance.

"That morning when you shot Dunscombe? Ellena's maid
saw you eavesdropping on Cale and Perriman. It must have
seemed the devil's own chance sent your way to rid yourself
of him."

For a moment, Hayland met his stare, gray eyes blank, only
the rapid flutter of the pulse in his jaw betrayed any emotion. Then he moved. Twisting the top of his walking stick, he
pulled the cane bottom loose. He stepped back, his short
sword hissing free, flashing dull in the pale, cold sunlight.

"Give me that stickpin."

Pulse lifting and muscles tensed, every sense focused utterly on Hayland, Terrance smiled. "But you weren't wearing it you said. So why does it matter?"

"Damn you. You had to come along at the wrong time, didn't you!"

"What would have been the right time? Whom did you want blamed for Dunscombe's death—or did you think that far ahead?"

Hayland stared at him. Terrance took a breath and readied himself to parry the small sword with his own walking stick.

A feminine voice, oddly fierce, interrupted. "Put the sword away, please!"

Both men turned, and Terrance's eyes widened as he saw Sylvain not six steps away, that blasted toy of a pistol clutched in her hand. At least she held it steady. She also stood with her feet braced wide and her body turned so she could sight down the short barrel.

Good girl—you learned that at least.

Glancing at Hayland, Terrance's instincts screamed for action, but he focused instead on waiting for Hayland's attack, for the opening he needed.

Before it came, the leaves overhead rustled and Waddington dropped from the oak, opposite Sylvain. Straightening, Waddington pointed his own pistol at Hayland. "Stand, sir! I must ask you to throw down your weapon and come with me to Sir Richard Birni, Chief Magistrate of Bow Street to answer inquiries as to the death of Myles William Oxenham Perriman, Baron of Dunscombe."

For a moment, Hayland did not move. Then he lowered the point of his stick sword and glanced at Terrance, his eyes as cold as the clouds gathering overhead. "Bloody bastard."

The next instant, he spun on his heel, throwing the stick sheath of his sword at Waddington and sprinting for Sylvain. She lifted her pistol, which she had lowered, but he pushed past her, swung his sword at her maid, which set that girl screaming, then he bolted for Piccadilly.

Cursing, one hand to his head where the stick had struck,

Waddington lifted his pistol. In two strides, Terrance reached him, pushing up on the man's arm as the Runner fired. The loud report echoed in Terrance's ears, and smoke filled the air with the sharp smell of sulfur. Waddington glared at him, but Terrance glared back. "You might have struck *her,* you fool!"

"Might 'ell!" Waddington muttered, Cockney flooding his accent. With a muffled curse, he sprinted after Hayland. Terrance watched a moment. Hayland had lost his hat, and his coattails flapped behind him as he ran eastward, no doubt hoping to hide himself in the city's traffic. Terrance almost hoped he would escape—no man deserved to hang for Dunscombe.

However, that would be Waddington's problem.

Pocketing the gold pin, he glanced at Sylvain.

She had lowered her pistol and had turned to quiet her hysterical maid. As if sensing his stare, she looked at him. Her bonnet had been knocked askew and shock lay pale on her skin, making the freckles on her nose stand out.

Striding over to her, he took the pistol. Then he scowled. "Of all the cursed—you left the blasted safety latch fastened!"

The color flooded back into her face as she scowled at the pistol. "Oh—oh, blazes! No wonder it would not fire." At a muffled cry from her maid, she turned back to the woman again. "Please, Doris—will you go and fetch a hack to take us back to Nevin House?"

Eyes enormous and hands still trembling, the maid glanced from Terrance to Sylvain. Then she bobbed a curtsy and fled.

Terrance tried to keep scowling at Sylvain—he really should not encourage her by showing the swell of pride that had risen in him. "So you tried to pull off a shot, did you?"

She sounded frustrated as she answered. "I had him perfectly in the sight—and you said I should aim to hit my target."

"Next time, first thing is to check your pistol, then your aim." He glanced at it. "Did you clean it and reload before you came here?" The tips of her ears began to redden. He nodded. "You're not going to make a marksman if you don't care for your pistol."

"Of all the—" Glaring at him, she folded her arms. "Some gentlemen might offer a word of thanks if a lady happened to their rescue."

"Only you didn't happen here at all. Were you following me?"

"How else should I meet you? But then Hayland arrived, and I would not have stepped in if not for that sword he drew."

"Yes, you would have. You seem incapable of allowing me to handle my own affairs!"

Her lower lip trembled.

Shocked by this, he stiffened. What had he said that she now looked so hurt and as if she might burst into tears?

She did not, however. Chin up, she glared at him. "That is because your affairs so often end with you utterly tangled in impossible difficulties!" Turning, she started to stalk away, but then she stopped and glared at him. "All I wanted was a thank you—a single, pleasant thank you!"

Turning away again, back straight, she strode away. His temper flared. So she wanted a bloody thank you, did she?

Ignoring the ache in his leg, he caught up with her, the blood still pounding fast in him from his brush with Hayland. He caught her elbow, spinning her around. She landed off balance in his arms.

For an instant, he held her there, hands tight on her arms, the words he had been about to pelt at her tangling on his tongue. She stared up at him, those blue-green eyes more green than blue, but huge as ever, with anger still snapping in them.

Her lips parted as if she had more words for him. But he didn't want that from her. And he no longer knew what to say.

So he did what he wanted—what every caged emotion in him demanded. He dragged her into a kiss.

She tasted not of peaches as she once had but of something more elemental, more female. And what he had intended lost its way as she softened. Wrapping his arms around her, he pulled her closer. She fit as if made for him, tucked perfectly in his grip, slender, pliant, vibrant. He teased her lips with his teeth and her mouth opened under his, and a new ache for more opened in him.

Dragging off her bonnet with one hand, he wrapped his fingers in her hair. He could drown in her scent, in those sweet curves now pressed against him, in the taste of her, and in those tempting soft moans escaping her which drove him to crave even more.

And then her curls came off in his hand.

Startled, he pulled back to glance at the curls, then at her.

Her breath came as shallow and ragged as his own. Face flushed, she would not look up to meet his stare. Her lips, reddened from that kiss, pulled his gaze, and he started to bend down to her again.

Snatching her false curls, she slipped from his arms, muttering, "I must get back."

She started to hurry away, and frustration welled inside him. With a scowl, he strode after her.

She glanced him then, but looked away at once and said, her tone stiff. "You need not escort me." She pulled up her bonnet by its dangling ribbons and jabbed it back on her head.

His mouth crooked. "Consider it part of my thank you."

Frowning, Sylvain slid a glance at him. So that kiss had been a thank you? Disappointment wove its way into the confused mix of feelings swirling in her—the panic, the mortification, and the pounding desire to throw herself back into another kiss.

But it had only been a thank you.

She had thought—well, her lips still burned, and for an instant she had . . . had dissolved.

Absurd, of course! Why should he, too, feel swept away when he went about kissing females at every whim! It meant nothing to him, and it meant . . .

She shied away from what it had meant to her. He had kissed her before, after all.

Only not like that.

Stuffing her false hair into her muff, she lengthened her stride, but Terrance kept pace.

At Piccadilly, Doris waited beside a hired carriage, and the maid's shocked expression set Sylvain's face to burning. With her hair disordered and her face hot, she must look as if . . . as if she had just been soundly kissed.

She thought Terrance would hand her and her maid into the carriage and that would be that. But after handing the maid into the hack, he turned to the driver, ordered it to Nevin House, and then tucked Sylvain's hand into his arm.

"We need to talk—and if you tell me even once that I should not walk so far with this leg of mine, I'll hop down the street on it to prove I can."

His words started a smile in her, and she pressed her lips together to hold it back. She would not smile at him. She was still angry with him for—well, she didn't know why. Only she did know. She was angry because she still wanted him to find as much in that kiss as she had.

But it meant as much to him as if he had shaken her hand. And it did not matter to him if he had instead shaken her world. Oh, why must she be a fool for him? Why could she not keep her promises to herself and her good intentions and remembered that he used that lethal charm and skill of his on every female?

Why did he have to kiss so very well so that her toes still tingled and even the memory of it could warm her skin and loosen her muscles?

Doris stared back at them from the carriage, a horrified expression on her face, so Sylvain gave what she hoped was a reassuring wave, and then she settled into step beside Terrance again, her steps less hurried.

Still too aware of him—of his warmth, of the spice of his cologne, of the strength in the arm that lay under her touch and his coat sleeve, she put on her best impression of Penelope's starched tones. "You wished a word with me?"

"You said you wanted to talk to me—but why in blazes did you bring a pistol with you to Green Park?"

"You ought to be glad I had it. I only brought it because I

did not want to take the time to leave it behind. Then I saw Mr. Hayland." She told him what Hayland had said the other evening, repeating his remark about not wanting to face his brother-in-law. "I thought you should know. But it seems as if you knew a few other things about him. Did he really shoot Dunscombe?"

"That's yet to be proved, but I suspect it will be."

"But why?"

He told her about Hayland's gambling debt. She listened, then she shook her head. "Did you stop to think that facing a man who had shot someone might prove dangerous?"

"Waddington was nearby. We had arranged that."

"Who is Waddington—that man with the red waistcoat?"

He explained about his meeting with the Bow Street Runner. "That's what this whole farce was about—pulling Hayland in, trying to make him slip up by making him overly confident that he was now safe." He dug out the gold pin and showed it to her. "I told him I'd found his pin that morning near Dunscombe's body. In truth, Waddington dug up a fellow who conveniently 'found' it within Hayland's rooms last night so we could use it today."

Stiffening, she glanced at him. "Do you even know how to tell the truth anymore?"

"And just what does that mean?"

But she only would shake her head. "It's nothing."

Terrance glared at her. Why had she become so quiet—so distant? He almost wanted to stop and shake her—only he rather thought that might end up with him kissing her again, and he really should not keep on doing that.

The things that a few minutes ago had seemed urgent to him vanished as he stared at her. What else did he have to say? Something about that kiss? Or something about the hunger for what it had released in him?

No—best not delve into that. He ought not to have kissed her really, but when had he ever resisted temptation? Except he was struggling to now, for he had the strongest feeling of something precious slipping away, only he could not quite pin down what that might be.

For a moment, he fought to put together what he did want to say to her—a real thank you. Yes. He owed her that, and quite possibly even his life. She had distracted Hayland. She had also been invaluable in getting him to London. Only somehow the words stuck fast, and left him scowling at her.

Then she was tugging her hand free from him. "This is Nevin House. But you need not come in."

Stopping, he looked down at her, ignoring the staid street of orderly town houses around them. With her bonnet askew and her curls peaking out in disorder from underneath, and her lips still red from that kiss, she looked not at all a proper young lady.

Desire to kiss her again stirred inside him. Just to see what she might do. Only he could hardly do so on Nevin's doorstep—not without either declaring for her or being ready to face a family member of hers at dawn. And he'd rather had enough duels just now, thank you.

Glancing at the house, he thought suddenly of the reception she would get—the maid was bound to have brought back God knew what kind of story. And that older sister of hers could be a shrew. Well, he could not allow her to face that on her own. He might be most of the things that were said of him, but he did not shoot people in the back, and he did pay his debts.

Taking hold of her arm, he told her, "Come along, then."

The porter swung open the door before he had his foot on the first step, and the maid's half-hysterical babbling carried into the street. He winced and hesitated. Then he glanced at Sylvain. She had her chin up and looked utterly calm. She had more courage than he.

Limping her up the steps, he took off his hat as they stepped into the house.

Her sisters both stood in the hall, bonnets and coats on as if they had just been coming or going. Well, one of them, he amended—the pretty blond Cecile or Celia or some such thing—actually sat in a high-backed chair against the wall, fanning herself with a gloved hand and looking as if she might be ill. The eldest, Penelope, stood over the maid, who sat in another of the high-backed chairs, looking ready to faint.

Beside them stood that half-Gypsy lord Penelope had married, and his cousin, Dawes. Both had that long-suffering look of men who would rather not be enduring an emotional display. Their faces tightened at the sight of him. Nevin even stepped forward, before Dawes laid a restraining hand on his arm.

No love lost there.

Another woman—sharp-faced with dark hair—knelt by the maid, waving something. Smoke twirled from it, filling the hall with the stink of burning feather. Then the woman turned and a jolt of recognition flashed into him. Mrs. Godwin. With Sylvain delivered to London, he had thought she would be long gone.

His jaw tightened as her eyes flew wide and she said, the words sounding startled from her, "My heavens—it's the footman."

Thirteen

Sylvain had forgotten about Mrs. Godwin. She had forgotten everything except that kiss, and now she saw her mistake. She slid a glance toward Terrance and noted the spark of irritation in his eyes and the belligerent set to his jaw. There would be no getting him to quietly slip away.

For a moment, no one spoke, and then everyone did.

Doris started babbling about pistols and the park and Bow Street Runners. Mrs. Godwin rose and Penelope pulled her aside to speak in urgent undertones, which started a knot in Sylvain's stomach. Nevin demanded an explanation from Terrance. And Cecila rattled off questions to Sylvain, alternating them with expressions of anxiety that her husband, Bryn, with one hand on her shoulder, sought to calm.

Easing a step forward, Sylvain put herself between Terrance and her family. They looked rather grim. Even Bryn, whom she had thought the sweetest of souls. He did not look so with that hard set to his mouth, which brought out his resemblance to his cousin. And Nevin's black eyes glittered with hostility. But then Terrance had once kissed Penelope, and Nevin seemed not to have forgotten or forgiven that.

Then Penelope stepped forward, commanding everyone in that daunting, regal tone of hers to quiet please. As the silence fell, Sylvain glanced at her sisters, apprehension tightening inside her. Penelope had that disappointed look in her eyes—the one that always tore into Sylvain. And Cecila's

blue eyes held a lingering apprehension. Guilt twisted inside
Sylvain, made worse by how ill poor Cecila looked.

She had failed them yet again. Of course. She had known she
would, and she had grown so tired of always doing so. Why
could they not accept that she had no fit place in society? Why
must her sisters forever try to pattern her after Cecila's grace or
Penelope's elegance? As if she had ever had either!

She edged closer to Terrance. At least he did not want to
remake her. Oh, he lectured her, of course, as he had today for
not checking her pistol beforehand, and for pushing into his
affairs. But he had not gone on at her about what a lady did
or did not do. Instead, he had kissed her.

Glancing at him, she found him watching her, but immediately his mouth lifted at the corner and the glitter in his
tawny eyes took on a wicked mischief. He gave her a wink
and the knot in her stomach loosened.

If he could find the humor in this, she could as well. The
worst that could happen, after the most thunderous of lectures, would be that Penelope would send her home. She
would not mind that—though it meant she probably would
not see Terrance again for a very, very long while. If ever.

Catching her lower lip in her teeth, she turned to her family.
Then she muttered, "I am sorry."

Face set, Penelope started forward, but Nevin came to her
side and took her hand. "Please. You should rest. Leave this
to me. Winslow—a word with you in private!"

Sylvain held out her arm to keep Terrance where he
stood. "Whatever you have to say to him, you may say in
my presence. None of this is his fault."

Penelope leaned toward her husband and spoke quietly
to him. His face whitened and his fists clenched. Sylvain's
heart began to thud. Mrs. Godwin must have told Penelope
everything.

After a cold glance at Terrance, Nevin turned his stare to
Sylvain. "So he traveled with you as your footman?"

For a moment, Sylvain held still. Then she nodded.

Terrance watched her. He would have been happy to oblige Nevin by stepping into another room. The half-Gypsy probably still fought dirty, but a good set-to just now would have dampened the restlessness that swirled inside him.

He would not allow Nevin, however, to turn an ounce of anger on Sylvain. Stepping around her, he came forward. "Can we sort out who is going to talk to whom someplace other than where your front door's open for the neighbors to gape."

Nevin's jaw clenched.

The absurdity of it struck Terrance and he grinned. He ought to be the last person to remind everyone of the proprieties.

Penelope seemed to feel the sting of his words, for she flushed. Then she took action. Blazes, but the woman could terrify with her organization. She recalled the gaping porter to his duties, bustled the maid off with the footman and butler who had come to gawk, ushered the rest upstairs to a rather attractive room done up in yellows, and even had the presence of mind to order tea.

"Though I do not expect you shall stay long," she added, looking at Terrance, her tone polite and ice in her stare. That put up Terrance's back. With a smile, he settled into a comfortable sprawl on the couch next to Sylvain. He would bloody well stay until it suited him to go.

Penelope lifted an eyebrow, but only said, "Mrs. Godwin, will you please repeat your story?"

The woman did. She kept to the plain facts about the journey from Somerset, not adding speculations on what sins might have occurred out of her sight. Terrance could have kissed her for that much. Instead, he watched the faces around him.

Sylvain's other sister, the blond one—what was her name? Cece?—gasped several times, her eyes going wide as lakes. Her husband, Dawes, shook his head and frowned, muttering something dire that sounded pulled from some play, but then the fellow always seemed to be quoting something literary. And Terrance decided that Nevin must no longer keep a knife up his sleeve as he once had, otherwise it would have been out and no doubt put to use.

He lounged, bad leg stretched out and aching, waiting for the inevitable condemnation of his actions. When they began sending disapproving looks at Sylvain instead, that stung like the sharp lash of nettles.

She sat with her hands folded in her lap, staring at the back of her gloves, her face pale and desperately guilty. As if she had anything to apologize for! She had had no say in his posing as her footman. What did they think—that she ought to have given him away?

Then Penelope spoke up, her tone sharp, "Do you have an explanation?"

Terrance glanced at her, ready to tell her to go to the devil. However, she stared not at him, but at her sister. Heat washed from his chest and into his face and he glared at the woman. "She doesn't have to explain anything!"

Everyone looked at him as if he had sprouted horns and a tail. Then Penelope said, "Really, Mr. Winslow! She is my youngest sister and no relation to you, so I fail to see how you have any say in the matter."

Temper lost, he glared back at her. "No say? Well, what if I were to tell you I have every say!"

"And what gives you any such right?" Nevin asked, tone dry.

Goaded, Terrance snapped, "Because she's my intended!"

The expressions around him shifted from narrow-eyed disapproval to blank shock. For a moment, the room filled with the sound of a clock ticking. Terrance clenched his jaw on the words that had stumbled out. He hadn't meant to say them. But looking at the stuffy faces around him, he was glad he had. Blazes, he owed Sylvain some protection in return for what she had given him. Only they stung him with guilt, for he didn't mean them. Why would she want such a bad bargain as himself anyway? However, he would not have this parcel of . . . of relatives telling him he had no say in this.

Only Mrs. Godwin smiled, the expression softening the

sharpness of her face as she murmured, "How sweet." Seeming embarrassed by her own words, she blushed and looked away.

Sylvain found her voice then, but only just, for her words came out half strangled. "Sweet madness."

He put a hand over hers, his stare urging her to follow his lead. "I've cleared my name today of any blame for murder so there's no need to keep this a secret any longer."

"Cleared!" Nevin almost choked on the word. "You've dragged your family name into the streets long before you added murder to your disgraces."

"As if you have room to talk—Gypsy!"

Nevin started forward, but Penelope's words checked her husband. "Gentleman, please. Let us not descend to name calling and blame. Mr. Winslow, regardless of what arrangement you think you have made with my sister, I doubt my father would countenance such a match. I certainly do not. Which means, it does not exist. Sylvain is not yet of age."

Sylvain sat up. "You know that if I told Father I wished this, he would allow it! And my age has nothing to do with this."

"It certainly does!" Cecila said, and then she glared at Terrance. "He is not a fit husband for anyone, and you are too young to see it!"

Sylvain glanced at her sister. "You are so wrong."

"What, do you think he may be 'plotting some new reformation'?" Bryn asked, sarcasm thick in his voice.

"And why could he not make a reformation?" Sylvain glanced at Terrance. He had acted on impulse—one he would regret, she knew. She saw that in his eyes already. Which meant that she had to offer him a way out. Ears burning with the lies turning in her mind, she faced her family. "We *are* engaged. And Terrance said that after he had cleared his name not a whisper of scandal would touch him until we wed next spring. If it does, I have told him that would mean an end to our betrothal."

Beside her, Terrance shifted on the sofa. He leaned closer, grating out the words between his teeth. "What are you doing?"

She ignored him. Of course, he would not be able to keep

out of trouble for so long. By then she would be back at Harwood House and the whole thing could be easily ended without him having to lose face in front of her family as he must if she exposed this as nothing more than his reaction to Penelope's imperious manner.

Nevin crossed his arms and lifted one black eyebrow. "Six months of him behaving to convince us he might do so for a lifetime? That should prove interesting."

"'Boldness is an ill keeper of promise,'" Bryn muttered.

"Is it now?" Terrance said, his collar tight again and damn irritated with this lot. He pushed himself to his feet. He started to stake a wager, then he glanced down at Sylvain and checked himself. The stakes had been set already—and this parcel of prudes thought him unable to succeed!

He had yet to back down from any challenge. And if it took six months—well, it had taken nearly four years to win the bet that he could kiss every female in the district. Besides, a few months of quiet living after the past fortnight seemed rather attractive just now.

Taking Sylvain's hand, he made a formal bow over it. "I'll call on you tomorrow, my dear, since we've plans to make." With a defiant glare at her relatives, he limped from the room.

Sylvain watched him go. Then she swallowed and braced herself for yet another lecture. Instead, Penelope came to her side. "Tea is what you need just now. And if he gives you one ounce of cause to regret this, he shall not have to worry about Nevin for I shall strip his skin from him."

"I do not regret anything that has happened with him, and I never shall." With that Sylvain rose and strode from the room.

Sylvain spent the rest of the day in the garden, declining an invitation from her sisters to take a light meal, and then one for tea, and one from Mrs. Godwin to take a stroll. She sat on a gray stone bench, although she would rather have been walking through woods. However, she had Trace for company, and she had had enough of parks and London streets for the day. She also needed time and solitude to think.

Only she found it difficult to remain detached and clear-headed—odd spurts of anger stirred, alternating with moments of gloom and then unrealistic spirals of hope.

How could he drag her into such a charade as this? Why had he thought of it? It would not last, not even as long as six months. But would she indeed have six months with him paying her court? A quick flush of pleasure chased through her, but she frowned.

"I have got to be sensible," she told Trace. The fox cocked his ear toward her, his focus locked on a sparrow perched in the honeysuckle-covered lattice behind the bench.

Sylvain tipped her head to the side and watched. Trace had eaten far too much earlier today to take his hunting seriously, but he was obviously stalking just for the pleasure of it. The pleasure of it? Was there not an opportunity for that here? Even in going through this just to go through it?

Her sisters certainly could not play matchmakers if they already thought her lost to Terrance. And they would be far more likely to be watching Terrance for any lapses in conduct than they would be interested in scrutinizing her behavior. But those were excuses. In truth, it would shock her family if they knew how desperately she wanted this fantasy to be real.

Trace scrunched down, then pounced, missing the sparrow, but startling the bird from its perch. It flew off, and Sylvain reached down to scoop Trace into her lap. He seemed not to mind that his prey had escaped. Panting now, he glanced around, as if looking for a new target, allowing her to stroke his wiry fur.

Wrinkling her nose against his familiar but pungent odor, she decided that if she were to be utterly honest with herself, then she had to admit that a danger also lurked in this.

What if she began to began to believe the fantasy too well?

Oh, but she did not want to worry over future problems. She glanced at Trace again, still happy. She might be far less so once her game ended, but why not at least enjoy herself while she could? Her lips twitched. That thought seemed worthy of Terrance himself. And not a bad way to approach life at all.

"What in blazes do you mean you want something out of this?" Terrance twisted in his seat, trying to both glance at Sylvain and keep an eye on his bays.

He had barely pulled up before Nevin House—the weather a bit chancy, what with clouds thick in the sky—when she had appeared, hurrying down the steps as if she had been waiting. She had on something in a greenish blue color with darker trim around the bottom, but he forgot the dress when she looked up at him and smiled. She looked different somehow.

Burke had jumped down to hand her up, since Terrance's leg had made it a bloody painful thing to climb into the curricle. Then, with the groom in his seat, Terrance had set off.

Now he tried to see just what it was that seemed different about her. Not the stylish gown, though it did draw the eye to that trim figure of hers. No, something else about her left him frowning and a little unsettled. Blazes, had she started to change from the Sylvain he knew into the lady he dreaded she would become?

She glanced at him, looking not the least cowed by his question. "I mean just that. Are you not a bit close to that milk wagon?"

"Might have a care for that gig comin' up as well," Burke said, leaning forward from his seat at the back of the two-wheeled carriage.

Knowing this for his manservant's twisted idea of humor—he took direction from no one on his driving—Terrance ignored the quip. However, he focused his stare on the traffic and waited until he could turn into the open expanses of Green Park. Then he slowed his bays to a walk and glanced again at Sylvain.

She stared back at him, picking up the conversation where they had left off. "Really, now. We both know that Penelope's attitude goaded you into this."

"Well, of all the——! Now who is being stingy with some gratitude? Or don't you care that I could as easily have said nothing and left you to your sister's less-than-tender mercy?"

"Oh, what is the worst—that Penelope might have sent me home? I should not have minded."

He gave a laugh. "What if she decided you compromised enough that you had to marry? I wouldn't put it past her to dig up some earnest young fellow, have her husband stick dowry enough on you and have a ring on your finger."

"She wouldn't."

"She would if she thought a babe due in nine months, and your family name at stake. She'd do it and think it all for your best—and you know full well she would. And if not that, there's the Continent to haul you away to, or she could have stitched some dragon-faced matron to your side."

"Oh, very well, so there were worse options. And I suppose I do owe you a thank you."

His mouth crooked. "What—no kiss to go with it?"

"If I go about kissing you in public, you shall have to admit that you could not behave even for a day. And I want this to . . . to go on for long enough that I might enjoy it."

She shifted in her seat so that she faced him, excitement almost shimmering around her. "You must know some interesting places in London, and I want to see them."

"I'm not taking you to a gaming hell, or a cockfight, or any of the places I know."

"You must know something other than that."

He thought for a moment. "No, that pretty well sums it up."

"Then you may buy a guidebook. As the future Mrs. Winslow, I have some level of freedom within my family now. Artificial, yes, but no one needs to know that." She glanced at Burke, as if just remembering him.

"Don't mind him," Terrance said. "He does as he's paid to, and he knows how to keep his mouth shut."

"Better than most," the manservant said, his tone dry.

Terrance glanced at him. He had already had words with

Burke on just how little humor there was in his having got himself not really engaged. Then he looked back at Sylvain. He had images of escorting her to dull balls, musical evenings, the theater even, and it all sounded an utter bore. And none of it was of any interest to his Sylvain—was it?

Well, he would just tell her no. He could make the occasional appearance at Nevin House for show, and spend the rest of his time letting his leg heal, and hunting with the Belvoir would start soon in earnest, taking him to Leichestershire for most of the autumn.

Then, voice pitched low, she asked, "Can you imagine what it is like to be a constant disappointment to your family?"

He checked his team as they sidled away from one of the milkmaid's cows, and then he wondered. How many years had he courted his father's disapproval? He had intentionally goaded the man, determined to show him how little his eldest son thought of him. His beloved father. The man who had driven off his mother with his temper and then lied to his sons about it.

The devil of it was, had he ever really gotten the reaction he had wanted? Had his father ever shown any regret? One moment of remorse? Yes, he knew how frustrating it could be to attempt the impossible.

He glanced at Sylvain. She sat very straight, looking about her as if interested in the scenery, but with a wistful longing in her eyes. He had not thought of how her family must view her—the sister who ran half-wild in the woods, the daughter who preferred the company of animals, the woman who could aim a pistol at a man without her hand shaking.

"Oh, I can imagine," he said at last.

Head tilting, she looked up at him. "Well, now they have you to watch instead of me. Just think on it—you shall be able to rub their noses in how wrong they were about you. And for once I will not be worried what they think of me. I cannot disappoint them any more than I already have—and I had no idea before this how glorious it would feel to realize I can give up trying to be what they wanted."

"And what was that?"

"A copy—a pretty, well-behaved, elegant, well-mannered lady who always knows how to say the right thing at the right time to the right person." She wrinkled her nose.

He laughed, and she glanced at him. "My sweet Silly, you have the wrong idea of your sisters if you think it's a good thing to be like either of them. Penelope is known for having the sharpest tongue in Somerset, and your other sister is a pretty flirt who lacks even half your sense."

"Am I to take that as flattery? Or ought I feel snubbed on their behalves?"

"Take it how you like—it's the truth. If I were to flatter you, I'd tell you that it would take me a lifetime of gazing into your eyes to decide if they are more green or blue." He looked at her, his eyes crinkling around the corners, the tawny depths warm, and his mouth curving. His voice dropped to a slow rumble. "A very pleasant lifetime."

Lips parting, breath shallow and fast, Sylvain stared at him. The laughter faded in his eyes, replaced by something hot that woke an answering heat in her. He leaned closer. Would he kiss her? Regardless of the challenge, of the milkmaids, of the nannies and the children, and the pair of older ladies who strolled in the park?

The carriage jolted as his horses broke into a trot. He checked them, then glanced at her, mouth crooked and his tone careless again. "That is flattery, my dear. Now, where do you suppose one buys a guidebook?"

They debated this until Burke leaned forward to say that most books ought to be found at a bookshop, such as Hatchard's. Sylvain glanced at the servant, but Terrance did not seem to mind his manservant's insolent tone, so she decided she ought not to either.

Setting Sylvain down at Nevin House, Terrance promised to find her both a guidebook and something interesting to do.

Deciding that she might as well tell him exactly what she did wish to see, she said, "A dungeon would be nice."

"Dungeon?"

"Well, one is forever reading about them after all."

He shook his head, made no promises, and drove away.

It took two days to come up with an armory, the best he could do instead of a dungeon. But as it lay in Carlton House and included a collection of boots and spurs from the time of Charles I, as well as models of horses said to be large as life, and a Chinese Tartar's war-dress, he thought it might do. The descriptions in the book he purchased actually had him curious.

She toured the Prince Regent's London house wide-eyed, interested in everything and blunt about her comments—she did not care for the grand staircase. "Can you only imagine how difficult the upkeep on all that gilt is!"

Amused enough, he agreed to take her not only to Drury Lane, but to an archery meeting she had heard about as well. He also found that he did not mind escorting her to a ball at Holland House, even if her relatives frowned at him—a decent game could always be had in the card rooms, and Sylvain showed an interest in whist. And when she asked for his escort to Sadler's Wells Theater, he found himself as entertained by the water spectacle as he was by her amazement.

The gossip started a week later. He heard it first from Burke, who woke him early, muttering, "Well, it's started."

Terrance rubbed his face and squinted at his manservant's lined face. "What in blazes has started?"

Burke poured a cup of coffee and handed it to Terrance. "Word is now that you not only shot that bleedin' Dunscombe, you've pushed off the blame onto Hayland to save your own skin."

With an oath, Terrance thrust the coffee back at Burke, sloshing the black liquid into the saucer. Then he threw back the covers. "If it's Perriman again I'll have his ballocks for bellpulls!"

"Don't know that it is. I had it from Saunders' cook who had it from Foster's man."

Terrance swore. Sydney Foster's tongue ran on wheels—malicious ones.

It took him half the day to track down first Saunders, at a coffeehouse in Lincoln Fields Inn, and then Foster at settling day at Tattersall's. A few quiet words impressed on Saunders the wisdom of allowing such rumors to die. Foster, however, seemed inclined to ignore Terrance's warning, until Terrance grabbed hold of the man's cravat and twisted. Pale and sweating, Foster at once seemed to forget everything he knew. Even the original source of the gossip, insisting in a strangled voice that he had heard it from a reliable fellow.

"Well, now you are hearing from me that I am unhappy, and if I hear any more such lies I shall be forced to demand satisfaction. And I can promise you, the bullet won't find your back, Foster—I can quite easily put it between your eyes."

Stuttering an apology, Foster begged pardon and fled as soon as Terrance released him.

The scene caused enough glances that Terrance decided he had best find out at once what might have reached Nevin or Dawes.

He learned from the porter at Nevin House that Lady Nevin had left with her husband and sister for Mrs. Cornely's musical evening. A grim prospect, but Terrance supposed it could be worse. It might have been Almack's. Then he grinned. Despite Nevin's title, that half-Gypsy lord was probably as unwelcome in that den of stuffy snobbery as he was himself.

Mrs. Cornely, a plump matron, looked shocked to see him, but he applied shameless flattery and dropped hints that he searched for a particular lady already known to him, which ignited a gleam of interest in the lady's eyes. She allowed him entry, and he bowed himself away from her as soon as he could.

He found Sylvain in a room filled with chairs, all facing a pianoforte. She brightened at once, and begged, "Please walk with me someplace—anyplace. Why is it that women's voices seem so shrill when they sing?"

"Yours isn't shrill."

"You've never heard me sing."

He teased her about that, playing extravagant compliments which had her wrinkling her nose at him. He even managed to stroll with her on the terrace under a chill moon, although Mrs. Godwin, glimpsing them, attached herself, keeping a few steps behind but close enough that it half tempted him to sweep Sylvain into a shocking embrace.

Walking home afterward, he found himself humming one of the songs and thinking about that. Even without Mrs. Godwin a step behind, he had been tempted to take advantage of his false betrothal. Blazes, what good was it if he could not so much as kiss his intended?

Only he really should not. He had made no promise to Sylvain, and bless her, she seemed inclined to take this for the lark it was. When he had proven that he could keep himself out of scandal and they called this off, it would probably be the only time he parted company from a woman on such friendly terms.

He stopped, oddly unsettled by the inevitable prospect of Sylvain returning to Harwood and him returning to his old life. With a shake of his head he started walking again. Must be the late hour—he had stayed far longer than he had expected at Mrs. Cornely's. However, he had assured himself that Foster's gossip seemed not to have spread far.

Blazes, but that bit of a gold-and-white dress Sylvain had worn tonight had seemed remarkably thin. What were her sisters thinking to tog her out so? He could swear he had glimpsed the silhouette of her legs when she stood on the terrace, the light of the rooms streaming around her. Or had he only pictured how those long legs of hers would look?

He frowned, turned the corner to the Albany, and stopped. Two ruffians who had been lounging against the wall came to attention, the larger one tapping his friend's chest. Burly and smelling of beer, they squared off at once, fists up. Ex-prizefighters, to judge by their crooked noses and the science in their stances.

For an instant, Terrance smiled. Then he remembered he was trying to stay out of trouble. "Look here—" A fist caught the rest of his words, cracking his head to the left, and snapping his temper to bits.

Fourteen

At one in the afternoon, Burke brought the note to Nevin House.

He had been instructed to hand the note directly to Miss Sylvain. But as he had a fair idea what the staff of any proper household would think about Terrance Winslow writing to a single female, rather than knock on the door, he opted to pace the street until the lady stepped from the house. When she did, he came up to her, doffed his hat, and gave her the note.

"What is this?" the older woman with Miss Sylvain asked, her voice as crisp as the sharp bite of autumn in the air.

Burke frowned at her. He hadn't much use for females, least of all this frosty-faced sort. So he gave her back a hard stare. "Well now, it might be a note, mighten it?"

The woman stiffened, but Miss Sylvain said, as she tore open the sealed sheet and scanned it, "It is only Terrance . . . Mr. Winslow writing to say he will be unable to escort me to the Hobbyhorse school tomorrow."

Surprise lifted the older woman's eyebrows. "He actually had the manners to write you in advance of this?"

Miss Sylvain did not answer but turned to Burke, worry clouding her eyes. "Would you take a note back to him please?"

Burke did not want to take a note back, but as the frosty-faced lady started on about how miss ought not to, he gave an immediate bow and agreed. Besides, with those wide green-blue eyes pleading at him, what choice did he have? Thankfully, as he followed her into the house, she asked Mrs. Frosty Face to wait in the hall.

But when the door closed behind them in the tidy study that she had led him into, she did not make for the desk, but swung around, asking, "What happened?"

Burke frowned. This had been no part of his instructions, only that worry haunting her eyes didn't sit at all well with him. "Nothin' much, miss."

She paced across the room. "Terrance never breaks a promise unless he utterly cannot keep it. So what has happened?"

Burke rubbed the back of his neck. "It's just his eye, miss. Right lovely shiner, he's got."

She sat down in the nearest chair. "How bad is it?"

"For him, or them?"

"This is not a joking matter."

"Weren't no joke. He's got an eye as would do that fellow Turner proud if he could get them colors on canvas, but them other two as set on him—"

"Two? Set on him? To rob him?"

Burke scowled. "Ain't my job to tell you more, miss."

"Should I ask Terrance then?"

Glaring at her, Burke stiffened. "You ain't the sort of female as ought to be going to a gentleman's rooms. Particularly not his."

"Then tell me what happened."

Sullen, Burke did so, thinking all the while that Terrance would skin him when this came out, and it always did. There was little enough to say—two ex-prizefighters, a lucky punch at the start, a broken nose, and some cracked ribs.

"Not his, theirs," Burke said as Miss Sylvain's face paled.

"And did he have these . . . these ruffians arrested?"

"I should say not. Not bad fellows, really. Just down on their luck. Didn't take more than makin' 'em a better offer to make 'em peaceable enough and willing to step up for a decent nightcap and to sort matters out."

"He gave them money—and a drink?"

"An' how else was he to find out they'd been—" Burke bit off the words, a guilty flush staining his face.

"Hired?" Sylvain stated, shock cold on her skin. She rubbed her arms and stared at Terrance's servant, and then her thoughts began to turn. One name leapt forward as someone who must wish Terrance only harm now. The man, after all, had killed once. Forcing her voice to remain steady, she asked, "Has Mr. Hayland not yet been apprehended?"

Chin down, Burke scuffed one boot on the carpet. "You got a note for me to take or not?"

Standing, Sylvain moved to the desk, a knot tight in her stomach. How stupid she had been to think this ended. Only Terrance had thought so as well, and had dropped his guard. Would he be any more cautious now until Hayland was caught? It sounded not—not when he ended by inviting the men who had attacked him to his rooms for a drink.

At least, with what sounded like a black eye to hide, he might stay in his rooms until he healed. But what happened then? Would he feel compelled to hunt for Hayland himself?

Sitting at Penelope's desk, Sylvain took up a quill, flipped open the inkwell, and drew out a sheet of vellum. But what did she write? *Please be more careful.* He would not, of course. With her lower lip between her teeth, she put quill to paper.

"Thank you for your note. I wish you would consider taking the waters someplace until you hear from Mr. Waddington that the situation is improved. That would prevent such circumstances as these occurring again. But I doubt you will heed this."

She read her words, then tore up the paper. Sound advice perhaps, but he had not even asked for it.

Putting down the quill, she turned to Burke. "Will you simply tell him . . ."

She let the words trail away. What could she have Burke say that did not sound as foolish? Tell him that she wished she could be there to look after him? That just the thought of him hurt brought on a physical ache?

Her situation prevented all of that. She was not really his

affianced wife. She had no right to say anything, other than polite expressions of sympathy, which Terrance would not appreciate.

Burke seemed to understand something of her feelings, for his expression softened. "Now, don't you fret, miss. He's a fellow as knows how to handle himself."

Cold, she hugged her arms. "Yes, but could not the same have once been said of Lord Dunscombe?"

"What in bloody blue blazes do you mean you told her?" From his one good eye, Terrance glared at his manservant. Bad enough to be cooped up in his rooms, unable to show his face without starting talk as to how he had had his eye blackened. Now he learned that Burke had not simply handed Sylvain the note.

Pushing away from the card table where he had been playing a depressing game of solitaire, he limped forward to glare at his servant, his dressing gown billowing around him, open over his shirt and trousers. His leg ached this morning, but less so than his head—that would teach him to try reason before fists with any man met on a dark London street.

Burke glared back, insolent as ever. "As if I had any say in the matter, what with her going on about askin' you if she had to! And she'd do it—never saw a female with such a stubborn chin as that. She'd show up here and I didn't think you'd fancy that much."

Putting a hand up to his swollen eye, Terrance swore. Then he turned to stare at his reflection in the mirror that hung over the mantel. The bruising had begun to yellow around his temple and cheekbone, but the skin just under his eye remained dark purple and it would be days before the swelling subsided.

In the mirror, he glimpsed Burke's glowering expression and swung around again. "You've something else to say?"

Burke held up his hands. "Not me, guv. Ain't my place to tell you that it's a bit harder to jump a fellow if he's in a hired carriage, not strolling the streets as if it were broad day. 'Course you might not care about the look you put on that Miss Sylvain's face when I had to tell her how you'd gotten yourself set on!"

Clenching his fists, Terrance glared at his servant. "I don't know why I don't turn you off!"

Burke snorted. "You don't 'cause I'm fair brilliant with horses I am—and there's few as would put up with your temper. Too much like your father, if you ask me!"

With that, he turned and stalked out of the room.

Fists unclenching, Terrance slumped. Then he glanced into the mirror, Burke's words echoing again.

Too much like your father.

He rubbed his sore temple. How had his life become this nightmare?

And was it true?

The voice—so like Terrance's—quickened Sylvain's step. She came into the drawing room dressed for dinner in a cream satin gown, and for a heartbeat she thought she imagined the scene. Her family laughing and talking to the tall, black-haired man who stood with his back to her, a black evening coat snug over his broad shoulders and black trousers outlining long legs.

Her throat tightened.

Then she noted that the shoulders were not quite broad enough, and while he stood over six feet, he lacked the towering physical presence she knew so well.

Not Terrance. Theo.

As he turned, Theo's blue eyes lit with a smile. Sylvain forced an answering one. So like Terrance, and yet so different. Lighter made, the lines of his handsome face more finely drawn, and lighter hearted, too. But while Theo drew the eye with his quick laugh and the dark Winslow looks, he did not dominate the room as did his brother. He also seemed on far better terms with her family.

Then she glimpsed his wife, Molly, seated near the fire, the candlelight gleaming from her red curls, and she came forward at once. She had liked Molly from the first meeting, over a year ago now, and she had not seen enough of her since Theo had married her.

"Sylvain, you remember Mr. and Mrs. Winslow," Penelope said.

"So formal, Pen!" Theo said, grinning. "Of course Silly remembers us. But, by heaven, I don't think we'd have known her—you haven't a leaf in your hair, or a tear in your gown, nor an animal at your heels."

"Her fox is in the garden," Penelope said, her tone dry.

He glanced at her, then gave a laugh. "So it is the same Silly we know. Come along, Molly has a dozen stories for you. She fell in love with Yorkshire—the pudding in particular—and heartily disliked Oxfordshire."

"Only because a decent meal could not be had," Molly added, smiling at Sylvain. Redheaded and plump, she looked utterly unlike what Sylvain would have once pictured as a wife for Theo. But watching him gaze now at Molly, Sylvain found it difficult to think anyone might have fit him better, for he obviously adored her.

It pleased her, too, to see Cecila and Bryn here, looking relaxed and comfortable. Strolling to Cecila's side, Theo began to tease her, acting more like a brother than a man who had once thought to wed her.

Sylvain watched them, her head tilted. Is that what love became when the hottest fires died? Did it become a deep friendship? It seemed a touch sad that it could. But then had there ever really been deep feelings between Cecila and Theo?

Before she could decide, Molly invited her to sit close by. "I'm to talk to Mr. Dawes tonight about writing a cooking book that Theo insists would make my fame—only it does seem to me as if Mr. Dawes would rather talk politics with Nevin than anything else. And I certainly would rather cook than write about it."

Sylvain sat down and glanced at her sister's husband, who was deep in conversation with his cousin Nevin. Then she looked at Molly. "Are you as happy as you look?"

Molly smiled. "Too direct as ever. I've missed you. But Theo says we might stay at Winslow Park for a few months, and I can't think of anything I'd like so well. His father even wrote us to come. But, tell me—what is this I hear about Terrance?"

Sylvain froze. Had her sisters mentioned the engagement?

Leaning forward, Molly said, "Even in Yorkshire, we heard that he had shot someone in a duel—only now it seems he did not. Theo laughed at the story, but then we kept hearing about it when we got to London, and I thought you might know the truth."

Sylvain relayed the story—or parts of it. She had to break off as everyone rose to go in to dinner, but she finished up afterward, when the ladies returned to the drawing room, leaving the gentlemen to their port and more political talk. Molly listened, asking no questions, her green eyes alert.

At last, she shook her head. "Theo will not like this. He won't admit it, but he does care about that brother of his. And I hate to think what Squire Winslow will say."

"That is not the worst of it, I fear," Sylvain admitted. "I think Mr. Hayland blames Terrance for suspicion falling on him."

"Who blames Terrance for what?" Theo asked, coming over to them.

His wife stretched up a hand to him. "Murder it seems."

He stared at her. "I hope you're joking, but with Terrance you never know. Did he really shoot someone?"

Molly leaned closer. "You had best tell him everything. But, excuse me, it looks as if Mr. Dawes does wish to talk with me about that cookbook idea."

Rising, Molly left them, and Sylvain recounted her story again. Theo's expression tightened as she spoke, and she began to wonder why she had thought him a lighter version of his brother. He looked rather too like Terrance in a mood just now.

"Blazes! I set off on my honeymoon, and looking for . . . well, looking about, and what does he do but manage this? Is it too much to hope Father's not heard?"

"He probably has," Sylvain admitted. "But this isn't done yet." Theo's jaw tightened as she told him about Terrance having been set upon. She took this as a good sign, and asked, "Could you—well, could you talk to him, perhaps? He might listen to you. Perhaps you could even get him to go with you to Winslow Park for a few days?"

He let out a frustrated sigh. "Poking my nose into this is a good way to get it punched. As to his going home—that would end with him and my father at each other again. You ought to have heard the row they got into at my wedding. But—well, I'll speak to this runner fellow you mentioned—what was his name? Waddington? He might be able to do something."

"Thank you."

Glancing at her, he flashed a smile and covered her hand with his. "Don't fret. He has the devil's own luck, you know. But, well . . . may I ask a favor from you in return? You . . . well, to put it in plain cloth, you're not like to face a leveler if you bring this up with my brother, and I am."

She smiled. "A leveler? I hope not. Do you need to ask Terrance for money?"

Looking appalled, Theo pulled back. "Certainly not. I've had nothing but relatives pushing money or property at me since I married—why is it everyone thinks a single fellow don't need such things? If my father had settled that bit of land on me two years . . . only never mind that. This ain't about my father."

Pulling a folded paper from his waistcoat pocket, he turned the note over, his long fingers manipulating it as if he had done this dozens of times. Worn and grayed, the edges spoke of such handling.

"Would . . . would you give this to Terrance when next you

see him? Molly wants to set out for Somerset tomorrow, and I can't say as I blame her. We've been jaunting about for too long, but that's done with now, only . . . well, tell Terrance he ought to see her. Tell him I mentioned his name, so he's expected."

He smiled, blue eyes brilliant. Then he pressed the paper into Sylvain's hand. "Tell him it's not half bad. He'll understand better afterward. But then I expect you'll know how to handle this. You're good with every other wild animal, so why not my brother?"

Sylvain took the paper, questions about it forming. She had no time to ask them, however, for Cecila came to them, suggesting a game of charades. Penelope overruled this as too exhausting, but agreed to have tables for cards set out, and the opportunity to ask anything more of Theo faded.

Not in a mood for casino or whist, Sylvain excused herself and gave everyone a good night. Doris helped her from her gown and into her night things, unpinning her artificial curls and leaving them on the dresser before she left. And then Sylvain sat on her bed, staring at Theo's note.

He had seemed oddly insistent about its delivery.

Tell Terrance he ought to see her.

Her? A former lover? A relative? It must be someone Theo and Terrance both knew. Curious, she turned the paper over. No writing to reveal any clue, and while she had an itch to open it, Theo had entrusted it to her for delivery, not for prying into.

Rising, she went to her wardrobe and tucked the paper into the satin pocket inside her velvet muff. Returning to her bed, she blew out her candle and slipped into the sheets, still heated from the warming pan Doris had slid across them.

She lay there, eyes open, staring into the darkness.

And she wished she had Theo's confidence that she knew how to deal with Terrance as easily as she dealt with Trace.

She did not see Terrance for four days, and she alternated between feeling disgusted with herself for noticing the time pass and worrying that perhaps something else had happened. He had, after all, promised to go with her, Cecila, and Bryn tonight to Sadler's Wells to see Grimaldi the clown. So she would certainly see him then—perhaps . . . she hoped. It did little good to tell herself that she would have had word if something really awful had occurred.

And the note remained in her muff, which she carried with her each day on the chance she might see him.

Distracted as she was, she did make a discovery—somehow, over the past week, she had stopped missing home. And she had started to enjoy London.

Terrance had given her that. His false engagement had freed her, and she noted that she had not since committed any huge social error—not stepped on her own hem, nor spilled a drop of wine or punch, not said the wrong thing at the wrong time. And she had acquired new friends.

Miss Beddington, whom she had met at Mrs. Cornely's, had come to call with her mother, and had even expressed an interest in meeting Trace, though she had wrinkled her nose at him and said, "He does rather smell. I didn't think foxes did."

She then went on to describe her ideal husband, asked Sylvain what she thought of London, and before she left, smiled and declared, "We simply must be friends, for you are tall and fair, and I'm short and dark, and we'll look stunning together!"

Sylvain did not care to be stunning, but Miss Beddington's endless flow of cheerful chatter took her mind off other things, and she liked that. She also rather liked Miss Beddington's brother, a sensible—if rather dull—young man, who not only talked to her, but also listened.

She was with the Beddingtons to watch a balloon accession at the White Conduit House when she next glimpsed Terrance.

Mrs. Godwin had gone with Miss Beddington to find tea, and Sylvain stood with Mr. Beddington as he read from a pamphlet he had about balloons. She heard only half the words about weather conditions and hot air, for her thoughts had drifted to worrying about Terrance. She really must stop that. Then, as if summoned by that, the crowd parted and she saw a familiar set of wide shoulders and a strong face above the crowd.

Her heart lifted.

She frowned and fought the reaction with critical inspection. He had his walking stick and still favored his leg, but he looked fit—no trace of puffiness in his face. His tawny eyes held a reckless glint as he gave her good day, and then he shot a glance at Beddington before offering her his arm.

"Damn cold out. Why don't we find someplace warm?" Beddington sucked in a shocked breath, and Terrance glanced at him. "Something wrong with you? Come on, Sylvain. Excuse us, Beddington."

With that he swept her away.

"I think it was your swearing," she said.

He glanced at her, puzzled. "What swearing?"

"Mr. Beddington—his surprise?"

He glanced back at the other man. "If that's all it takes to shock the fellow, he ought to stay in the schoolroom. What in blazes are you doing here? Shabby-looking sort of place. And who is that fellow anyway?"

"Miss Beddington read about the balloon going up—I don't think she has your guidebook. And that, as I told you, is her brother."

He frowned. "Just who are these Beddingtons?"

"They are friends. My friends. And Miss Beddington is a very nice girl, so you are not to swear at her if you meet her. It would more than shock her."

"Sounds dull."

Feeling insulted, Sylvain bristled. "What is dull is the sort of person who goes off for days without a word to anyone!"

Looking down at her, he grinned. "You missed me then?"

She looked away to watch as six men still struggled to lay out the silk of the balloon on the ground. Two yapping dogs and the tug of the wind hampered them. "Not at all. I just was uncertain if you still planned to go to Sadler's Wells tonight."

He leaned closer. "Your ears are pink."

Wrinkling her nose, she glared at him. "I am sorry I ever told you about that."

"Oh, I would have figured out eventually what gives away your lies. Must we stay?"

"I came with the Beddingtons, and it would be rude of me to leave. But you can go if you wish."

For a moment, he thought he would. It would be a different matter to be going up in the balloon himself—and taking Sylvain with him—rather than watching someone else have all the fun. However, he had already gone to all the fuss to find her. And he rather fancied how the wind pressed the material of her dress against her legs—quite shapely, long legs.

He glanced back to note that Mr. Beddington trailed behind them—no doubt looking at Sylvain's legs as well. Irritated, Terrance glanced at Sylvain. "You seem to have acquired a watchdog."

She glanced back at Mr. Beddington, and smiled at him. That deepened Terrance's frown. A deep dislike formed for the earnest, young Mr. Beddington. What the blazes did Sylvain want with that sort of dull dog?

"Skinny fellow isn't he? Does he suspect me of having designs on you? Should I tell him we're engaged."

"No! What—are you jealous of him?"

"Me? Never."

He looked away from her, uncomfortable with such a direct question. And with the emotions stirring in him. Jealous? Impossible. And yet . . . he glanced down at her, and then at Beddington, disliking again how the man's stare remained fixed on her.

But it wasn't jealousy. Not in the least. Absurd notion! But, well, blazes, her sisters had rigged her out in fine style. He liked this pale green dress and short jacket trimmed in black braid that she had on today. Not too fancy, but the lines somehow managed to add a sophistication he had not noticed before. They also emphasized that trim waist, and the attractive swell of her hips, and breasts that would nicely fit into his palms.

Where in blazes was this Mrs. Godwin of hers to look after her, instead of leaving her to the gawking stares of the likes of Beddington?

"I thought of coming to visit you in your rooms," she said as they strolled through the crowd gathered to drink tea and watch the hot air balloon.

"A fine thing that would be. Here now—do you want that badly to be rid of me that you'd force a scandal on me?"

"Oh, come. You might not care to lose Penelope's challenge, but it would free you of any more responsibility towards me. You could go off whenever you like then for however long you like without having to tell anyone anything."

"Back on that again, eh? I left for Newmarket—I had to go someplace or go mad, and my face wasn't fit to show. But you must have known I'd be back. Besides, did you ever happen to think that I don't mind having some of that responsibility?"

"Don't mind? That certainly sounds as if it appeals so very well to you!"

Irritated now, he stopped and turned to glare at her. "What in blazes is wrong with you today?"

"Wrong? Why should anything be wrong when you have only had two ruffians set on you, and there's a murderer still loose who has reason to hate you!"

"Oh, for—you don't have to be worried for me."

"I know I do not—but I am."

She stared up at him, her breath ragged with emotion and her eyes troubled. Astonished to see her this way, he reached out to brush a red-gold curl tugged loose from her bonnet. He didn't know how to deal with this. So he tried a grin. "Honestly, you must think me as green as Beddington there."

"I spoke to Theo the other day—the people who care about you do worry for you. That is what happens when someone lov—" Turning away, she broke off her words. But then she looked back. "Your brother loves you, that's why he worries."

"Oh, rubbish! Theo's a good sort, but love? That's a fiction from your brother-in-law's poetry books! Theo's just worried I'll leave him on his own, he is."

He grinned at her, trying to lighten the mood between them. But anger flashed in her eyes. "How dare you belittle his feelings!" Dragging her hand from her muff, she thrust a note at him. "Theo gave me this for you. He said you should go see her. That you are expected. And he is worried for you!"

Taking the note, Terrance snapped the wax seal and opened it. He scanned the lines, and as he did, his mouth flattened into a grim line. "What else did he say? Well, what else?"

Sylvain stepped back, shocked by that sharp, sudden anger in his tone.

As if he had been hovering close by, Beddington came forward, asking, "Miss Harwood, is there some trouble?"

Caught off balance, she glanced at him and started to tell him to please go away. But Terrance also turned on his heel, looking ready to throttle the poor man. She stepped between them, changing her words at once. "Thank you, but would you mind finding Mrs. Godwin and telling her I should like to go?"

He shot a hard look at Terrance, but something in Terrance's face must have made him think better of saying anything, for he only gave short bow and strode away.

Sylvain looked at Terrance, her chest still tight. He had pulled off his hat to run his hands through his short, black hair, so that it stood up in spikes. His face had paled, and the glitter in his eyes left her wondering if she ought to say anything more to him.

Glancing at the note in his hand, she saw an address in Islington for a Julia Kendall.

An old lover, she thought, lips pressed tight and a sickening twist in her chest.

Why had she thought herself up to any of this? New gowns and haircuts did not make a new person. Under it all still existed the grubby, skinny Sylvain who had grown up next to a man who never looked twice at her.

Looking up from the note, eyes bleak and voice dull, Terrance asked again, "What else did he say about our mother?"

Fifteen

A chill shivered across Sylvain's skin, and she knew from his tone that he asked because he had no intention of using the address given him. Though she had seen her answer in his eyes, she still asked, "You do not plan to see her, do you?"

His jaw tightened, but he said nothing. Turning, he stared at the six men still struggling with the now partially inflated balloon, its brilliant, red-and-blue vertical stripes contrasting with the green of the trees and the gray sky, its wicker swan gondola still on the grass.

She stared at him, watching the fortress rise around him. "How can you be so cold to those who love you—how can you say their feelings do not exist?"

How can you not go?

He glanced at her. "It's love to leave your sons, is it?"

She met his stare. "You won't know—not unless you ask her." She turned away, oddly empty inside. Then she glanced back at him. She had no right to say the words, but she had to say them. Not for him. For herself. She would never forgive herself if she left them unsaid. "Please. Do not make your father's mistakes, Terrance. Look how it has taken him years to start to learn how to forgive—and what misery that has cost everyone around him."

The glitter sharpened in those tawny eyes to searing hostility, and she almost flinched.

He said nothing, but turned and strode away, his walking

stick clenched in his hand, his shortened step not hampering his stride in the least.

Glancing down, Sylvain saw the slip of paper. She bent down and picked it up, then folded it and tucked it back into her muff.

Would he ever make peace with the ghosts of his past?

And would he ever have a future until he did so?

"And why must I push myself into everything with him?" she muttered, hating herself and the fact that she could not be one of those fascinating, bewitching beauties who could capture more than his frowns.

Staring up at the building, Terrance tried to think what he was doing here. He had dropped that damn scrap of paper, but the numbers trickled through his thoughts over and over again. His aimless wandering had taken him here, and he knew they had not been as aimless as he had thought.

What was he doing here? He had not thought of her in years. Julia Kendall. She had taken back her maiden name even though his father had not divorced her. How could a man divorce a wife whom he had buried?

Turning, Terrance started to walk away. She ought to stay buried. Then he stopped.

He glanced at the building again. A mean, narrow house of brick with bright red flowers in a box on the windowsill of the first floor, lace curtains, and a door painted blue and set with a brass knocker.

How had Theo found her? Eyes narrowing, he remembered that his mother's family had actually been from Oxfordshire. Had Theo gone there—and where else had he gone looking for her?

You should go see her . . . you are expected. Sylvain's words echoed in his mind. How could he be expected? He scowled. He still did not care that she had left him and his brother. She had probably not even had a thought beyond escaping his father. But why had she run off as she had, with the pretense of going to some spa to take the waters, and then creating that fiction of her death He wanted that question answered.

Gripping his walking stick tighter, he limped toward the door. A maid in a tidy white apron and cap set over a sober dark blue dress answered his knock.

"Julia Kendall," he said. The words croaked in his voice, and he could get nothing else out.

Eyes widening with curiosity, the maid held open the door, letting him into a sparse hall with only a side table and an oak stand to hold hats and canes. Two hats already stood there. His made three.

The maid led him up the uncarpeted stairs to a parlor that overlooked the front. Like the hall, the furniture looked functional: bare oak chairs, solid and scarred by age, a high-backed settee, a rocking chair, a worn carpet, its colors faded by sun and years. He glanced around. The only real bit of color came from a vibrant watercolor of what looked remarkably like sunrise at Winslow Park.

He stepped closer. It was his home—and the view from over the old garden, eastward.

Uncomfortable, he turned away and folded his hands behind his back. A coal fire burned in the grate. The house had a maid, so was it by choice she lived so Spartan? And who else lived here? Relatives? A new, not-quite husband?

He'd been a damn fool to come, and he started for the door, then checked his step as it opened and she entered.

For an instant, he did not remember. Then the faint scent she wore reached him. Roses. Memories flooded him. How she'd held him, singing something calming during thunderstorms. Her leaning down to brush a hand through his hair, or tug his collar straight before sending him off to church. How her face had looked after an argument with his father—tight, pale, those finely arched brows creased and her hands shaking.

She had something of that in her face just now, only now he was of an age to lay a name to the emotion—anxiety.

She said nothing as she stared at him, with eyes the color of a good tawny sherry. Eyes too like his own. Silver streaked her black hair, a wing of it was wound into the thick mass worn pulled back and up in a crown of braid. The silver somehow enhanced the dark, lustrous color. She had to be in her fifties, yet only the faintest wrinkles fanned from her eyes, and those lines around her mouth looked to come from smiles.

Dressed in a plain, dark gown, she came forward, but did not hold out her hands. She did smile, however, creasing the lines on her face, and then she said, in a melody of voice he would have known anywhere, "Terrance."

Resentment swelled in him, bitter and harsh, almost choking him as the words stumbled out. "Why did you go? Didn't you love us enough to stay?"

She stopped and he regretted saying anything. He sounded a petulant child, not a man grown. Turning around, his breathing fast and ragged, he sought for self-control. Blazes, why had he come? He must be mad.

He heard the rustle of her skirts as she moved to the fire and then that soft voice of hers answered, no recrimination in it for his outburst, no regret for the past. Simply a calm acceptance that tore into him, stirring his anger again like a poker in the flames.

"It was never a matter of love enough to stay, but love enough to leave."

The words startled him and he looked at her. She gazed at him, hands at her sides. "I couldn't bear to have my feelings turn to hate, Terrance. I know it is difficult to understand, but having a concern such as this meant I must act as I was led?"

"Led?" Frowning, he pulled back.

She sat on the wooden settee and folded her hands in her lap. The gesture seemed oddly calming, and then he realized that it reminded him of how Sylvain often sat when she faced a difficult task.

"It took a long time to reach my decision, but I knew from

the start that I could not take you. That would have killed your father. You . . . you and Theo . . . you were—and I think you must still be—his life."

"But you left! You walked away from your vows."

"I am a Quaker, Terrance. I recognize no authority but the spirit that lives in me—in each of us. And so I must act as I am called—as we all must. I married your father in love. I lived with him in love. And I bore you from love. But I would not watch that love become a lie. I would not live a life of miserable deceit, and I could not see him tear my feelings to tatters with an anger he could not seem to control."

Terrance's mouth twisted. "So you died to us?"

Her mouth tightened and he saw a flash of anger in her eyes. Something in him relaxed that he could shatter that calm around her. He did not want to be the only one raging here. He did not want to be alone in his anguish.

"I do not approve that Basil pretended I had died. I did not expect that of him. I left letters for you and Theo for him to give you. But . . . well, I do believe he acted in your best interest."

"Oh, did he now! Such nobility from everyone!"

"Terrance, such scorn is unworthy of you. Your father would never see you harmed—and neither would I."

"But still you left!"

"I did. And it is my own flaw I confess that I am not strong enough to offer love even in the presence of anger. I would that it were otherwise—but I could not bear it. And so my choices were to stay and die, or to leave. And God called me to leave. Oh, yes, I could have taken you—and the Lord knows I was tempted. The Friends would have hidden us, I knew that." Tears wet her eyes. "And had I feared for you, I would have. But to do so would have killed him. And I couldn't. I couldn't hurt him. I'm sorry."

Standing, she moved to the door. She stopped, her back to him. "I understand if you cannot forgive me. Theo was so young, I doubted he noted my presence or lack of it. But—

oh, I find I am furious with Basil for not telling you the truth.
And I should not be."

He went to her then and took her shoulders to turn her
around. For a moment, he could only stare at her, too many
words struggling in him, too many feelings. He wanted to strike
at his father—but as he stared at her, the anger began to fade.
As did the pain. And only ashes of regrets seemed left.

What had Sylvain told him—not to make his father's
mistakes. Damn her for being so right.

Struggling for what might pass as a smile, he said, the
words sounding rough to him, "He always was a pig-headed,
arrogant proud fool. And so am I."

Shaking her head, she put her hand to cup his cheek. Tears
glistened on her lashes. "My baby . . . oh, God, I missed you."

Burying his head against her shoulder, he put his arms
around her and pulled her close, and then he stood there, her
tears wet on his cheeks, holding her close, eyes shut tight. He
stood there until his leg began to ache, and her tears dried, and
then he still did not let go.

At last, she shifted in his hold and he pulled back, asking,
"Do you mind if I throttle my father?"

"Not even in jest—I am a Quaker still. I cannot hold with
violence. It is my gift and my curse that such makes me ill."

Terrance winced—blazes did not the Winslow temper run
through him as strong as in his father?

Immediately, her hand came up to touch his face. "What is
it? Do you fear yourself? You did look so like Basil when I
walked in." She smiled. "But you have my eyes."

Taking her hand, he kissed her palm. "Only not your calm
nature. I'm the very devil, I fear."

She shook her head. "No. We all carry the light of God in
us, Terrance. Perhaps yours is just a little more obscured by
clouds. But you can look past them—I have faith in you.
Now, come and sit with me and tell me about your life."

He stiffened, and sought for excuses, but she insisted, and
so he found himself sitting next to her on that hard settee and

stuttering though words like a schoolboy. Things he thought
he could not mention to her came to mind, and though he
tried to skirt them, she pulled out more than he wanted to say.
But she never gasped, nor showed the least anger toward him,
nor any condemnation.

He thought again of how much Sylvain reminded him of
her, or was it the other way around? Both such calm women.
So self-contained. And it flashed into him with the cut of
lightning how unbearable it would be to have what lay between himself and Sylvain turn into something ugly.

Blazes, no wonder his mother had left. No wonder he
feared the change that seemed to be taking place between
Sylvain and himself. The thought startled him. And led to the
topic of Sylvain.

He found himself talking about what it had been like to be
her friend as she grew up, and of coming with her to London.
His mother listened to everything, her hand resting on his, a
smile in place, watching him, almost as if she could not take
in enough of him.

The room darkened, and a servant knocked and then entered to light the candles.

"Will you stay to dine?" she asked.

He started to say he would, and then he remembered that
he had promised Sylvain to take her to the theater—and how
unhappy she had been with him earlier today. How worried.

"I cannot. I'm sorry. But I will come back."

Her smile lifted again. She walked with him to the front
steps, and stood there as he strode away, his thoughts jumbled,
but oddly lighthearted. He glanced back once, but saw only
her dark silhouette framed in the door.

Then he turned and started to walk again, frowning, his
stare on the pavement, trying to sort through a muddle of
emotions, which pricked and stung like a muscle fallen asleep
and woken.

Was he furious with his father? He ought to be—for the
lies, the lost years. But had the squire told those lies to save

his pride? It had seemed so to Terrance. He had been certain
that his father had not been able to bear others thinking that
his wife had left him.

But what if she was right? What if his father had lied with
the belief that he somehow could protect his sons from his
own anguish and loss? A small shift, but everything looked
different from that angle.

Love.

He had scorned the notion earlier, but now it seemed as if
everyone in his life had acted from that emotion. And gotten
themselves and those around them into a bloody great mess,
as well, because of it.

He kept walking, his attention inward.

He would see her again. He had to. But what did he now
say to his father? Blazes, but he could throttle the man. Only
his mother would not approve. A Quaker? How had she ever
ended up with a man like his father?

His mouth quirked. Well, Sylvain would certainly be smug
tonight when he—

Pain cracked into his head, spinning the thoughts away.
Pavement rushed at him, slammed into him. He lay still, his
mind screaming but muscles limp, struggling to hold on to a
thread of consciousness.

Anger surged in him. Damn, damn, damn. Why had he not
taken a hack? Damn Burke for being right. Not now. I don't
want this now!

Someone—a man—muttered something about drunken-
ness. A drunk friend. Who the hell was drunk? Was he?
Blazes, his head felt like it. Hands caught his arms and lifted
him. Struggling to turn his head, he managed a groan. Pain
slipped into blackness.

"We really must go."

Sylvain glanced at the ormolu clock, and then at Cecila,

who wore ice blue tonight, and who for the first time in days did not look white and ready to bolt for the nearest basin.

"Are you certain you feel well enough?" Sylvain asked. The color in her sister's cheeks told that she was, but where was Terrance?

Cecila smiled, and turned to glance at her reflection in the mirror, pulling loose a curl so that it curved around one white shoulder. "For a blessing, it's the first time I do. And I am not going to spend the evening waiting for Terrance Winslow. He can meet us at the theater if he wishes."

Sylvain nodded and rose, taking up her pink evening cloak. She hated pink, but Cecila had picked it out for her as a special gift.

Coming to her side, Bryn took the cloak and held it for her. "Have faith, little one. Grimaldi is said to be quite the most comic clown in England. He will bring you a smile."

Sylvain nodded. But she kept thinking of how harsh she had been with Terrance. No wonder he had kept away tonight. Only why had he not sent a note? Oh, she had been no better than either of her sisters, telling him what he ought to do, thinking it only for his own good.

She would beg his pardon. If he came.

Why has he not sent a note?

It seemed to take forever to arrive at the theater. As they stepped from the carriage, Sylvain scanned the glittering ladies and gentlemen clad in black coats, looking for that pair of broad shoulders which could always be glimpsed towering over all others. Lanterns cast flickering pools of yellow, making the shadows dance, but she knew she would not mistake him in any light.

Inside, Bryn took their cloaks and left them with a maid at the cloakroom, then escorted them to Lord Nevin's box. Nevin and Penelope dinned with Nevin's sister, Lady St. Albans, and her husband the earl.

"I really do not like clowns," Penelope had confessed.

"Besides, St. Albans has promised to mix me my own perfume, so I must go and be nice to him."

Sylvain had smiled at her sister's confession—Penelope had so few flaws, her distaste for comedy seemed almost a blessing. But Sylvain could only be grateful she had not had to attend dinner with the earl, for his sharp wit and his knowing smiles left her feeling utterly provincial.

In the theater, the crowd settled, the music began, and the curtain rose. Sylvain saw nothing on the stage. Searching the audience, she looked for Terrance.

By intermission she had given him up, and a knot had settled low in her stomach. She wanted to go home. However, laughter flushed Cecila's face and Bryn had not looked so relaxed since she had arrived in London. Rising, he offered to fetch them champagne.

Cecila made a face. "I am not taking anything this evening—it is not worth the risk that it will want to come up again. But do take Sylvain for a stroll. I want a word with Lady Manning, for I haven't had a good gossip with her in weeks." With a smile she waved them off.

In the corridor, Bryn took Sylvain's arm and led her down the stairs, to a room with velvet-covered chairs. Seating her in one, he brought back two glasses of champagne, and then he asked, "You're not really enjoying any of this, are you?"

She forced a smile. "I just thought . . . it's not like Terrance to ever break a promise."

He sat down next to her. "Perhaps you expect too much from him?"

Glancing down at her glass, she said nothing.

"Cheer up. It could be worse."

She glanced at him. "How is that?"

"Well, let me tell you a story. There was a fellow who once loved words—loved them so much, he thought they could do anything. But then he tried to make a business of them, and he found he really did not like that at all. He had expected too much of them."

"What did he do then?"

"Well, he looked at the words, saw that what he really wanted was to use them—to make others hear him. To make a difference. And he decided to chuck the business and better employ himself."

Shaking her head, Sylvain found herself smiling despite her mood. "What does that have to do with this possibly being worse for me?"

He took her half empty champagne glass. "The story illustrates the glimmering hope of the chance to change your mind. You are not yet married to Winslow. You may cry off without anyone saying anything other than that you are a wise young lady."

Her smile twisted. "Why is it that the wisdom of the head and the wisdom of the heart so often disagree?"

"Because most of us have stupid heads that think about silly things such as the opinions of others—trust your heart, my dear. It's the best advice I can give you, and if you like I shall give you a dozen quotes of others who would say the same."

Holding up her hands, she shook her head. "Please no."

"Then may I fetch you another glass of champagne?"

She agreed to this, and watched as he made his way across the room, thinking how very lucky Cecila was to have fallen in love with such an easy gentleman to love.

Glancing around the room, she tried to pretend to herself that she did not still search for Terrance.

Her head lifted and she stiffened as Lady Dunscombe stepped into the room, emeralds glittering around her throat and at her wrists and ears. Looking around the room, the lady gave Sylvain the smallest of smiles, and then turned away.

For a moment, Sylvain sat still. She ought not to do anything. But Lady Dunscombe seemed to be remarkably close to her brother. Was there not a chance she knew something of his whereabouts, or his intentions towards Terrance?

Face hot, but unable to sit still, Sylvain rose and wove her way through the crowded, stuffy room to the lady. Stopping beside her, Sylvain hesitated, then touched her arm. The lady turned to give Sylvain a startled glance. "I beg your pardon? I—"

"Please, I must speak to you. It's about your brother."

Sixteen

Lady Dunscombe stiffened. With a smile, she turned to the lady and excused herself. Taking Sylvain's arm, she led her to a small alcove. "What of my brother?"

Glancing around, Sylvain saw Bryn talking to a heavy older man. She turned her attention to Lady Dunscombe. "You must know that he is wanted for the murder of your late husband."

Face flushed, and eyes narrowed, she shook her head in denial. "I don't believe he killed Myles."

"Well, now he may wish harm to Terrance."

"We have nothing more to speak of!"

She turned, but Sylvain caught her arm. "I believe that he paid two men to set upon Terrance. And tonight, Terrance was to meet me here, but he has not come. Can you honestly say that you know where your brother is, and that he has nothing to do with Terrance's absence here?"

Again, she shook her head, her emeralds glinting in the candlelight. Doubt crept into the lady's brown eyes, but she drew back, throwing out her words like a challenge, "You little fool. He does that to all of us. Tires of us and simply leaves."

"I am not discussing his leaving—I am speaking of his not having keep his word to be here. Did he ever once make you a promise that he did not keep?"

Eyes narrowing, Ellena started to answer, and then she checked her scorn. Had Terrance ever made her a promise? She searched memories that she had not wanted to look at, and she realized that he had never once said that he loved her, nor had he made her the vows she had longed for.

Lifting her chin, she regarded the girl before her. A sweet child, but far too innocent for the likes of Winslow. She stepped closer.

"My brother has done nothing wrong, and Terrance . . . well, you would be wise to avoid such a man."

A stubborn set came into Miss Harwood's mouth. Then she said, "How can you be so certain that your brother is not guilty? He certainly acted so when he threatened Terrance with a sword, and then ran away."

Ellena glanced around. Others in the room had started to move back to their seats. She looked again at the girl, fear crowding her. "Edwin—it is not his fault. He must hide because of that slander."

"Then why not help him—and me? You swear he is innocent, but do you not want to be utterly certain?" Sylvain saw the hesitation in the woman's eyes. She took her hand. "If you care anything for your brother, you must help."

"Just what do you mean? You want me to betray my brother to you. To tell you where—" Face pale, the lady cut off her words.

Sylvain straightened. "You know where he is, don't you? You have seen him? Can you go to him tonight? You must try to convince him that revenge upon Terrance will not gain him anything. Please? Will you do that much—if not for Terrance, then for his sake. More blood on his hands will not save him!"

Pulling her hand away, Lady Dunscombe stepped back. Then she turned and started for the stairs that led back to the theater. Sylvain's hands clenched and she fought the urge to chase after the woman. She could do no more.

Slowly, the woman's step faltered, and then she turned and came back, uncertainty haunting her eyes. "I cannot help you. Edwin was betrayed once to the authorities, and now you ask me . . . I will not see him hang for shooting a man who was brutal to me, and to everyone else in his life!" She pulled the sleeve of her gown back from her shoulder, revealing a pink line of scar. "Myles gave me that—and if Edwin had not shot him, I might have done it myself."

Sylvain stared at the scar, and then looked into Lady Dunscombe's eyes, which were glittering as brightly as the hard stones around her neck. She watched as the woman realized that she had just admitted knowledge of her brother's guilt.

Again, the lady turned away, but when she turned back, the emeralds trembled. "I don't want my brother to die. He is all I have left!"

"Then help me—take me to him and perhaps we might stop any further bloodshed."

He had the money for a better room than this dank hole, thanks to Winslow's bank draft. Edwin smiled, drank back his whiskey, then poured another glass. But even with Winslow's five hundred, he could not afford to show his face in London. Not with a bloody Runner searching for him and his reputation now that of a criminal.

That changed tonight. Tonight Winslow settled the accounting.

Putting down his glass, he pulled forward the sheet of paper that lay on the scarred table. Did it look enough like Winslow's hand? He had kept the bank draft for days, copying the signature endlessly before he had crept out, hat low and collar turned up to risk taking it to Winslow's bank. They had given him the money. And that had given him the idea.

This would work. This had to. He glanced toward the bed.

The room had no more than a narrow cot, a table, and single wooden chair and a lopsided shaving stand. It smelled of chamber pots from the other two rooms for let, and ale from the taproom below, and the stink of the London docks seemed to hang in the thin curtains that dangled limp from windows too dirty to show any light.

He'd been lucky to find the place—the landlord had asked for payment in silver in advance and no more questions than that. And he'd had even better luck to lay Winslow cold with a single blow, so that now he lay trussed up like a Christmas goose waiting to be served.

Smile twisting, he splashed more whiskey into his glass. God help him, he hoped he never had to pull off such a thing again. There had been that Runner to deal with first.

He had almost stumbled over the man as they had both trailed Winslow to Islington of all places. His stomach clenched on the whiskey as he remembered the sound of his sword stick cracking against the Runner's skull. He'd had to catch the man as he slumped, and drag him into an alley before anyone came across him. He'd taken the Runner's pistol, but he had left the man breathing.

Perhaps that had been a mistake. Perhaps he ought to have slit that damn Runner's throat. Only it had grown dark by then and Winslow had stepped from the house.

Edwin's stomach soured. He threw back the whiskey, hoping it would settle the knots in his guts. Winslow's fault, all of it. He wouldn't have had to hit the Runner if Winslow hadn't deceived him. And he wouldn't have had to shoot Winslow now.

He read the note again, looking for flaws. He could not afford another mistake.

This had to work!

It had so far. The hackney driver had not blinked an eye after he had clubbed Winslow with the Runner's pistol, and then called for the hack, claiming Winslow was a drunken friend. For an extra shilling, the fellow had even left his hack, stumbling up the narrow stairs with Winslow between them.

There had been a damn awkward moment when Winslow moaned and seemed to be coming to, but he'd slipped back after muttering some name.

Rubbing his thumb across his glass, Edwin stared at the man. Why couldn't he have kept out of it? He could have left the country and no one would have cared, least of all himself. But, no, he'd had to ruin everything.

Edwin read the note over again. Was it desperate enough? Full of sufficient guilt? Would the blame now shift back to Winslow for all of it? Throwing the note down, he ran a hand over his face. Yes, it would work. If it looked like a suicide.

He ought not to have drunk so much, but he needed the drink. He had not needed it to shoot Dunscombe. He'd had hate to drive him. And desperation. He had that again now, but though he wanted Winslow dead—and his own life back—he'd tried twice to pull the trigger, only to end up sweating and sick with it.

Pull yourself together and get it done!

Sloshing more whiskey into his glass, he downed it, then rubbed the back of his hand across the stubble on his chin. Another few drinks—that's what he needed. Then Winslow moaned.

Edwin walked to the bed, careful not to get too close. He didn't trust the damn fellow even with his hands and feet tied.

"Get it over with. Get it done," he muttered to himself. Striding back to the table, Edwin picked up the pistol and turned back again.

Terrance heard the muttering and turned toward it. Fractured images struggled to fit together. His head ached. There had been a carriage. The rest swirled in confusion. Stairs? What else? His stomach heaved.

Prying his eyes open a crack, he blinked at dim candlelight. The smells of tallow burning, of saltwater, and the stench of an ale house set his stomach churning. He tried to pull away—only he seemed to be hampered. Dampness hung in the air, cloying and cold. A cramp twisted his leg and he tried to stretch. Something caught at his ankles. He tried to lift a hand to his head.

Then he heard a pistol cock.

Opening his eyes, he stared into the bore of pistol. He looked up from it into a face from hell.

Hayland hadn't shaved in days. Red rimmed his blood-shot eyes, as if he had not slept in as long. The hand holding the pistol shook, so he slammed his other one on it. His cravat hung loose from his neck and wrinkles creased his coat and breeches, which seem to have been worn for too long without laundering.

A wrong word, or movement, and Hayland would pull that trigger. He could see that in the man's eyes. He could also see Hayland trying to work up the nerve for it. He might have a chance.

Hayland pulled the back of his hand across his face. Wiping away tears or sweat or both? He screwed up his face again, then muttered, "Oh, hell."

Stepping closer, he pushed the pistol to Terrance's temple.

Terrance croaked out his words, "Dunscombe—you could've claimed that an accident. You'll hang for this."

"Shut up! Damn you, shut up!"

Terrance swallowed, his mouth dry. Sweat broke out on his palms and upper lip. Had he judged wrong? If he had, he'd end with a bullet in his head.

He didn't want that. Blazes, he had too much left undone. Things unsaid. Urgency rose in him, and instinct urged him to struggle against the ropes. He fought the craving for freedom. He needed his wits, scrambled as they were.

If he ever needed to act with care, this was the time. Though he still wished he had his hands free and wrapped around Hayland's throat.

"Bloody all, Hayland—don't make this a bigger mistake. I should know. All I've done with my life is make mistakes."

"Shut up!"

"Why? So you can scatter my brains across the room? For what?"

"It's all your fault you're here! You took my name—my life! I'm going to have it back—for you're going to take the blame for everything! A tragic end to a tragic life!"

Terrance clenched his back teeth, then said, "Yes, it is my

fault. But how will you explain rope burns on my wrists? Think, man! Waddington already thought you guilty when he came to me. He'll see this as another reason to hang you. He wants to make a name for himself, and it'll be a better one if he brings in a man who killed twice!"

Sniffling, Edwin pulled back. He wiped at his face again.

Terrance pushed for his advantage. "Think, man. We're not all that different. We've both bloody well about ruined our lives—but there's still a chance for us. It's not too late. It can't be. So what if mistakes have been made. Learn from them. Hell, I've done nothing but make more of them. Is that what you want? To go on making mistakes until you make one too big to undo?"

Shaking his head, Hayland started to lower the pistol. "I made that already. I wouldn't have shot him, but he—God you have no idea how he could be."

"Oh, I do. A bloody bastard."

"The worst. He wanted me ruined. And he'd have done it." Tears streamed down Hayland's cheeks. "It's all gone now. I'm ruined anyway. Bloody bastard. Christ, I ought to shoot myself!" He started to turn the pistol to his head.

"Hayland! Listen to me. Don't be an idiot. Do you want to tear the heart out of your sister? You will if you shoot yourself. She's no one now. Will you leave her that way? Abandon her?"

"Like you did! Bastard!"

"Oh, for—she wasn't in love with me so much as she was with the idea of having someone who might take her from Dunscombe. She wanted me because she thought I just might shoot Dunscombe in a duel for her."

Leaning against the wall, Hayland slumped against the floor, muttering and sniffling, "No one to love her. No one to love me. No one. Just got each other. Always have."

Terrance strained against the ropes; they cut into his skin and held fast. If only he could get a hand free. Hayland still held the pistol, but it lay loose in his fingers now. If he dropped the thing, half cocked as it was, no telling what he'd hit.

Desperation welled in Terrance. Then his jaw tightened. He was not about to die. He'd spoken to Hayland to distract the man, and had ended up saying more truth than probably either of them wanted. But it was the truth.

Starting to sob, Hayland slumped onto the floor, sprawling there, tears streaming and his face buried against his arms.

Cursing, Terrance struggled against the ropes. He hoped Sylvain would forgive him for not getting to the theater with her tonight. He wished he had.

He'd managed to almost work one hand free when he heard light steps on the stair. Stilling, he glanced at Hayland. Had he heard as well? What in Hades would the man do if someone burst in? He still had that damn pistol.

Muffled, drunken sobs still came from him, but Hayland lifted his head, eyes puffy and bleary. Oh, blazes!

Then the door opened, and Ellena burst into the room, Sylvain a step behind her. "Edwin!"

"Easy. He's a half-cocked pistol in his hands!"

Sylvain halted, but Ellena went down on her knees beside her brother, murmuring his name over and over. Cautious, Sylvain stepped closer and eased the pistol from his slack fingers. The man wrapped his arms around his sister.

"What do I do with it?" she asked, glancing at Terrance.

"Just put it down over by me, and then find me a knife."

She set the pistol down on the floor near the bed, but instead of leaving to go in search of a knife, she sat down beside him and started tugging on the knots, explaining how she had arrived here in a rapid flow of which he only caught only half.

He wanted to watch her. He wanted to grab her and hold her as tight as he could—blazes, he was worse than Hayland. However, he kept a wary eye on Hayland. The man was too drunk and too dangerous to trust.

Feeling the knots ease from his wrists, he sat up to rub them, then he winced as his head spun. He touched a hand to the raw skin around his wrist as blood tingled into his fingers again. Sylvain moved to his feet, but he set her hands aside, and dragged off the ropes himself. Then he stood. He had to wait a moment for the world to settle before he limped over to Hayland.

Ellena stared up at him, eyes wide and face tear-streaked. "Please, don't harm him."

"Harm him? That lunatic almost murdered me!" He glanced at Sylvain. "Fetch the landlord. We'll need to send to Bow Street."

Looking troubled, she came to his side. "Terrance, I—I promised her I would not betray her brother."

Startled, he stared at her. Then he turned and limped for the door. "I didn't promise."

Hurrying forward, Sylvain grabbed his arm. "No, but I gave my word that if she brought me here no harm would come to her brother. Promises matter—you know that."

Frustration simmered in him. "I am not going to turn him loose so he can have another go at me! Or some other poor sod!"

Lady Dusncombe looked up at him. "Please, please let me take him away. We'll . . . we'll go abroad. We'll never return. I swear it, for there's nothing for us here."

Terrance looked from Ellena to Sylvain, one pair of eyes pleading, the other challenging. Then he glanced at Edwin, still crying, but now with his head in his sister's lap.

And his words to Hayland—about still having a chance—came back to him.

Maybe chances had to first be given to others.

With a curse, he strode from the room.

He came back to find Ellena anxious and white-faced, but she had gotten Edwin off the floor and onto the bed and had stopped his drunken tears. Sylvain watched him, eyes calm, a trusting look on her face.

He frowned at them. "There's a ship leaving within the quarter hour. You'll need money for passage."

Reaching up, Ellena unfastened the emeralds from around her neck and held them out. "Take this."

Terrance shook his head. "I'm quite aware that your brother cashed a bank draft that he took from me. If he has any of the money left, that'll have to do for you."

She nodded, then turned and rifled in Edwin's pockets, finally pulling out a roll of bank notes from his coattail pocket. She handed these to Terrance.

Sylvain came to his side. "What must I do?"

"You ought to go home, only I can't send you there alone. So stay close." She nodded and forced a stiff smile. He flicked a finger across the tip of her nose, then asked, "Do your sisters know you're here? No, forget I asked that."

Sylvain's smile relaxed. At the theater she had sent a footman to tell Bryn and Cecila that Lady Dunscombe would take her home and that she wanted them to stay and enjoy the performance. She winced. She had told more lies in the past few weeks than she had in all the years prior.

Then she glanced at Edwin Hayland. There were worse things than lies.

Edwin swayed as Ellena pulled him to his feet, but he managed the stairs and made it to the dock, stumbling only a little over the cobbled streets. Sylvain kept close to Terrance, as he had asked, shivering under the light evening jacket. She had left her pink cape behind. But she would have stayed close even had he not asked, and even if it had been a blazing hot summer day, not a chill autumn night.

On the docks, the water lapped against the quay, and a ladder led down to the water. Two rowboats, one of them manned just now by a scruffy, rough-looking man, bobbed in the inky water.

"These them passengers for the *Orion*?" the man called up.

Terrance glanced down. "They are—hold a moment."

Ellena looked at Sylvain then turned to Terrance. "Thank you." Standing on tiptoe, she kissed his cheek. Then she came to Sylvain and took her hands. "I shall never forget you." She pressed something into Sylvain's hand. Then made for the ladder and started down it.

Her brother looked down at the rowboat, then he glanced at Terrance. Words slurred, he asked, "You mean that—what you said? About chances? Mistakes?"

Terrance nodded. But he doubted Hayland would see the gesture in the dimness of the moonlight, so he said, "Go on, Hayland. Waddington will be after you still, but I'll do what I can to discourage him. Just remember it won't be wise to come back to England."

Hayland nodded, then started down the ladder, his face pale. Shivering in the night air, Sylvain stepped closer to Terrance. His arm came around her.

"Will the Runners still hunt him?" she asked.

"They've been known to go abroad for their man. However, Waddington may not be so keen on that. Particularly if I can impress on him just how disliked Dunscombe was—and that society has as much value for a Runner who knows when to look the other way."

She frowned. "It seems both wrong to let him go, and yet wrong to allow him to be taken and hung. Why are there no easy choices in life?"

Turning, he snuggled her close against him, fitting her into his arms. "Some are easy. Life is. You're even easier."

"Me?" She stared up at him, her features indistinct in the moonlight.

The shrill of a watchman's whistle, shouts, and the distant pounding of boots rose behind them. Terrance glanced around. "Oh, blazes. Waddington, unless I miss my guess— he must have caught the trail somehow. Only I don't want to talk to him just now."

Leaning over the dock, he glanced down, then he looked at Sylvain. "Do you trust me?"

She took a breath, then nodded. He swung her up over his shoulder, startling a squeak from her. "Terrance, after all you've been through!"

He grinned, and started down the ladder. She held still, thank heavens, for his head was swimming and he settled her in the rowboat as he sat down heavily. He probably shouldn't be doing this, but blazes he wasn't about to start being a sensible fellow now. Finding the mooring rope, he loosened it and pushed off with an oar.

"Am I being abducted?" she asked, head tilted to the side.

"No reason Ellena and that brother of hers should have all the fun—don't you want a moonlit boat ride?"

She scooted closer to him on the wooden bench. "In summer, perhaps."

Hearing the scuffle of boots and angry muttering, he glanced up at the docks. He would have to talk to Waddington soon. Then he looked down at Sylvain.

Moonlight turned her red-gold curls to pale strands. She had no bonnet on, and no gloves. Her hand came up to his chest. His throat tightened. He had come too close to losing this—to losing everything. That near sense of loss sharpened his world, crystallizing emotions that had seemed so confusing earlier. His world seemed as crisp as the stars above.

Letting go of the oars, he let the tide carry them as he turned and kissed her, long and hard and full. Her lips met his, her mouth opening, yielding to his. The touch of her tongue to his quickened his blood. He caught the back of her neck and tilted her head to deepen the kiss, claiming her. She opened to him like the sweetest flower, pressing her breasts to him.

Pulse ragged, breathing hard, he pulled back, then demanded, "Marry me. I don't want a pretense with you."

Her mouth curved and the warmth of her breath brushed his face. "Is this to save my reputation?"

"No."

"Because you feel obligated now?"

"Oh, I'm obligated. I'm obliged, in fact, to want you. Blazes, I've lived a shadow of a life far too long, and I want something better. I want to find love—and I want to find it with you."

"But I thought you—we . . . ? Why me?"

His grin flashed in the moonlight. She sounded delightfully confused—as if she could not think herself anything special. He knew otherwise. His head still spun from his kiss, from having his arms around her.

"Why?" she said again.

Sylvain knew she ought not to ask this. Only with her blood pounding, and his arms tight around her, she wanted to know. She had to. For the moonlight and the danger had left her reckless with her heart.

"Because, my sweet Silly, you ask just such questions. Because if I don't, I might miss my own chance. Because I've made enough mistakes, and I'm not making one now."

She parted her lips to ask more questions, but he covered her mouth with his. With a sigh, she gave it up.

Wrapping her arms around his neck, she pulled him closer. Perhaps this would not last. Perhaps she would become another woman he left. Or perhaps not. Had he not just said something about missing a chance?

"I'll marry you," she managed to say as he moved his kisses to the hollow of her throat and his hands to her waist, and before he dragged her down in the boat, his arms wrapped tightly around her.

Epilogue

"If you tug any more on that neckcloth, you'll ruin it," Theo whispered, leaning closer to his brother.

Terrance shot him a glare. "It feels a blasted noose."

Theo grinned. "Just keep thinking of her—it's how I got through my own wedding."

Terrance glowered at him, and then at the faces gathered in the small, stone Norman church. All the blasted village of Halsage seemed to be here.

I am mad!

Spring flowers—bright, smelly things—decked the church. Though Mrs. Harwood had not been deemed well enough to attend, she had tucked a handkerchief into Terrance's pocket this morning when he had called on her, telling him, "I know you'll be good for her."

Blazes, but he wished he knew that.

For six months he had managed to stay out of trouble—well, mostly. There had been the small matter of a bet to settle as to if it was possible to drive a pair of bulls in tandem harness. It was—but only just. And it had not been his fault that that opera dancer he had once known had decided to throw herself into his arms smack in the middle of Bond Street.

But his being respectable—or mostly so—did not keep Nevin from frowning at him now. Thank heavens Sylvain's sisters could not attend—for one had a new babe, and the other was too close to her time to travel. That at least spared him their glowers.

He had asked Sylvain if she wished to put back the date so that her sisters could be there, but she had only stared at him and then asked, "Why? Cecila will try to dress me in white and then she'll cry—she always does at weddings. And Penelope will want us to marry in London!"

He had kissed her for that.

Only now he wished she had put the date back—years back.

He glanced over to his side of the church, stuffed with relatives, most of whom, he suspected, arrived with expectations of scandal or because they had never believed this event would occur. The squire beamed at him—blue eyes bright with delight and looking dapper in a new, dark blue coat for the occasion. And no doubt already naming his grandsons.

And then Terrance caught sight of the heavily veiled lady in the back. He relaxed. She had come. He had thought she might feel too awkward, but she had come.

Then Mr. Harwood started down the aisle, Sylvain on his arm, and everyone rose. Terrance froze with terror.

What in Hades am I doing?

She looked enchanting, done up in gold and creams and yellows. "Without any floaty bits," she had said, wrinkling her nose when she had described her bridal gown to him.

She came to him, blue-green eyes bright, brimming with happiness, and Mr. Harwood put her hand in his. She had not worn gloves—neither had he—and at the touch of her skin, he grinned.

It swept over him then, a sense of such rightness that he wondered how it had taken him so long to find this. And why had he looked everywhere but in the home woods?

Relaxed now, he turned to face the vicar, even able to put up with his dour disapproving glances.

Sylvain noticed the tension ease from Terrance and some of it fled her as well. She still dreaded that she might do something awful—she had insisted on a simple gown for no better reason than to reduce the risk of tripping.

For courage, she glanced at her wrist. The emerald bracelet that Lady Dusncombe had given her sparkled. She had had only one note from the lady—a short letter of thanks, with no address for an answer.

She smiled. Chances to change mattered.

And then the vicar called on her to give her vows. She looked at Terrance as she pledged to worship him with her body. The giving of love welled inside her like life's very breath.

The vicar droned on. *Almost done*, Sylvain thought, giddy now and light-headed.

The scream shattered her mood, rising from the back of the church in a shrill shriek, followed by muttering and hasty movement. Sylvain turned to glimpse Trace's bobbing red form as he skittered out. Mrs. Peyton fainted then, taking three gentlemen with her bulk. Others rose to hurry to her.

Biting her lower lip, Sylvain glanced at Terrance. Had she ruined this day? She ought to have locked Trace up at home, but it was such a beautiful day—and she had rather encouraged him to follow by inviting him up into the carriage with her.

Terrance frowned as he stared at the back of the church, eyes narrowed and disapproval darkening his tawny eyes.

Then he looked at her.

With a wink, he grinned, eyes lightening.

He glanced at the vicar, but she had already guessed his thoughts. She had her skirt in her hands as he bolted with her hand clasped in his, heading for the woods, laughing as they left disaster behind.

Nearly breathless, he stopped when they gained the first wood and pulled her against a tree. Then he glanced back at the church.

"You are barely proper," she said, her arm around his neck.

"Me? And whose fox started the commotion?"

"Mine. Ours." She grinned.

"Too right. As to proper . . ." Another glint darkened his

eyes. "My darling, there is nothing proper about how I feel about you."

"Good. I am not certain I could live with anything other than a barely proper marriage to an impossibly improper man."

"Thank heavens for that!" he said. Then, still grinning, he dragged her down in the grass to prove her right.

Author's Note

Prior to the mid 1700's London had no police force—highwaymen rode the main roads, gangs looted rich houses, and to walk the streets was to risk one's life. While an organized police force existed in other countries, the English feared such a force might lead to a loss of civil liberties. However, in 1748 Henry Fielding became police magistrate at Bow Street and organized his "Runners." His small group—only eight men—began to establish police records, patrols, and became the first organized detectives in England. They continued as a small group—usually less than a dozen, and their work might include guarding royalty, acting as a watch against jewel thieves at a masquerade, simply being on call, or investigating murders.

Runners could and did travel abroad to capture criminals, but permission had to be obtained from the other country's government.

Most Runners wore "plainclothes," but they could wear the scarlet waistcoat of a man on patrol, or the blue of a patrol conductor. They generally carried a wooden tipstaff or truncheon, usually about a foot long and made of ebony or some hardwood with a handgrip on one end and a brass crown on the other. Being hollow, this could hold a warrant for arrest, and served much like a modern policeman's badge.

As it was customary for private individuals to reward a Runner on the successful completion of a case, some Runners retired rich. But not all Runners served the law—John Sayer married the widow of a member of a gang who had robbed a bank in Scotland, stealing twenty thousand pounds, of which only twelve was returned. After Sayer died, the remainder turned up in his effects.

Finally, in 1829 Robert Peal—who had fought for years to establish an organized police force—was allowed by Parliament to found the Metropolitan Police. And London had her "Pealers" or what we now call "Bobbies" after Bob Peal.

I do enjoy hearing from readers about my books, present ones, past ones, or future ones, so please write or email, and don't forget to ask for a free bookmark: Shannon Donnelly, PO Box 3313, Burbank, CA 91508-3313, read@shannon donnelly.com.